FIRST

F-BOMB: SEALS LOVE CURVES, BOOK 3

MARY E THOMPSON

First

F-BOMB: SEALs Love Curves, book three

Copyright © 2019 Mary E Thompson

Cover Copyright © 2021 Mary E Thompson

Cover Photo from depositphotos, Copyright © stetsik

Background from depositphotos, Copyright © yupiramos

Flag from Pixabay, CC0

Published by BluEyed Press, All Rights Reserved

No part of this book may be reproduced in any form or by any electronic or mechanical means, including information storage and retrieval systems, without written permission from the author, except for the use of brief quotations in a book review.

This is a work of fiction. All characters, businesses, locations, and events are either products of the author's creative imagination or are used in a fictitious sense. Any resemblance to real persons, living or dead, is purely coincidental.

Ebook ISBN: 978-1-944090-72-2

Print ISBN: 978-1-944090-73-9

Audiobook ISBN: 978-1-944090-66-1

❀ Created with Vellum

F-BOMB: SEALS LOVE CURVES

Welcome to the world of F-BOMB where a group of former SEALs have come together to protect the curvy women they love and the country they call home from the dangers of the world. They have the training and the knowledge, and they have the ability to kick some ass when needed. And it'll be needed.

F-BOMB: SEALs LOVE CURVES

Freedom
Fiancée (subscriber exclusive)
Forgotten
First
Failure
Friends
Family
Forbidden
Future
Finally

SUBSCRIBE NOW AT MARYETHOMPSON.COM

For that first love… whether they're the one who got away, the one you set free, the one you stayed with forever, or someone else, may you always remember the joy of falling in love for the first time.

For my first and only love, thank you.

1

———

The truth was the most important thing to Pilar Luna. She valued it above everything else. Trusting that the people she loved told her the truth was not always easy.

The truth was a funny thing. Most people would say the truth sets you free. That it's a balm on your soul. It can release you from pain and heartbreak and misplaced devotion.

But the truth can also do the opposite. The truth can destroy you. It can cripple you. It can take your heart and smash it into bits.

That was why the truth was so important to Pilar. She had been there. More than once. She knew what it was like to find out the truth about someone and have it ruin everything you thought you knew.

"Why are we here?" she grumbled to her brother.

He turned back to her with a wide grin. His dark hair had bright blue tips, something new for him. It had been a long year for him, always checking behind himself. It was nice to see him smile, and she couldn't help the tug at her own lips.

"Because parades are awesome. We didn't do stuff like this at home, hermanita."

"That's because the cartel didn't approve of celebrations or anything that would bring the people together. They wanted us scared and separate," Pilar snapped.

Juan's smile faded, and she immediately regretted her words. Juan, or John as he'd changed it to when he moved to Niagara Falls, spent more than his fair share of years as a falcon for the Castillo cartel. He didn't realize what he was getting into when he was young, and by the time he understood, it was too late to get out.

But he did. She was proud of him for walking away. It took guts. Guts Pilar had to use when she found out the man she fell for on one of her breaks from school was further up the chain than her brother and involved in things she couldn't even think about, let alone be a part of.

"I'm sorry," Juan whispered, squeezing her hand. His dark brown eyes showed how much he meant his words.

She smiled at him and squeezed back. "It's not your fault. I'm tired. It's been a long week."

His eyes brightened, and his grin returned. He stared over her shoulder and held up a finger. "I know what will make you feel better."

He took off before she could ask him where he was going. She tried to follow him through the crowd, but between the people lining the streets to watch the parade and the vendors selling everything from sausages to light up necklaces, he vanished far too quickly.

Panic flooded Pilar's veins as she rushed down the street, scanning for his blue tipped hair and bright red shirt. The sea of red surrounding her swallowed up her brother like he'd never been there at all.

Pilar pushed ahead, blindly running. She had to have missed him. She turned back but kept moving forward.

She ran smack into something, backing into a hard... body. Arms came around her, hands gripping her biceps. Her panic was real, potent, a thing surrounding her as surely as the stranger's hands.

She tried to step away, but the hands tightened on her arms.

"Are you okay?" he asked in a smooth, deep voice that set off every nerve ending. Male. Commanding. Calm. If she weren't so terrified, she might have found the voice sexy, but she could only think of getting away.

"Fine," she said, again trying to push away from him.

He finally let her go. "It's crazy here, isn't it?"

She turned and looked at him. His accent said he wasn't a local, but he wasn't Mexican either. His skin was too light and there was no hint of Mexican in his tone. "Yeah, busy."

She scanned the area again, needing to find Juan. He couldn't have gone far.

"Are you looking for someone?"

She nodded. "Yeah, my... cousin," she stammered, remembering their cover story at the last second. She kept their mother's last name when she made the move to the States permanent, but her brother chose a whole new identity. Something she wasn't willing to ask how he knew how to do.

"Maybe I can help you. What does he look like?"

Pilar shook her head. "It's okay. I'm sure he's around here somewhere."

He shrugged. "If you're sure. But I don't mind helping. My friends are grabbing food. I was saving our spot so we can see all the festivities. I'm a newbie at all this. Never thought I'd stand on a street and throw my sausage around."

Pilar's eyes bugged out. "What?"

He held up a raw sausage. "For the parade. Are you a Dyngus Day virgin, too?"

The conspiratorial grin he flashed her had her fighting her own smile. "I am," she admitted. "And I'm going to stay that way if I have to leave to find my brother."

His eyes narrowed. "I thought you were looking for your cousin."

"Oh, um yeah. We're just really close. I always thought of him as more like a brother."

The guy's eyes narrowed but stayed warm. He was looking at her a little too closely for someone she just met on the street. And he was being friendly.

"Um, I need to go."

Pilar turned and came face-to-face with the last man she ever wanted to see.

"Hola, amore," Carlos Ibarra said with a menacing grin and eyes only for her. His black gaze scanned her body, pausing at her breasts and between her thighs.

There was a time when seeing his eyes heat the way they did made her a puddle at his feet, willing to do almost anything he asked because she loved him. He twisted that love, and he turned it into something disgusting that shamed her to her very core when she found out who he really was.

"You don't have a kiss for me?" he asked.

Every muscle in her body seized, unable to function. She wanted to slap him, or kick him, or do something that would bring him the same kind of pain she experienced, but he was invincible. The kind of man who couldn't be hurt because he had no heart. No emotions. No feelings.

A hand slid around her waist and tugged her close to a firm body. "Sorry, man. She saves her kisses for me."

The guy she ran in to. He was holding her and pretending she was his.

She belonged to no one, but the last thing she wanted was to let Carlos think she was alone. Vulnerable.

Carlos's eyebrows winged up and a vicious grin turned his lips up. "Ah, that won't be for long." Carlos moved to walk away, then turned back. "I'll let Juan know you're being taken care of. He was pretty pissed at us for leaving you all alone. Of course, I can take you to him."

"Where is he?" she cried, breaking free from the stranger's grasp to get up in Carlos's face.

He growled and shoved her back. "Don't you ever come at me again, or you'll get to share a resting place with your brother. Adios."

And just that fast, the truth knocked Pilar on her ass all over again.

Jack Farrell didn't know what to expect from the woman in front of him but collapsing on the sidewalk definitely wasn't it.

He should have. She just found out her brother was kidnapped. But it still shocked the hell out of him.

He reached for her arm, gently placing his hand on her. "Hey."

She immediately jerked away from him and scrambled to her feet as though she just realized what was going on. Her dark gaze scanned the crowd, but he was gone.

"Where did he go?" she demanded.

Jack shook his head. "I don't know. I was more worried about you. Are you okay?"

She shook her head, slowly at first, then quicker. "My brother. They took him."

Jack's face hardened. "Who was that?"

She laughed softly. "The man who's going to kill me."

"I'm not going to let that happen," he promised her. She had no clue who he was, but that didn't matter to him. He was going to keep her safe. He wasn't losing her. Too many people in his life had died.

Not that she was in his life, but she was standing in front of him. She was there. And he was going to keep her safe.

"Come with me," he said, reaching for her hand and starting down the street in the direction she initially came from.

She tugged out of his grip, causing him to stop. "I'm not going anywhere with you. I don't know who you are."

Jack grinned. "I'm the man you're saving all your kisses for, remember?"

A ghost of a smile crossed her lips, but it didn't last long. Fury replaced the fear with determination on its heels. "I have to find my brother."

Jack nodded. "I'll help you."

"Why?"

Jack grinned. "Because it's what I do."

"Who are you?" she asked, taking a step back.

Jack shook his head and followed her, doing his best to look innocent. "I work for a company that helps people."

"Smooth," the sarcastic voice in his ear muttered.

Jack pasted on a grin, ignoring his friend and boss, and hoped it would help convince Pilar to go with him.

She turned back to where Carlos disappeared. "I have to find my brother."

Jack nodded. "I know. My company can help you. And keep you safe so what you said doesn't actually happen."

She laughed mirthlessly. "Unless you're some kind of superhero, it's going to happen. Now that Carlos knows where to find me, he'll either take me back or kill me. Maybe both. Definitely both."

Jack's grin slid onto his lips easily. He opened his mouth to tell her he *was* a superhero when the voice was back.

"Don't you fucking dare, Squirrel. Just bring her in."

Jack scowled at the voice in his head and vowed to make sure Pres knew exactly how much he appreciated being called Squirrel.

"What's your name?" Jack asked, pretending he didn't already know.

She drew in a ragged breath, one that hitched in the middle. She faced away from him, but he could still see her profile. Full lips, one clamped between her teeth, caught his attention first. He'd always been a sucker for a woman with soft, plump lips. Her dark eyes held pain and fear, but that damned determination was still there. Her arms were crossed, one hand pinching her chin as if that made it easier for her to figure out what to do. Her curves dragged his eyes down, making sure he took in every dip of her body from the swell of her breasts to the slight narrowing of her waist, then out again to her wide hips, then curvy legs down to the sandals on her feet. It was still cold for sandals, but her bright pink toenails told him she didn't care. She was ready for fun and sun.

"Pilar," she whispered, as though testing it out.

He nodded and stuck out his hand. "Jack Farrell. It's nice to meet you, Pilar."

She stared at his hand for a long moment. Long enough that he felt like an idiot and wanted to pull his hand back. But he waited. She had to trust him if she was going to go with him. There was no way in hell he was letting her get in her own vehicle. Not when she was in danger.

She was smart not to trust him, but she had no way of knowing that. All she knew was her brother was gone, and she had no one else to trust.

Finally, she extended her hand and slid it into his. A zap shot up his arm and settled in his dick, bringing it to life. If that wasn't surprising enough, Pilar tugged his hand, catching him off guard and yanking him to her. She glared up at him, her eyes as dark as midnight. She was so close he could feel her breath on his cheeks as she growled, "If you're lying to me, I'll castrate you. You got me?"

Jack fought a grin as the assholes in his ear hooted and hollered that he'd finally met his match. All Jack could do was nod, because if he opened his mouth, he risked a laugh coming out.

Or something much worse. The truth.

PILAR COULDN'T BELIEVE she threatened the hot guy who was trying to help her. Even more than that, she couldn't believe she actually accepted his help and went with him.

She knew she was safest at the parade, surrounded by thousands of other people, but seeing Carlos shook her. More than she expected it to. She never thought she'd see him again. Or maybe she just hoped she'd never see him again. He was the stuff of her nightmares, and coming face-to-face with him after three years of hiding was the most terrified she'd been since the day she found out what kind of monster he was.

She slid a glance at Jack. Jack Farrell. If she was smart, she would have sent a text to a friend with his picture in case she ended up in a ditch somewhere in a few days. Except she didn't really have any friends. A few acquaintances, sure, but no real friends she trusted with the truth. One of the many consequences of living in fear. She didn't get close to anyone and didn't let anyone close to her.

As she sat in a truck with a stranger, going back over the Grand Island bridges toward Niagara Falls, she wondered if she'd live to tell anyone. He could easily pull into a warehouse and she'd never be seen again. Or anything. She had no clue who he was or what he was going to do with her.

"I promise I'm not going to hurt you," he said softly.

Her head snapped his way, meeting his gaze. He pulled the sunglasses he wore down so she could see his eyes. They were a dark green, so dark she wasn't sure what color they were at first. They reminded her of a forest, with hidden depths and secrets around every turn. And for some reason, she believed him.

"Where are we going?" Pilar finally asked. She hoped she didn't sound as terrified as she was.

"My office. It's up in the Falls."

"In?"

He laughed softly. "In the city. We do a lot of work with the border so we like to be close."

"What kind of work?" she asked, eyeing the man next to her. He was big. Much taller than her or Juan. He was thin, but he definitely didn't lack muscle. He looked like a soccer player with long, strong legs and a narrow frame. Pilar always had a thing for soccer players.

"It's a task force, F-BOMB. We work to keep our borders safe."

Pilar choked back the snort that rose in her throat. If he only knew who she was. She chewed her lip. He was the kind of person she should have gone to when she first found out who Carlos was. But it was too late for that. It was too late for her. Carlos was back, and he had Juan.

"Do you really think you can get my brother back?"

Jack took the exit onto Robert Moses Parkway toward downtown Niagara Falls. He kept his gaze focused on the curvy road as he wound around toward the Upper Niagara River, but Pilar was sure he was paying her attention, too. Nothing got by the man next to her. Which made her wonder again why was she trusting him.

"We'll do our best," Jack said. He glanced at her again, then reached over and squeezed her hand.

And again, she found herself believing him.

2

—————

JACK CATALOGUED EVERY MOVE PILAR MADE FROM THE moment he said "F-BOMB" to when they arrived at the massive building they housed their office in. He eyed her when he drove under the building and parked his SUV in the designated spot for company vehicles. And he watched her as she processed where they were.

Either she was a damn good actress, or she was clueless.

"You work here?" she asked, scanning the underground parking structure. "You're kidding right?"

Jack shrugged. "No. Why? Not fancy enough for you?"

She rolled her eyes and got out. Jack scrambled to follow her and hear what she had to say. "There are tons of places for people to hide down here. On top of that, there are multiple entrances, which means escaping is easier. And there aren't any cameras, so if something were ever to happen down here, no one would know. This place is a criminal's dream."

He narrowed his eyes at the curvy beauty and wondered how she knew all the weak points. They were the same things the team talked about when they rented the office space, but it was nondescript and provided them with anonymity to operate without having to deal with anyone else.

Jack nodded and turned toward the elevators. "Then how about we head upstairs so we're a little less vulnerable." He added one of his grins to encourage her even more.

She rolled her eyes at that, too, then stalked off to the elevator without him.

With her arms crossed, she waited for Jack to swipe his card to give them access to the elevators. The only way up was with one of the security cards every employee was required to use. Each card gave them access to one floor only, the one where they worked. Jack was pretty sure English hacked his card and could visit any of the floors in the building, but Jack's only went to the F-BOMB offices.

Pilar was silent as she stood in the corner and chewed on her lower lip. If it wasn't already tempting him, the slick, red flesh was making Jack rethink his personal vow to stay away from women for a while.

The doors whooshed open, revealing the sterile entryway of their offices. He held the door open for Pilar and followed her out, her tension radiating through the small space.

"Pilar, you're safe here."

She shook her head. "I'm not safe anywhere."

"Good, you're here," Dunn said, walking through the secured doors that led to the bowels of F-BOMB. He turned to Pilar with faux surprise and said, "I don't think we've met. I'm Daniel Dunn."

Pilar barely acknowledged him, shaking his hand and turning back to Jack. "Are you going to help me?"

Jack nodded. "Yeah, and so is Dunn. He's in charge

around here. You need to tell him everything that happened, Pilar."

"Okay, well, I was walking down the street with my... brother."

Dunn held up his hand. "Let's get you inside. How about a cup of coffee? Or some tea?"

Jack shook his head as Pilar's eyes lit up. She thought it was a coincidence that Dunn offered her tea.

"Tea, please. Thank you. I appreciate it," she said with a grin.

"Of course," Dunn said, leading Pilar through the doors and into the conference room they used for visitors.

Jack started to move past them, but Pilar called out to him. "Aren't you staying here? I thought you were going to help me."

Jack turned back and nodded. "I will. You need to tell Dunn everything first, though."

Dunn swung his gaze between them and gave Jack a tight grin. "Maybe it would be best if you joined us," he said carefully, offering Jack no room to argue.

Jack wanted to distance himself from Pilar, to ignore the attraction he felt for her and pass her off to someone else, but he was the one she knew. Sort of.

Jack finally nodded and moved into the room behind them. Pilar watched him until he claimed a seat, then took the one next to him. Dunn, the son of a bitch, smirked and sat across the table from them. He thumbed out a text to someone, probably asking for Pilar's tea, then looked up at her.

"Okay, Pilar, right?" he asked.

She nodded.

"What's your last name?"

She hesitated. "Luna."

Dunn wrote it down on the pad in front of him. "And your brother is missing. What's his name?"

She took a deep breath. "Juan Rios. He goes by John, though."

Dunn nodded. "Rios? You have different last names? Are you married?"

She shook her head. "I've never been married. My brother and I both changed our names when he moved to the United States. For me, it was years ago. My degree is in my name."

Jack sat up straighter and leaned toward her, offering her silent support.

"Is there a reason?" Dunn asked.

"Carlos Ibarra. He's the man who took my brother. I... I was involved with him years ago, and I didn't want him to find me. Juan was the same. Didn't want Carlos to know where he was."

Dunn nodded, taking notes as she spoke. His earpiece was quiet, but Jack knew English was listening, too. Typing in everything she said and recording the conversation. Everything would be checked and double checked. It was the only way for them to do their jobs.

"Why didn't you want him to find you?" Dunn asked softly, looking up at Pilar. He was giving her the power, submitting to her. It was all a mind-fuck, a game to get her to trust him. To think he cared. And it was pissing Jack off. He wanted Pilar to trust *him*, not Dunn.

"He's dangerous. When I called things off with him, he was angry. He told my brother I'd pay for it."

"Your brother was friends with," Dunn pretended to check his notes, "Carlos?"

Pilar half-shrugged. "They worked together. That was how I met Carlos. He came with my brother to our house once. I was home from school for the summer and Carlos showed up. I was... stupid."

Dunn smiled with her.

"I'd never known anyone like him. He had a way of making me feel special."

The wistful look in her eyes had Jack ready to go hunt the bastard down and strangle him with his bare hands. Usually that was a job for Archer, whom they called Hulk, but for the first time, Jack understood the rage it took to kill someone up close and personal instead of from the other end of a sight at a few hundred feet.

"I'm sorry for what you went through, Pilar. I have to ask, though, what does this have to do with your brother missing now? If this Carlos was upset with you before, why is he now here and why would he take your brother?"

She shook her head once, enough to shake off the old memories in her eyes, then looked up at Dunn. "When Carlos threatened me, Juan said he decided it was time for him to find something else to do. It took him a couple of years before he could get out, though. Their boss wouldn't let Carlos leave Mexico to come after me, but when Juan disappeared, I guess things changed."

"How so? And how do you know that? He just disappeared an hour ago." Dunn was good. He even sounded sincere.

Pilar shook her head. "No, I don't mean when he was taken. He left his job a year ago. I was working in Texas, a few hours from the border. Juan showed up on my doorstep on the last day of school. He was done with the cartel and wanted to get as far away from Mexico as possible. We came here because our parents visited Niagara Falls on their honeymoon and constantly told us how beautiful it was. We wanted to be close to them. They died a few years ago."

Dunn reached across and grabbed her hand, smiling up at her. "I'm sorry for your loss."

She smiled back at him, then glanced at Jack. He didn't know what she saw, but the hitch in her breath said it wasn't good. He unclenched his fist on the table and worked at smoothing the anger from his face. He was always cool under pressure. It was a requirement for being a sniper, but sitting in the same room as Pilar and Dunn, and watching Dunn play her, had him ready to tear into his boss.

"Anyway," Pilar continued, "once Juan left Mexico, it was only a matter of time before Carlos found us. We knew it, but I guess we got complacent."

She glanced at Jack again. He hated that he couldn't tell her what was really going on, but until he got the word from Dunn, he had to stay silent.

"You believe Carlos took Juan in order to get to you?" Dunn asked.

Pilar nodded. "I know he did. He told me he did. You heard him." She turned to Jack for confirmation.

Jack shook his head. "He didn't specifically say that. It was clear he wanted her to know he was the one who had her brother."

"Why else would he take Juan, and why tell me, if he wasn't after me, too?"

"What kind of work does Carlos do? That Juan used to do?" Dunn asked. He sounded bored, as though the question was simply a way to connect them.

"They worked for an import and export company," Pilar said stiffly.

"With the borders?" Dunn asked.

Pilar shook her head. "Not always. Packaging and making sure everything had the right paperwork to pass customs. Stuff like that mostly."

Dunn scribbled something on the paper, and there was finally a sound in Jack's ear. "Clueless or hiding?"

Dunn caught Jack's eye and lifted an eyebrow. Jack lifted two fingers against his chest, signaling the second option. Dunn nodded in agreement.

"Unfortunately, I'm not sure if we are going to be able to do anything," Dunn said, leaning back in his chair. "There isn't a whole lot to go on. This Carlos guy doesn't have a motive for taking your brother, especially if he's really after you. I have no way to track them, and if they're not from here, I have no known associates to use to find them. This is probably something you're going to need to report to the police."

Pilar's eyes filled, her tears spilling out onto her cheeks. "Please, Mr. Dunn. Don't do this. I need your help. Jack said you would help me find my brother. Carlos will kill him. He's a ruthless murderer, and he won't hesitate to kill my brother if he thinks it'll get me to go to him. He wants me back, and he doesn't care if he has to keep me in a cage. He will, and I can't live like that. I'd rather die than ever be with that monster again."

Dunn leaned in, his eyes sharp. "Do you have any kind of proof that he's killed people?"

Pilar shook her head, but her gaze slid to the side. Definitely lying. "I did, but it was destroyed. Juan... my brother is a good man. Growing up in Mexico isn't easy. And Juan ended up getting involved with the wrong people."

"So you're saying you had proof of Carlos killing people, but your brother took it and destroyed it, and now you want us to save him from the man he was protecting? Your story sounds more and more like Carlos isn't involved with your brother's disappearance at all. Are you sure your brother didn't just get lost in the crowd? That he's truly gone?"

Pilar full out sobbed at Dunn's accusation. Jack grabbed a box of tissues from the sideboard behind him and slapped them down on the table in front of her. "We'll give you a minute," he growled, then jerked his head to the door for Dunn to follow him.

Dunn raised his eyebrows at Jack, but he stood and followed him into the hallway, closing the soundproof door behind them. The recording devices in the room would pick up anything Pilar said to herself and any calls she made.

Dunn crossed his arms over his chest and waited for Jack to speak.

Jack paced a short distance up and down the hallway, his gaze falling to the door more than once. "Why did you go after her like that?" he finally hissed.

"Do you believe her?"

Jack nodded. "Yes. She thinks her brother's gone. You heard Carlos. He made it pretty damn clear they took Juan."

"We knew they were going to meet," Dunn said slowly.

Jack sighed. "I know, but we were supposed to have eyes on Juan at all times. He wasn't supposed to disappear. What the fuck happened?"

Dunn raised that damn eyebrow again. "Situations change. We all know this. We couldn't stay on Juan and not have Pilar aware of our presence. We had to give him some space. He demanded it."

"Do you think he double crossed us?" Jack asked.

Dunn shrugged. "Hard not to think that's exactly what happened. He came to us with this whole thing. He was the one who set it all up. And when we're closing in, all of a sudden he vanishes."

Jack shook his head. "I just find it hard to believe he would leave Pilar. They seem to be really close."

Dunn's neutral expression slipped, just long enough for

Jack to see the anger and distrust Dunn carried with him for the last two years. It had only gotten worse since their Commanding Officer and supposed friend betrayed them all almost a year earlier. Brady Williams was Dunn's mentor, and he took the betrayal hardest, especially since he was already burned by an informant he thought he loved.

"People aren't always who they seem. Juan grew up and became one of the go-to people for the Castillo cartel. He and Carlos were side-by-side through all of it, even though Carlos rose higher and faster. We've been suspicious of Juan from day one."

Jack knew it was the truth, but the way Pilar broke down said she truly thought her brother had changed. That he was a good man. "I don't think she knows anything about this."

Dunn shook his head. "No, but she knows something. We need to keep her close. If Carlos gets them both, it's likely he'll kill them. She's our new informant. Until we can get what Juan promised us, we need Pilar."

Jack nodded. "What are we going to tell her?"

Dunn gave Jack a hard glare. "Nothing. You got me? She stays in the dark about everything going on. We will tell her we believe she may be right about her life being in danger, and that we will find Juan. After that, there's nothing she needs to know."

"Are you serious?" Jack asked, incredulous.

Dunn nodded sharply. "Yes. And if you can't handle that, I'll put someone else on her."

"Whoa, wait. You want me on her?"

Dunn looked at him like he was crazy. "She knows you. She obviously trusts you. If she didn't before, she definitely does now since you dragged me out of there after I attacked her. Good move, by the way. If you can get her to trust you, she might offer up whatever information she has on Carlos and the rest of them."

"I didn't do it so she'd trust me," Jack grumbled.

Dunn narrowed his eyes at Jack. "There better not be another fucking reason, Squirrel. We all need our heads in the game with this one. Think with the head on your fucking shoulders, not the one you usually use."

"Fuck you, Pres," Jack said.

Dunn's glare hardened. The two men stood in the hall-way, staring at each other. Their breath came in rapid pants, tension ramping up higher and higher. Jack was ready to start swinging if he had to. Happily.

"Both of you pull your fucking shit together and get back in there. Now."

Ryker Hamilton. Known as Dex to them. The voice of reason in their ears.

Dunn and Jack tossed each other another glare, then headed back into the conference room.

3

———

PILAR STARED AT HER PHONE AND WILLED IT TO SEND HER A text. For Juan to ask where she was and say she disappeared when he went to get whatever the hell it was he thought would make her happy.

He was constantly doing things like that. Little things that made her smiled. She knew he regretted introducing her to Carlos, even though he never intended for them to get involved. Pilar kept it from her brother because she knew he'd be pissed. He never wanted her to date any of his friends, but Carlos was charming and it didn't take much convincing for her to go out with him.

When Juan found out they were together, he went nuts. Pilar didn't understand why. She had her head buried in the sand when it came to her brother and his involvement with anything illegal. She suspected it, but he always denied it when she worked up the courage to ask him.

That was the night he sat her down and told her the truth about what he did for a living. How he was paying for her to go to school in America.

Pilar was so angry with him that she ran. She believed

he was lying and went straight to Carlos to laugh about the lengths Juan was willing to go to keep them apart.

She wished she'd just believed her brother because what she witnessed when she got to Carlos's was worse than any imagination could have dreamed up.

The door opened to the small room where she was being held, jerking her back to the present. A present that involved her missing brother and her evil ex.

Mr. Dunn walked in first. He was a commanding presence, a man who was hard to ignore. He was attractive, with dark brown skin and eyes that matched. His muscles were much bulkier than Jack's, but he was definitely a good-looking man. What bothered her about him was he obviously didn't believe her. Although why, she had no idea.

Jack defended her and Juan, which made her want to trust him. She couldn't completely, but if she had to pick between the two men walking into the room, it was definitely the second one.

She glanced at Jack and had to fight the urge to leave the room. He was glaring hard at Mr. Dunn, his eyes drilling holes in the back of his boss's neck. The pure hatred in his gaze had her rethinking trusting him at all. She'd only seen a look that harsh once in her life. In the eyes of the man who wanted her dead.

Jack swung his gaze to her, and it softened immediately. She wasn't sure what to make of that. Which man was he?

"I apologize for upsetting you, Ms. Luna," Mr. Dunn said. "That was not my intention."

Pilar nodded. She didn't know where he was going with his apology, but she wasn't going to give him more ammunition to use against Juan. She needed his help to find her brother, not accuse him of working with Carlos again. Juan wouldn't do that. He promised her.

"We need time to look into all this. Since you believe your life is in danger, we'd like to keep you in protective custody for the night, at least."

"Protective custody? You're joking, right?"

Mr. Dunn shook his head and raised an eyebrow. "I'm not kidding. If you're in danger, I don't understand why you wouldn't want someone with you at all times."

Pilar swallowed the lump in her throat. She knew it was the smart thing to do, the logical thing, but being watched was going to wear on her. It also meant she couldn't go looking for Juan.

"Pilar," Jack said, drawing her attention. "What are you thinking?"

She took a deep breath and glanced at Mr. Dunn. He was watching her with interest, but no longer glaring at her like she was guilty. "I'm just worried about Juan. I want to go look for him. What if he's home? What if it's like Mr. Dunn said and we just got separated?"

"We'll go there first. Check out your place and make sure Juan isn't there. Then we'll go somewhere safe."

"You're going to go with me?" she squeaked. She wasn't sure she could handle that. A man like Mr. Dunn, a man who would protect her but keep her at a distance, was safer. A man like Jack, someone who plied her with jokes and made her want to trust him, he was dangerous.

"I don't have to, but that was the plan. There are others who can go with you," Jack said calmly.

Her gaze flickered to Mr. Dunn, who sat back and watched their exchange. Of course, he saw her looking at him.

"We assumed you'd be most comfortable with Jack since you allowed him to bring you here. If you're not comfortable with him, I can assign someone else to go with you."

Pilar thought about it for a second, then shook her head. It made sense. She trusted Jack more than she trusted Mr. Dunn, and she hadn't met anyone else. She would have to keep her walls up. She had very little doubt part of his task was to find out everything he could about Juan and Carlos. If she was going to get her brother back alive, she needed to make sure that didn't happen. There was no way men like them would be interested in saving a cartel falcon.

JACK HELD the door for Pilar while she climbed back into the SUV. He scanned the parking area, making sure no one was there with them, then closed the door quickly so he knew she was safe.

He jogged around to the driver's side and climbed in, then started up the vehicle. His own truck was parked a few spots away, but he wasn't taking any chances. The company SUVs were equipped with bulletproof glass and GPS. He knew the GPS was a risk because it could be hacked, but it was worth the risk to make sure his team always knew where he was.

He backed out of the spot and was about to leave the garage when he remembered he shouldn't know where Pilar lived. "What's your address?"

She rattled it off for him to key into the vehicle. He hit go and listened to the automated voice tell him what he already knew.

Pilar was silent for a few minutes. Jack watched her out of the corner of his eye. He debated saying something to her, but he didn't know what. He wasn't known for being a great conversationalist. He could make people laugh, but he didn't think that was what she needed at the moment. She wanted reassurances that her brother would be okay, and Jack couldn't give them to her.

"Do you think he was right?" she finally asked softly.

"Who?"

"Mr. Dunn. Do you think he's right about my brother? That he's working with Carlos again?"

Jack started to shake his head, but that could reveal too much. He fucking hated having to lie to her. Jack was a lot of things, but a liar wasn't one of them. Not usually. "It's a possibility. You seem pretty sure he's not, though. Why are you asking me?"

Pilar shrugged and leaned against the door. "Nothing about this feels right. Juan has been so careful since we moved here. Everything he's done has been under the radar. Until today when he wanted to go to the parade. It doesn't make any sense."

Jack squeezed the steering wheel. If he told her, she would feel better, but she wouldn't trust him. In order for them to get what they needed, she had to trust him. So he kept his mouth shut and said the only thing he could. "Maybe he thought the threat was over. That Carlos wasn't going to come looking for him." He paused, debating his next words but knowing he had to ask them. "Do you really think Carlos is here for you?"

Pilar's gaze jerked to his. She hesitated for a second, then nodded. "I do. Juan said Carlos never stopped trying to find a way to come after me. He knew where I was during school and my first year working, but their bosses wouldn't let him leave the country. It was too big of a risk. When Juan left, it pissed them off. I guess the risk became worth it."

"But you think Carlos's boss sent him up here to find you? Not your brother?"

She narrowed her eyes at him. "You think they were after Juan? But why?"

Jack shrugged, playing his part. If she pieced everything together, she might be able to figure out what Juan was going to turn over. She might be able to turn it over to them. As much as he hated the idea of not going after Juan full force, they hadn't established a level of trust in him that said he wasn't planning the entire thing all along. Jack had to operate as if Juan could be playing them.

No matter what his beautiful sister thought.

"Do you think he could still have the proof I gave him? Is it leverage to keep them away from us?" she asked, her voice hushed and scared.

Again, Jack shrugged. "I have no clue. I'm just surprised that Carlos grabbed your brother if he was really after you. He could have taken both of you, or just you, if you were his target."

Pilar stared out her window again and chewed on her lip. She stayed that way until Jack pulled up in front of the four unit condo building she lived in. He hadn't ever been inside, but he'd seen enough pictures of the place to know every inch of it.

Jack got out and went around to Pilar's door. He opened it and smiled at her when she finally met his gaze. The emotions were starting to pile up on her. Exhaustion was sneaking in around the edges of her eyes and tightening her mouth. It had been hours since her brother disappeared, and she was feeling it.

Jack held out a hand for her to take as she slid out of the tall SUV. She was tiny standing next to him, almost a foot shorter than his six-four height. He'd never had the desire to wrap a woman in his arms and take away all her fears, but when Pilar looked up at him, her dark brown eyes searching his gaze, he ached to do just that.

"Let's go inside," he said instead of acting on his desire. She was getting to him. It was supposed to be the other way around, with him getting to her. He was the one who needed information, not to fess up to all his secrets. But she disarmed him with every look, and fighting his attraction to her wasn't easy.

He just needed to get through the next few days. They'd find Juan and get what they needed to take down the whole operation, then Jack and Pilar would never have to cross paths again.

She nodded, breaking the connection between them, and led the way to the building. She unlocked the front door and headed for unit three upstairs on the left.

Jack scanned the building the entire time, checking for anything out of the ordinary. The other units were closed with no signs of forced entry. The hallways were quiet. A muffled TV played in the unit across the hall from Pilar and Juan's, but there was nothing that concerned Jack.

Pilar unlocked her apartment and stepped inside before she turned on the lights, then gasped.

"Shit," Jack breathed, taking in the space. Every cushion on the couch was sliced. The TV and computer on the dining room table were both smashed. Papers were scattered everywhere in the small space. It was a mess.

"Stay with me, Pilar," Jack said, moving into the apartment. He closed and locked the door behind them and drew his gun. With it pointed toward the hallway, he moved toward the only bedroom.

Pilar pressed close to him, her breathing rapid and loud as he strained to listen for movement in the bedroom. The closer he got, the closer she pressed to him until her breasts squished against his back and distracted him from what he was doing.

Jack stopped and grabbed one of her hands with his. He wrapped it around his waist, letting her get as close as she needed to be. Her breath hitched, her entire body pressing to his back, and she wrapped her other arm around him.

They moved as one, slowly walking toward the back of the apartment. Jack held his breath to stop breathing her in and keep his focus, measuring every step so he didn't tip off anyone who was still inside.

The bedroom was dark, but thankfully empty. The shower curtain fluttered, but when Jack whipped it aside, no one was hiding there either. Pilar still held on to him, her body trembling as they moved through the space. He went back to the kitchen and checked the laundry room, then slid his gun back into the holster and took a breath.

"No one's here, Pilar. You're safe."

That was all it took for her to finally breakdown. She collapsed on the floor and sobbed, the sound shredding his resolve to keep his distance from her. Jack dropped next to her and reached for her, pulling her onto his lap and holding her while she cried.

He didn't know how long they sat there, but the voices in his ear said he needed to make a call before they all showed up and scared her even more. He pulled out his phone and tapped the screen to bring it to life. Seven texts and three missed calls already. He tapped the first one and held the phone to his ear.

"You fucking answer me when I call you," Dunn growled at him.

"Someone was here, boss," Jack said, not tipping Pilar off that he was still connected to the team through the listening device in his ear. "No signs of forced entry, but the place is trashed. Couch is sliced, everything tossed. They didn't go for subtle."

"Something is there. Or they found it and we'll get a body," Dunn said, swearing.

Jack glanced at Pilar, who was still crying, and hoped she couldn't hear the other end of their conversation. "Agreed. We're going to get some clothes for her and go. Send in a team to search the place."

Dunn agreed to send a team in and hung up. Jack rubbed Pilar's back. She'd quieted, but he knew she wasn't done being upset.

"You want to grab a few things and we can get out of here?" Jack finally asked.

She nodded, moving back and out of his arms. She stood stiffly, her actions wooden and awkward. She glanced back at him when she went toward the bedroom and nibbled her lip. "Will you, um…"

"You want me to come with you or do you want privacy to get your stuff?" he asked, reading her thoughts.

"Will you come with me?" she whispered, her voice raw and shaky.

Jack nodded and followed her, glancing around the room as he went. Normally, he'd be one of the guys sent in to clean up a place like this. English would be there to scan for any surveillance, but Dunn and Dex were likely to be the ones searching the place. Going through every item and hoping something crucial was overlooked.

Jack followed Pilar into the one bedroom. A double bed sat in the middle of the room, one he knew she slept in alone. Juan stayed on the couch so he could keep his sister safe. There were definitely things about him that made Jack trust him, or at least not distrust him entirely.

Pilar grabbed a duffle bag from the closet and tossed it

on her bed. She glanced up at Jack and asked, "How long should I pack for?"

Jack drew in a breath and shrugged. "I don't know. Let's say a week and hope it isn't that long."

Her breath hitched again, likely imagining her brother gone for that long and the things Carlos would do to him. Jack could only hope she'd see her brother alive again. He knew the chances weren't great unless Juan was working with Carlos. Neither option was good.

Pilar grabbed a few items from her closet and added them to the bag, then moved to her drawers. She started at the top and screamed when she opened the first one, dropping to the bed with her hand over her mouth.

4

———

"WHAT HAPPENED?" JACK ASKED, MOVING TOWARD PILAR with a hand on his hip.

She couldn't speak. Her eyes watered as she sat on the edge of her bed, fear flooding every vein in her body.

"What the hell is that?" Jack asked.

"It's a cactus flower," Pilar said, finally finding her voice.

"What's a cactus flower? And why is it in your drawer?"

"Carlos," she whispered. "He used to bring them to me. He always told me they reminded him of us. Something beautiful from something ugly. I never understood why he said that. Not until I found out who he really was."

"Fuck," Jack breathed. He looked around the room. "We need to get out of here, Pilar. As soon as possible."

She nodded and slammed the drawer closed, leaving the offending flower, and all her underwear, behind. She couldn't bring herself to pack anything in that drawer. Not when Carlos could have touched any of it. She couldn't bear the thought of him ever touching her panties again.

"I can't," she stammered. "I don't know what to bring."

"Tennis shoes. Sweatpants. T-shirts. Comfortable clothes. It's going to be really boring."

She nodded, realizing he had no clue what she was talking about. She went to the next drawer and grabbed the first few t-shirts, barely seeing which ones they were, then snatched pajamas and tossed in a few pairs of socks. She hated going without panties, but she preferred that to wearing anything Carlos might have had his hands on.

Pilar grabbed the book from her nightstand and her Bible from the shelf, then on instinct, grabbed the book Juan gave her for Christmas. She hadn't read it yet, and if she was going to be locked up for a week, she had time.

She added a charger for her phone and her toothbrush and a bag of stuff for the shower and decided she was ready. She zipped up her bag and threw it over her shoulder. She was really looking forward to sinking into her bed after the day she had, but she knew she wouldn't sleep. Especially after finding Carlos's flower.

Jack grabbed her bag and led the way out of the building, pausing before every corner and acting like someone was going to jump out at them. The sad thing was someone might.

Pilar stayed close to Jack and was more than a little relieved when he walked her to her door and stood there until she was closed inside the shiny black SUV. He jogged around to his side and tossed her bag in the backseat before he started up the vehicle and drove off.

"Are you okay with one stop before we go?" he asked after a minute.

Pilar nodded. The urge to laugh bubbled up inside her. She was at his mercy, literally. She blindly put her trust in a guy she met on the street and was allowing him to take her to a safe house. He was driving her around, had been inside her home, and was protecting her. Now, he was asking if she minded if they made a stop. What if she said no?

The laugh inside Pilar popped out of her mouth with a muffled snort. Jack glanced sideways at her, his eyebrows narrowed. The look made another bubble pop.

She tried to push it down, but it kept coming. One little burst led to two and six and twenty, and before long, Pilar was heaving for breath as she rocked with her laughter.

"Are you okay?" Jack asked. His voice was concerned, and when she looked at him, he looked terrified.

Which only made her laugh harder.

Pilar couldn't talk. She couldn't even breathe. The entire day had been a complete mindfuck, and she was sitting in an SUV with a complete stranger who thought she was unhinged.

She probably was. And the whole thing made her start laughing all over again.

Jack finally pulled the SUV to a stop and turned in his seat. "Pilar? What's so funny?"

She shook her head, unable to explain it to him. But the longer he looked at her, that crease between his eyebrows and his down-turned lips, lips she wanted to kiss, the less funny the whole thing was.

Then reality came crashing down on her again. She was the least trusting person on the planet, and she put all her faith in a man who insisted he could be trusted. She was doing the same thing with Jack that she did with Carlos. Buying all his lines without finding out for sure if he was the good guy he claimed to be.

She saw the way Jack looked at Mr. Dunn. He said he was his boss, but what person spoke to their boss the way he did? Were they really Carlos's people? Was he leading her into a trap?

Everything came down on her at once, and she went from laughing to panicking. She struggled to draw a breath. The events from the day flashed through her mind. Juan's smile. Carlos's sneer. Jack's narrowed eyes. The flower. The conference room. The SUV.

"Pilar?" Jack said again, his voice louder but muffled.

She glanced at him. That crease was deeper. His mouth opened, but no sound came out. He reached for her, but she couldn't let him touch her. She didn't know him.

She scrambled for the handle and threw herself out of the SUV. She nearly smashed her face on the asphalt in her rush to get away from him. The handle. It was still in her hand. She let go and pushed away from the vehicle. She had to get to safety. She had to find Juan. Stop Carlos.

Lights. She saw lights and moved toward them. People. Shopping carts. Red. She liked red. She went toward it. He couldn't get her with so many other people around.

Except Carlos took Juan in the middle of a parade. A fucking parade. How did someone get kidnapped at a parade? Unless he was working with Carlos again. He went willingly.

No. She shook her head. Juan wouldn't do that. He said he was done. He wouldn't lie to her. He knew how important it was to her that he not lie. After Carlos, she couldn't handle lies. Juan wouldn't lie.

Pilar wandered through the store, barely seeing anything as she went. Food. Yes, she was hungry. She grabbed something frozen and clutched it to her chest. She needed to eat. An umbrella. It was going to rain tomorrow. And sneakers. She needed sneakers, but she couldn't remember why. They were pretty. Pink and sparkly. She liked them.

She went to the front door and stared at it. There was

something else she was supposed to do, but she couldn't remember what it was.

She walked outside again. Now what?

JACK FOLLOWED Pilar through the store. She was in shock. He understood it. She wasn't someone used to the things she faced that day. It was only a matter of time before she broke.

He should have gone straight to the safe house when she started laughing, but he didn't realize how bad she was until she ran from him.

He didn't understand why she picked up the things she did, but he didn't question it. He grabbed a sweatshirt from a rack on their way in, then saw a pair of basketball shorts in their lap around. He could wear his jeans for a few days if he had something to sleep in. There were clothes at the safe house, but he wasn't sure exactly what. Thankfully, there were baskets with multipacks of underwear near the walkways. He grabbed one for each of them, hoping he got the right size for her. He'd never bought a woman underwear before.

When she headed for the door, he grabbed a cashier and asked her to scan everything before Pilar left. Thankfully, she was quick on her feet and grabbed one of the things people used for a gift registry. Jack added the few things he picked up and paid cash for the whole thing, leaving the change behind when Pilar walked outside alone.

It was only a matter of time before she passed out completely. Jack managed to get her to the SUV and into the front seat. He buckled her seatbelt and slid into his seat.

She stared straight out the window at the blackness surrounding them. Jack stayed quiet. He didn't know if she was afraid of him or just overwhelmed, but he had to assume it was both. If she heard his voice, she could freak out again.

He drove north, away from the city of Niagara Falls and into the quiet country town where the safe house was. Everything was dark, but Jack knew the way well. Every week, one of them was up there to check on the house. They all knew how important it was to keep a safe house safe, but that meant they had to make sure no one was there who shouldn't be.

Jack pulled onto the road cut in the middle of the trees. It was small enough that if you didn't know it was there, you'd miss it. The trees closed in around them, swallowing up the bright headlights as Jack drove away from the highway.

A mile down the road, a small cabin came into view. It was rustic and looked worn down, but both were by design. The security system surrounding the cabin was state of the art, as was the solar system that ran it. They couldn't take a chance with the house being on the grid, so they created their own power supply. The cabin also had well water and satellite internet. The only TV was a collection of movies and an old DVD player.

When Jack first went out there, he never imagined the cabin would feel small. He loved being surrounded by nature and the cozy feel of the place. He grew up on his parents' soybean farm in a huge home that always felt like it was for show. Behind closed doors, his parents were simple people, but they had appearances to keep up. Jack never understood it and got out as soon as he could.

Jack shook off thoughts of his parents as he grabbed Pilar's stuff and his shopping bag from the backseat. He left the lights on so he would be able to unlock the front door, then turned off the truck and climbed out. He ran to the door and jammed his key in the lock. He turned it just in time, the door opening as the SUV's lights blinked off, plunging them into darkness.

Pilar's scream was audible from outside the truck. Jack tossed their stuff inside and ran back to get her. He yanked open her door, but she fought him, pushing away from him and kicking at him. She landed a blow to his stomach and got in a good slap on his jaw before he managed to wrap her up in his arms.

"Shh," he whispered in her ear, his lips pressed against the shell. He tried hard not to breathe her in, but failed. "I'm here, Pilar. You're safe, honey. Shh."

She stopped fighting him after a second, slowly going limp. He held her, rocking her back and forth until she was weightless in his arms.

Jack scooped her up and grabbed the things she was holding on her lap during the drive. He kicked the door closed and locked the SUV, then headed for the house.

He took Pilar straight to the bedroom after locking the front door. He eased her onto the bed where she immediately curled onto her side. He debated taking off her shoes or covering her up, but eventually decided against both in case the movement woke her up. She needed her sleep.

Jack left the bedroom, closing the door enough that she would have privacy and quiet but leaving it open a crack just in case. He put away the things they picked up at the store and dug out his phone.

More missed calls and texts. Fuck.

Before he could listen to messages or reply to texts, his phone rang again. "Yeah?"

"If it wasn't for English, I'd think you were dead. What the hell is going on?"

Jack sighed. He knew Dunn was just doing his job, but the guy had lost it since Williams turned on all of them. They used to trust each other to get the job done. Now, Dunn was constantly questioning all of them like he was waiting for the next betrayal.

"She freaked out. All of this finally hit her. She walked around Target like a damn zombie and walked out without paying for things. And that was after she laughed hysterically for a good five minutes."

"Shit," Dunn breathed.

"Yeah."

"How is she now?"

Jack glanced at the door. "Passed out finally. She tried to kick my ass."

Dunn snorted. "Did she succeed?"

Jack huffed a laugh. "No, but she got in a few good blows."

"You probably deserved it for something," Dunn joked.

Jack nodded, knowing his boss was right. A few hits were the least of what he deserved for his sins.

"Are you in for the night?" Dunn asked.

"Yeah. I'm going to grab one of the meals in the freezer and cook some dinner, then a movie and try to forget I'm in the middle of nowhere and standing guard over a woman who doesn't trust me."

"Sounds good."

"Hey, did you find anything at the apartment?"

"Not what we need. They tore the place apart, though. I'm guessing since we don't have a body, they didn't find what they were looking for."

"So, what's next?"

"Try to find him," Dunn said, sounding more than a little pissed off. "We have no leads. Cameras in that area didn't show anything with all the people around. They blocked Juan from every view we had."

"Almost like someone knew?" Jack asked.

Dunn drew a breath. "Yeah. We have to consider it. We've been at this for months and he hasn't given us much to go on. Never enough to bring them down."

"We've stopped a few shipments," Jack defended.

"Yeah, but not in over a month. And stopping shipments is small compared to everything else. They can re-route trucks and we have nothing. We need the rest of the info from him."

"All he wanted was a guarantee of safety for his sister," Jack growled. "Even if he died." At the time, he was one of the ones who debated if it was worth it. Juan said he had enough information to take down the cartel and their US aid, but making guarantees was tough when there was no proof.

"Well, now he has it," Dunn said.

Jack sucked in a breath and glanced at the door to the bedroom again. Dunn was right. Juan got exactly what he wanted. Pilar was in protection.

"We don't know what's really going on. She seems like she's in the dark, but if she had proof about Carlos, she probably knows more than we realize. If Juan is gone, she's our new lead. You have to keep her safe."

The thought of anything happening to her made Jack squeeze his fist shut. He would protect her with his life.

"I got it."

"Yeah, I know you do. We'll keep you posted. And Slade's on call tonight. He'll be watching you all night. Keep the monitors on."

Jack looked at the desk set up in the living room. It ran the security for the entire property, from sensors at the road to motion detectors through the woods surrounding their cabin. If anything moved out there, they'd know about it.

"Got it," Jack said. "We'll be fine."

"I know. And thanks, Jack. I know this is the last job you wanted, but you're the best option."

Jack nodded. "Hooyah."

5

Sausage. Spices. Pasta. Mmm, it smelled good.

Pilar grinned in her sleep, surprised and thrilled that her brother was cooking. Juan was always happy to let her do it all. She never minded, though. She was just happy to have him with her again.

She rolled over and looked at the clock, then jolted upright. Her clock wasn't on her nightstand because her nightstand wasn't there. The room she was in had wood paneling instead of soft gray paint. There was a metal shelf with sheets and a bin of toiletries instead of a dresser full of her clothes.

Her dresser. The one with the cactus flower in it. Carlos. It wasn't a nightmare. Well, it was, but it was also her reality.

Which meant Juan wasn't the one cooking cajun sausage and pasta. It was her new roommate and protector. Her sexy new roommate and protector, but that didn't matter. They were only there until he found her brother.

Juan.

The sharp pain through her heart had her clutching her chest. She couldn't lose her brother. She thought he was gone years ago, when she found out who he was and stopped talking to him. It broke her heart, but she refused to turn her head. He swore to her he'd changed. She couldn't lose him again.

A soft whistle reached her ears, a tune she vaguely recognized. Her lips curled up in a grin that finally had her climbing from the bed. Her shoes were still on, and her clothes were rumpled but all present. It was one more thing that made her smile, especially when she really wasn't sure how she got into the room in the first place.

She walked out into the main room of the small house, glancing around at the space. She could see all of it from where she stood, from the front door through the tiny kitchen and across to the couch in front of a TV playing Die Hard. A fireplace crackled with a low burning fire, giving the place a cozy feel. Curtains were drawn over dark windows.

"Hey, you're up," Jack said from the kitchen with a grin. "Darn. I was hoping I could eat all this by myself."

Pilar looked at the pan on the stove where he was stirring what looked like enough food for four people instead of just two. She smiled, still feeling out of sorts. "I don't eat much."

He shook his head. "Then we need to change that. I can't have you getting too skinny on my watch."

Pilar ran a hand down her hips and rolled her eyes. "Not much chance of that happening."

Jack snorted. "That's good. I'd hate to let down men everywhere by taking away all your curves."

"Are you flirting with me?" Pilar asked, narrowing her eyes.

Jack shook his head, his smile fading. "No. I apologize. I've gotten in the habit of telling the truth and sometimes it's too much. I didn't mean to offend you."

Pilar smiled faintly. If he only knew how much she wished he was hitting on her. She was the nerdy kid growing up, the girl who wore glasses and had her hand up first for every question the teacher asked.

Nothing changed when she finally talked her parents into getting her contacts and she learned to let someone else feel smart. She was already awkward and shy, especially around guys.

She took enough psych classes in college to understand that was part of why she was so drawn to Carlos. He flirted with her and made her feel beautiful instead of awkward. He wanted her, a feeling she'd never experienced before. She shouldn't have fallen for it, but she did. He was so easy to love. He made sure of it.

"Listen," Jack said, bringing her back to the room she was standing in the middle of, "I know we don't know each other, so why don't we start from scratch here. Get to know each other. We're going to be stuck sharing a bathroom and with only each other for company for a little while. We might as well make the most of it. I promise not to hit on you, and you can promise not to..."

He trailed off like he was waiting for her to come up with something. She definitely didn't know him well enough to know where his buttons were, but he had badass bachelor written all over him.

"I promise not to tell all your friends that you put the toilet seat down to pee."

His eyes widened comically before a grin split his face. The dark stubble on his cheeks made him look older, but when he smiled, his green eyes lit up and he looked a decade younger than she assumed he was.

"You're cruel. I can't have them thinking I piss sitting down, so I'll take that deal." He added a wink to let her know he was in on the joke, then waved her over to the stove. "I grew up in Georgia, and we have a tendency to over-spice things. I tried to go easy on it, but most of the guys tell me my food is too hot. I can make something else if this is too spicy for you."

Pilar smirked at him. "You're just hoping you can get the whole thing for yourself. Nice try, amigo, but I like spicy foods. Caliente."

Jack shook his head and lifted an eyebrow. "Well then, dish it up, Ms. Luna."

Pilar grabbed one of the bowls next to the pan and scooped a healthy serving into it. Her stomach rumbled at the scent, and her mouth watered, ready for a taste.

She glanced around the room as she made her way to the couch, the only seating in the place. She took one end of the couch, tucking her feet up underneath her as she settled in to watch the movie.

Jack joined her a minute later and handed over a bottle of water. She smiled in gratitude and blew on the bite she had ready.

She felt the weight of his stare as she slid the bite into her mouth. The pasta was cooked to perfection with just the tiniest crunch to it. The sausage melted in her mouth, a crisp on the edges giving her something to bite into. The flavors were unique but delicious. And definitely spicy. She loved it.

"Stop looking at me," she said through her teeth. "I'm not running to spit it out."

Jack chuckled and finally settled back on his side of the couch and dug in to his dinner.

They ate in companionable silence while Bruce Willis worked his way through the skyscraper to find all the hostages and bring the bad guys to justice. Pilar never saw much appeal to the movie when she was younger, but she couldn't help but hope the man sitting next to her had some of the same skills and could kick ass as well as Bruce did.

"We'll find him," Jack said after he finished his second bowl.

Pilar nodded. "I hope so."

Jack gave her a small smile. "Tell me your favorite memory of your brother from when you were kids."

Pilar smiled, picturing Juan's floppy dark hair and goofy, crooked grin. He was always getting into trouble, skipping school and doing things she would never dream of doing. Where Pilar got straight A's and followed every rule, her brother was lucky if he passed and broke more rules than Pilar knew about.

"Juan's three years older than me, so when I was in my first year of high school, he was a senior. He was always trying to get me to break the rules with him, but I refused, so one day, he walked with me to school, but when we got there, he left. Halfway through second period, I got a phone call from the office that said I was needed at home right away. It wasn't unusual for kids in our town to be pulled out of school, but it hadn't happened to me yet, so I was nervous. I was on my way home when he pulled up next to me in our neighbor's tractor. He stole it and made me go with him to the stream that ran behind our property. We spent the whole day playing in the water and dreaming about our future."

Jack was silent for a long minute. "That sounds like a great day."

Pilar nodded. "It was. I never skipped school again, but it was a perfect day."

"Did your parents ever find out?"

She laughed. "No, they didn't. Juan took the tractor back, and we walked home, and our parents had no clue."

Jack stared at the credits rolling up the screen. "You were lucky to have him growing up. He sounds like he was a great brother."

Pilar nodded. "He still is a great brother."

Jack nodded sharply. "That's what I meant."

Pilar pressed her lips together and nodded. She hated that he sounded like Juan was already gone. She couldn't believe that. She couldn't have Jack believing that either.

"You will find him, right?"

Jack met her eyes and nodded. "We'll do everything we can to find your brother, Pilar. I promise you that."

She drew in a breath and closed her eyes. That was all she needed to hear.

JACK WASN'T sure what to do with Pilar. Cooking dinner was a matter of survival. Watching a movie was easy since there was nothing else to do. At least, nothing he thought was a good idea.

But when the movie ended, and they were sitting there talking, he didn't know how to handle himself. He was the idiot who said they should get to know each other, but with every word out of her mouth, he wanted to know even more.

"Did you like growing up in Mexico?" Jack asked.

Pilar shrugged. "I didn't know any different. It wasn't like I saw what people outside my town grew up like. Not until I went to college. And even then, I didn't get into people's personal lives."

"You seem like you're pretty quiet."

Pilar nodded. "I am. Although, I'm surprised you think that after how many times I've yelled at you today."

She laughed, a sound that tightened his chest. He hated lying to her. He hated lying in general. Lies cost people things. "True, but this is a high-stress situation. You withdraw a lot. When you're thinking or processing. That's not a bad thing."

She cocked her head and looked closely at him. "I have a feeling you're the same way."

A smile tilted his lips. She was perceptive. "Most people don't see that."

She grinned. "I'm not most people. I'm an occupational therapist. My job is to see the things people don't always want me to see."

Jack nodded. "So, in other words, I won't be able to hide anything from you."

She started to grin, but it fell just as quickly as it began. "I don't like people who withhold the truth. I had enough of that with Carlos and my brother."

Jack nodded solemnly. The last thing he wanted to do was remind her of Carlos, but he had a job to do. He had to find out if she knew anything.

"I wouldn't do that to you." He paused, as though gathering his thoughts. He understood psychology, too. "Obviously you and Carlos were close."

She scoffed. "I thought we were. I never really knew him, though."

"So you weren't involved in his business?"

She shook her head quickly. "No. Of course not. I told you, I had proof of what he did, but Juan took it."

"What did he tell you he was going to do with that?"

"The video?"

Jack nodded, carefully keeping his features neutral. She

didn't reveal it was a video before. That was good information.

She shrugged. "He didn't say. He just said he'd take care of it."

"But he never did."

Pilar shook her head. "No. But he shipped me back to my aunt and uncle the next day, and told me never to return to Mexico. To our home."

Jack shifted closer. "Why?"

She drew in a breath. "When Juan found out about Carlos and me, he flipped out. He told me I needed to stay away from Carlos. When I told him..." She looked away and drew in a ragged breath. "When I told him I was in love with Carlos, he told me to leave Mexico. That Carlos was an evil man who would have me killed if I ever decided to leave him, but he couldn't touch me if I left the country."

"Did he say how he knew?"

Pilar nodded. "He told me he was the same as Carlos, and that it wasn't safe for me to be there. That if I didn't leave, I would be dead. It was the first time Juan admitted to me what he was really involved in."

Jack blew out a breath and ran a hand through his hair. He'd seen some shitty stuff in his time with the Teams. He'd taken more lives than probably Carlos and Juan combined. But he took out people who were a threat to innocent civilians and the world at large. He slept well at night knowing the people he killed were researched and targeted for a reason.

Killing was a sport for the cartel. It was something they used to train new recruits. Targeting innocent families and betrayers. Juan was right to get Pilar out of the country, but she never took any precautions after that. She didn't go to the authorities and ask for help. Because her brother took away the one and only leverage she had.

"Anyway," Pilar continued, "I haven't been back to Mexico since. I didn't see my brother for years. When he showed up again, I thought I was imagining him. It was the happiest day of my life."

"And he said he was out? That he was done with all the cartel stuff?"

Pilar nodded, a ghost of a smile on her face. "He did. He was free. He said he'd paid off some debt to them, and he was able to go on and live his life without fear."

He was lying.

Jack hated the thought, but it was the truth. There was no paying off the cartel and getting away with your freedom. The only way out was in a body bag. Something Jack had a feeling Juan and Pilar were going to learn before the whole thing was over.

"If that was true," Jack said gently, "then why did they take him?"

She shook her head. "That's why I know Carlos is really after me. He knows I'd do anything for my brother. I'll even trade my life for his, if he asks me. I'd go with him if it meant Juan was free and safe. So I know they're here for me. There's no other reason."

Jack nodded, but he wanted to shout. This woman, this sweet, beautiful, amazing woman, was willing to give up herself, her life, her body, her mind, to save the brother who betrayed her over and over again.

Dunn was wrong. Pilar wasn't in on any of this. She was completely in the dark about everything Juan was doing. When he came to them, he said no one else was involved, but he demanded protection for his sister, whether he was alive or dead. Dunn dragged his heels, assuming Pilar had the same knowledge, but she was innocent. The only thing she did was fall in love with the wrong man.

Just like Meredith when she thought Jack was a man who could actually love her back.

Jack was no better than Carlos. He was a killer who didn't deserve the love of an amazing woman. But Jack would do anything in his power to keep Pilar safe. He couldn't save Meredith, but he could save Pilar. He would save her.

6

———

Jack watched Pilar's back a little while later as she disappeared into the bedroom. He wanted to call Dunn and tell him what he found out, but she could overhear the conversation. Instead, Jack settled for a quick text that he hoped would explain everything.

She doesn't know anything.

He tucked his phone away and set about cleaning up the kitchen. It was a pet peeve of his that things were left for morning, something ingrained in him since childhood. When he was done, he grabbed a bottle of water from the fridge and went back to the couch.

Without the option to flip channels, Jack put on another movie and tried to lose himself in the Adam Sandler comedy. His mind kept returning to the things Pilar said. All the tiny pieces of information they didn't know.

She loved Carlos.

Juan lied to her.

Juan told her to leave the country.

Juan was tight-lipped about his sister, and for good reason. They all assumed she was as mired in the bullshit as he was, but Pilar was just a woman who made a bad choice in a guy. Jack couldn't fault her for that anymore than he could fault any of the woman who'd fallen for him. He knew how easy it was for a woman to believe what she wanted to believe about a man, especially when the man wasn't trying to convince her he was wrong for her.

And even if he was.

Jack rested his head on the back of the couch and closed his eyes. Meredith had haunted his dreams for months. She wasn't particularly memorable when they were together, something he knew was shitty to think, but it was true. He never bothered to distinguish one woman from another. He never got involved with more than one at a time, but he never got attached either.

Meredith had different plans, though. She thought she was the one woman who could change Jack. She joked about it, and he was stupid enough to think she really was joking.

When he told her he was leaving, and not to wait for him, she was upset. She cried and begged him to come back to her. He thought she was worried about him. He was placating and said he'd be fine, but she pressed.

She told him she loved him, and he laughed it off. When he left, he knew he'd never see her again. He ignored her calls and deleted her voicemails, knowing it wouldn't do her any good to hang on to him. A clean break. He always went with that.

But Meredith was different. He didn't realize it until it was too late. Until he found out she suffered from depression and had taken her own life.

That deployment was the worst one of Jack's life. Not

only was he dragging around Meredith's ghost, but Rodney died and the whole Team seemed to fall apart. He imagined himself a lifer, but when the others decided to walk, he was more than willing to go with them.

A loud laugh on the screen drew Jack's attention back to the present. Thinking about Meredith always meant he was going to have a sleepless night, and with a woman to protect in the next room, Jack couldn't afford that.

He longed for a beer to take the edge off, but that was dangerous when he was the one in charge of making sure Pilar was safe. It wouldn't have mattered, though, because they didn't keep beer in the safe house. Team rule. They couldn't risk losing focus, so they kept all temptation away.

The door to the bedroom opened, and temptation herself walked out. Pilar wore a dark t-shirt that was so thin it was nearly see-through. A pair of shorts peeked out from beneath. Jack had gone far too long without bringing a woman to his bed, and Pilar was definitely testing his resolve.

Right until he looked at her face.

"What's wrong?" he asked, standing and moving toward her.

She nibbled her lip and shook her head. "Nothing. I'm having trouble sleeping is all."

"You look terrified."

She swallowed roughly. "I am," she whispered as though the admission cost her.

He cupped her elbow, ignoring how soft her skin felt in his palm, and guided her to the couch. Then he grabbed a fresh bottle of water and brought it to her. She smiled up at him and took the water, sipping at it.

"Want to finish the movie with me?" he asked, returning to his seat.

She settled against the cushions and nodded. Jack pulled the blanket he intended to sleep under over their legs, a move that felt more intimate than he intended. She smiled in thanks and pulled the blanket up to her chin.

Jack watched Pilar almost as much as he watched the movie. She laughed softly at the funny parts, like she was afraid to feel real joy. At one point, she turned to Jack, her eyes wide with fear.

"Do you think he'll find me here?"

Jack immediately shook his head. "No. This place is safe. No one knows it's here."

"Are you sure?"

Jack reached under the blanket for her hand and found her leg. Their eyes locked, and a flash of desire ignited between them. Jack pulled his hand out and held it out, palm up, for her to place hers in his.

Pilar drew in a breath and set her hand in his, her gaze flicking from their joined hands to his eyes.

"I promise you, Pilar, I'll keep you safe."

She nodded once, then leaned toward him, his hand still clasped in hers.

They sat like that on the couch, holding hands, until the movie ended. Since neither of them were asleep, Jack put a new movie on and went back to his spot on the couch.

They both reached for the other's hand once he was settled. Jack grinned at her. Her hand felt right in his, her small palm enveloped in his larger one. He wanted to pull her closer and wrap her up in his arms and tell her no one would ever hurt her again, but he wasn't the man for that job. He was horny and lonely and had a mountain of guilt piled on top of him. Taking care of a woman for longer than a few days was the last thing he could promise.

Slowly, Pilar's hand went slack in his. Her head rested

against the back of the couch, her mouth open slightly. Jack took the time to stare at her. Long lashes looked even longer in the late night shadows. Her olive skin glowed. Her lips were a delicate bow, and plump and perfect. Even her nose was cute.

The blanket slipped off her shoulder, exposing the edge of her neck down to the line of her t-shirt. He could tell she wasn't wearing a bra, and the knowledge made him hard. She was his type. Short and curvy. He loved a woman who would sit at a restaurant with him and actually eat dinner. He exercised constantly, and he wouldn't say no to a woman that wanted to run with him, but he also didn't mind a woman who stayed in bed waiting for him to come home from his run.

But none of that mattered because he wasn't going to have any woman in his bed. Not until he knew he wouldn't end up with another dead ex on his conscience. Because it didn't matter what anyone said, he was to blame for Meredith's death. And he couldn't handle losing Pilar, or anyone else.

Jack tugged the blanket back up on Pilar, covering her again. She snuggled closer to him, her head falling to his shoulder. He knew he should take her back to the bedroom, but he couldn't bring himself to move her.

He was selfish. For the first time in far too long, he felt like he was doing something good for a woman. Instead of hurting her, he was helping her. He'd protect her and bring her brother back. And then they'd take down the cartel and she would truly be safe.

He leaned his cheek against her forehead and closed his eyes. Just for a minute, he'd let himself enjoy her. Then he'd get up and take her to the bedroom. And walk away.

CARLOS WAS NOT A PATIENT MAN. It was one of the reasons he was so good at what he did. He didn't wait for things to happen. He made them happen.

"Who was that man?" Carlos asked calmly as he stood over his former associate.

Juan was a low level nothing. He never had a stomach for the real work. He ran for them, transporting product on occasion and cozying up to the police, but he didn't like to get his hands dirty. Carlos saw it as a part of the job, a part he had no problem doing because the bosses liked him for it. He kept them from being involved, and Carlos had enough connections that no one ever came after him.

"I don't know," Juan muttered. He spit blood to the side, narrowly missing Carlos's boots.

"I'll break your jaw if you get blood on my boots," Carlos growled.

"Fuck you, Carlos."

Carlos stepped forward and backhanded Juan. The other man groaned and dropped his head to the side. There was a reluctant part of Carlos that was impressed Juan hadn't given up everything he asked for. He hadn't expected Juan to hang on so long.

"Where is Pilar?"

"Somewhere you'll never find her."

Carlos lifted an eyebrow. It was the closest Juan had come to admitting he knew where she was. "Why do you say that? Because you told her to hide?"

Juan shook his head. "Nope. I didn't tell her anything."

"So you set up a meeting with me and didn't tell your precious sister? You had to know I'd be coming for her, too. She was a sweet little thing. So tight and pretty when I fucked her the first time. I'd never been inside a woman like her. Better than a hit of the stuff we sell every day."

Juan glared at Carlos, but with his hands behind his back and his legs zip-tied to the chair, he couldn't actually do anything.

Carlos got up close to him, close enough that he could smell the reek of piss and sweat from the other man. "When I get her back, I'm going to fuck her until she bleeds. Make sure she knows better than to ever leave me again."

Juan jerked his head up quickly, narrowly missing smashing Carlos's nose. "Keep your dirty fucking hands off my sister! You stay away from her! I'll fucking kill you if you touch her!"

Carlos punched Juan in the stomach, knocking the wind from him so he stopped yelling. "You'll do no such thing, because you'll be dead by then. You thought you were so smart, but we knew where you were all along. Andres has been following you. He has people everywhere. You know this."

"My sister has nothing to do with any of it."

Carlos tsked. "But she does. She's my woman. I'm the one who took her virginity. She gave it to me willingly. She stained my bed with her blood, and no other man will ever have her."

"If you think she hasn't slept with another man, you're fooling yourself. She couldn't wait to get away from you and erase your tiny little cock from her memory."

Carlos drew in a breath. It wouldn't do him any good to lose his patience with Juan. He needed information from him, and Carlos was nothing if not a good soldier.

"Pilar hasn't been with another man. I know that. You didn't know I'd been fucking her for months, so why would I believe that you have any clue what she's doing now? No, she's mine alone. But that's not the only reason we're here. What did you do with the information you stole from us?"

Juan shrugged. "What information?"

"You know what information I'm talking about. We know you're the one who copied all of it."

Juan shook his head. "I don't know what you're talking about. I was just a falcon. And not a very good one, according to you."

Carlos grinned. "You weren't. I told Andres you couldn't be trusted, but he thought you were loyal. Now, he wants a gift."

Juan swallowed roughly, the cockiness finally gone. "What?"

"Oh, we'll get to that, eventually. First, you need to tell me what you know, what you've already told the authorities, and what you plan to share."

Juan shook his head. "I don't have anything."

"You're lying, and you know how I treat liars."

Juan's eyes widened comically. Carlos would find the whole thing amusing if his ass wasn't on the fucking line. Andres sent him to handle Juan after their shipments were picked up because the intel he got said the leak came from Juan's location. That info was being funneled through them. Andres blamed Carlos for fucking Pilar and pissing Juan off. He said it was all Carlos's fault.

He knew it wasn't. Juan was the fucker who couldn't handle his shit. He led him right to Pilar's bed when he brought Carlos home and introduced them. There was no way Carlos was going to pass up a chance at a sweet piece of ass like Juan's little sister. Juan was the asshole who created the whole mess.

But Carlos was smart enough not to tell Andres that. He had to clean up the mess, which meant Carlos had to get all the information from Juan and make sure their operation was safe.

"I didn't do anything," Juan said, quieter this time.

He was breaking down. His resolve was fading. Pilar was the one and only thing Juan cared about. Which meant Carlos had to find her. If she was no longer out there, free and available, then Juan would tell Carlos anything he wanted to know.

"I wonder if your sister would agree. Does Pilar have any information, I wonder? Maybe I should bring her here and ask her."

"Stay away from Pilar."

Carlos grinned. "I don't think I can do that. I love your sister, and I think it's time for our reunion. I've missed her. None of the other whores I've fucked have been nearly as satisfying as Pilar. My Pilar. I'll let her know you said hola, though. After I remind her who she belongs to."

"No! You can't! Leave her alone!"

Carlos laughed as he walked away, leaving Marcus and Cal to shut him up. He had a woman to find.

7

PILAR WAS HOT. UNBEARABLY. LIKE MEXICO ON A SUMMER DAY with no breeze kind of hot. She tried to move, but she was also pinned down.

And not alone.

Alarm flipped her eyes open. She didn't want to alert whoever was holding her down so she carefully scanned her surroundings. She was still in the small cabin in the woods with Jack.

She sucked in a deep breath and got way more than she bargained for. Spicy male scent flooded every cell in her body and instantly changed her alert from fearful to excited.

Jack. He was what was holding her down. Except it wasn't because he was trying to hurt her.

A loud rumble echoed around her as he drew in a loud snore. His breathing paused for a second, then he exhaled softly.

Pilar tried to ease her way off the couch, but they were linked. His arm was around her, his hand on her hip. One of her arms was around his waist, her elbow resting on his thighs. Her head was on his chest, his tilted back on the couch. One of his legs was in front of her, keeping her from rolling off the couch.

She was stuck.

She tried to move, hoping she could slide out without waking him up. She pulled her arm back first and accidentally brushed against the hard ridge in his jeans. Her cheeks flamed, but Jack didn't move. Thank God.

With her arm unwound from him, she hoped she could push herself up to kneel, then climb over his outstretched leg. The only problem was she had to put her hand between his legs on the couch in order to get leverage.

She closed her eyes and recited a Hail Mary, praying her patron saint would help her out and get her out of the mess she was in.

Pilar took a deep breath and set her hand between his legs, connecting with the soft cushion. Before she could think about it, she pushed back and swung her top leg over his, balancing on one knee and the other foot.

She looked up at him to make sure she didn't wake him up and gasped, nearly falling back to the couch.

"Nice moves," he said. His voice was all rough and raspy like men's voices were first thing in the morning.

It was more than a little sexy, and coupled with the erection now very visible since she'd dragged the blanket off him, she was in serious trouble. "I was trying not to wake you."

"I'm already up," he said, his gaze not leaving hers.

She wasn't so strong. Her eyes moved to his crotch, then quickly away. "Um, sorry. I didn't mean to..."

Jack stretched lazily and groaned. "This couch sucks. I was going to carry you back to the bed, but I must have fallen asleep. Sorry about that."

Pilar scrambled up, putting much needed distance

between her and the man doing all sorts of dangerous things to her insides. She crossed her arms over her chest to hide her embarrassingly hard nipples from his view.

Jack balled the blanket up and tossed it to the other end of the couch, then stood. He reached his arms over his head and stretched again, twisting one way then the other and rolling his head. "I need a run. Shit."

He turned away from her, taking the tent in his jeans with him, and headed for the bathroom. He closed the door, giving Pilar a blissful few minutes to herself to pull her shit together.

She went back to her room and grabbed a sweatshirt. The fire died out overnight, and it was colder inside than when they went to sleep. Pilar could hear a fan running, but the heat blowing into the bedroom was minimal.

She walked barefoot to the kitchen, wishing she thought to pack slippers. Barefoot was a way of life when she was growing up. She was so used to it that moving to a place where it got so cold was a harsh reality for her. She had to wear shoes year round in Niagara Falls since even the summer was cool for her. Plus, it was a city, not the country like she was used to.

Pilar started the coffee and opened the fridge. It was stocked with water and a few other things, mostly condiments. It left a lot to be desired. The freezer was a different story with frozen meals and enough food to last them a few days.

"We don't use this place much," Jack said, scaring her when he came up behind her. "No fresh food because it goes bad too quickly. We have a pretty good collection of canned and frozen stuff, though. What do you usually eat for breakfast?"

She forced a smile for him. "Eggs?"

He laughed. "Of course you do. We don't have any eggs."

"I know. It's fine. I can eat something else. What do you have?"

Jack gestured to the freezer, then opened a cabinet door to reveal a stock of non-perishable foods. "You're welcome to anything, but I'm happy to cook if you'd rather relax."

Pilar shook her head. "I need to do something. I'm kind of going crazy here knowing my brother is out there somewhere, and I'm just sitting here. Hiding."

"You're staying safe," he defended.

She smiled at him. "We both know I'm hiding. Your team is out there looking for my brother, and I'm in here, with the curtains drawn in a cabin off the grid where no one I know would ever think to look for me."

"I'm not going to let anything happen to you, Pilar."

She nodded. "Thank you. I appreciate that. Now let me cook something. Maybe you can try to get the fire going again. It's a little chilly in here."

He adjusted himself and nodded. She thought she heard, "I hadn't noticed," but she wasn't sure. Jack went outside, leaving her alone again to breathe and think. And cook.

JACK STOOD OUTSIDE and sucked in a deep breath. He'd never lived with a woman. Sure, he'd spent the night with more than a few, but moved in and lived together? Nope.

He knew that wasn't what he was doing with Pilar, but it was the closest he'd ever come. They were sharing a space, cooking for each other, brushing up against each other, sharing looks and touches and all sorts of things he hadn't shared before.

Like waking up with her arm resting on his hard cock and a hell of a peek down the front of her t-shirt. Jesus. He almost blew right then. Her up on all fours, ready for him to move behind her.

Fuck.

He ran a hand through his hair and tried to push the memory from his mind. He almost jerked off in the bathroom after that, but he knew he couldn't keep quiet if he did. There were things he was not willing to share with the strangers he was tasked with protecting. Like how fucking good her name would taste on his lips. Or any other part of her on his lips.

Nope. Not gonna happen. Not only would it jeopardize his job, but getting involved with her was a bad idea for a host of other reasons. The first of which was she already had enough baggage.

Jack scanned the small cleared yard for movement even though none of the alarms had gone off. He was sure they were blissfully alone, except for Slade watching his every move.

Jack lifted a hand to wave and took a deep breath. He walked around the side to where the wood for the fireplace was stored and found the pile pitifully low. He groaned and shook his head. As much as he loved to run, chopping wood was something he hated. Sure, it was rhythmic and monotonous, but he didn't get to go anywhere. It was standing in one place and swinging an axe.

Since going for a run was out of the question, Jack accepted his fate and grabbed the axe. He headed over to the stack of logs neatly piled at the edge of the clearing. A stump covered in a thin layer of dew was right in front of the stack, ready for him to beat to hell with every swing of his axe.

Jack had just put the first of the logs on the stump when his phone buzzed in his pocket. He wanted to ignore it, but he couldn't take the chance it was Slade calling with an issue or Dunn with an update.

He tossed the axe down and dug out his phone, sighing when he saw Dunn's name on his screen. "Yeah."

"We found something."

Jack's heart rate kicked up in anticipation. He wanted some action, and needed it to be of the variety he got shooting things, not losing himself in the curvy beauty who slept curled up in his arms all night. "What is it?"

"One of the guys they picked up on one of the runs. He talked. Said there's been chatter about Juan and finally bringing him to justice. The guy made it sound like they've been watching him for a while."

"How is that possible?" Jack asked, glancing toward the house. He knew Pilar couldn't hear him from inside, but he couldn't have her sneak up on him and overhear something she didn't need to know.

"We don't know that yet. When the first truck got picked up, they started to get anxious, but he said they were watching their routes and going after anyone who might have leaked them."

"All his intel is a year old. Are they really so stupid that they didn't change anything in a year? Especially after someone walked?"

"I guess. But if they had eyes on him at all times, they didn't need to worry about it. They knew where he was so if anything came out, they'd know it was him. That wasn't all the guy had to say."

Jack hated the way Dunn parsed out info, like he was toying with them. "What?"

"They have someone on the inside working with them. Alerting them."

"Well, we figured that."

"Yeah, but this guy gave us a name. Gerald Sloan."

"Do we know him?" Jack asked, trying to place the name.

"No, but someone does. They're going after him today. He's in DC."

"Good," Jack spat. "Fucking asshole betraying his country."

"Agreed. Hey, listen, the guy also said this Carlos guy is after Pilar. That he has some twisted infatuation with her and that he's been talking about getting her back. It sounds like he's not leaving until he finds her. At least, that would be my guess."

Jack sighed. "I can't say I'm surprised by that. She said things were pretty heavy between them until she found out who he was."

"And you still think she had no idea what's going on now?"

"Yeah. She was scared, man. When she saw that flower, she freaked out. She's afraid of him."

"I've heard that before," Dunn grumbled.

Jack pinched his lips shut and kept in the angry retort. He understood that Dunn felt guilty for trusting the wrong woman. His mistake got their teammate and friend killed when they walked into a trap. Since then, Dunn hasn't trusted a woman.

"Anyway," Dunn continued, "I think we need to up our monitoring. We have to assume they have more help than we're aware of and that anyone can find you up there."

"We have the alarms. We're good here."

Dunn blew out a breath. "Still, stay sharp. Be vigilant with her. We can't risk losing everything we worked for. If Juan doesn't come back, Pilar is our only shot at getting the intel we need to bring the cartel down. We've put too much into this to lose it now."

Jack nodded, not trusting himself to say anything.

"We'll talk soon," Dunn said when Jack didn't reply.

"Yep."

They hung up, and Jack closed his eyes for a long minute. He worked to steady his breath, something he'd trained himself to do for years. First, as a kid when he was trying to hide in the fields instead of doing his chores, then later as a sniper when hiding meant life or death.

When his heart rate returned to normal and Jack could breathe in and out without clenching his fists, he opened his eyes and took in his surroundings. Nothing had changed in the time he was out there. They were in the middle of almost twenty acres of woods with one road in and out. If anyone was going to come at them, he'd know. They were alone.

Jack grabbed the axe again and tossed it over his shoulder. He spread his feet to stabilize himself, then swung, splitting the wood with a satisfying crunch.

He set up the next log and swung again, the slice of the axe through the wood driving him on. He was angry. Dunn accusing Pilar of being involved. Dunn thinking Juan was double crossing them. The idea of Juan double crossing them. Carlos being after Pilar. Pilar being involved with Carlos. Meredith. Rodney. Williams.

Stack. Swing. Slice. Stack. Swing. Slice. Stack. Swing. Slice. Over and over, Jack went through the motions. He lost all track of time and all ability to focus on anything around him. When he started to sweat, he stripped off his shirt and wiped it across his face, letting the cool April breeze chill his exposed skin.

Jack let his anger fill him and overflow into the axe. He imagined each crunch was a blow delivered to another person. One to Williams for betraying them. Another one for killing Rodney. A third for kidnapping Jaymes and Lily. One to Juan for double crossing them. Just in case. One for himself for hurting Meredith. Then Carlos. For sleeping with Pilar. For getting her to trust him. For terrorizing her. For taking Juan. For all the people he killed.

For making Jack look in the mirror.

He knew he wasn't any better than Carlos. He was a killer. He was a man who hurt a woman. He was a man who let women trust him and love him, then destroyed their trust, and them. He was no better than Carlos.

Stack. Swing. Slice. Stack. Swing. Slice. Stack. Swing. Slice.

It was rhythmic. Soothing. It calmed him. He was doing good. Helping Pilar. He wasn't hurting her. He was helping. He wasn't like Carlos. He couldn't be.

"Jack," reached the edges of his consciousness.

Stack. Swing. Slice.

"Jack," a little louder. Meredith? Calling to him. Needing him. Like the phone call after she took the pills. When she told him what she did and asked him to help her. The one he ignored because he was with another woman. He wasn't going to go back to her, so the message didn't matter. He deleted it, but not permanently. It stayed in his deleted messages until he found out she was gone. Torturing him with the knowledge that he could have saved her if he was a better man.

"Jack," she said again, a hand on his arm.

He dropped the axe and spun. Pilar. Not Meredith.

She gave him a tentative smile, her eyes scanning his body. They lit with desire, and he hated himself. He was just like Carlos, except everyone knew Carlos was a monster. No one knew what Jack did.

8

———————

"Are you okay?" Pilar asked. The first two times she called him name, he didn't answer. She assumed he was just finishing up his work, but when he finally turned and looked so lost, she was concerned.

Of course, she was also trying to hide the fact that she was turned on beyond belief. Walking out and seeing him swing that axe, the muscles of his back bunching and twisting with his every move, got her more than a little excited. She'd never had such a strong, physical reaction to a man before. She wanted him. Badly.

"Jack? Are you okay?"

He nodded and shook off her hand. "I'm good. Just wanted to get this wood together."

He had two piles that would have kept them warm a full winter instead of a few days. Unless he thought they were going to be there a lot longer.

"How long are we staying?"

He shrugged. "There's no way to know."

She followed him with her eyes as he moved to the stack

of logs where he'd left his shirt. He tugged it back on, then started picking up pieces of the chopped wood to carry inside.

"Can I help you?"

He shook his head. "I got it."

She stepped back, wondering what happened while he was outside. He changed. He was funny and kind and friendly before, but now he was distant.

Pilar followed him around the house and inside the front door. He stacked the wood neatly, then added a few logs to the fireplace and lit pieces of newspaper to get the fire going.

Once the flame started to lick at the wood, Jack stood and turned toward the bathroom. "I'm going to take a shower."

"Oh, um, breakfast is ready," Pilar said lamely.

"I need to take a shower," Jack said, ignoring her and going straight to the bathroom.

Pilar nodded, watching him go and wondering what in the hell was going on.

The water turned on a minute later, and she did her best not to imagine the stream sluicing down his chest, racing over the muscles she ached to touch. After the feel she got of him that morning, she was sure the rest of him would be just as stunning as his chest was.

She shook her head. She'd never know. She was a job to him. A task to complete. She wasn't the woman of his dreams, or even the woman of the moment. Not that she really wanted to be, but it was nice to imagine for a minute that she might have been the reason Jack woke up hard.

She rolled her eyes at herself and stifled the tears that sprang up. Jack was a sexy, badass, former SEAL. He could have any woman he wanted. There was no way he'd be interested in a woman like her. Murderous ex-boyfriend or not, Pilar didn't fit with a guy like Jack. And it was definitely time she got that through her head so he didn't have to keep brushing her off. That was obviously why he changed outside. He was pissed that she was rubbing up against him and didn't sleep in her bed, and he didn't know how to tell her to back off.

Message received, Jack Farrell. Message received.

JACK STOOD in the shower and let the lukewarm water trickle onto his back. He would have given his left nut for a hot shower to beat the hell out of him, but well water and a small water heater meant he had to take what he got.

Which was a whole lot of nothing.

He closed his eyes and slowed his breathing. He survived months in the desert. In his mind, he needed to go back there. Where being cold seemed like a faraway dream.

Instead of imagining the desert, Pilar popped into his mind. Her dark eyes searching his. Her breasts swinging free beneath the t-shirt she wore to bed. Her laugh. Her grin. Her curves.

He was hard in seconds. He wanted to fight it, but he couldn't. If he had to suffer through knowing he was only going to hurt her if he touched her, he had to alleviate some of the pressure building in his cock.

He stroked himself once, biting back a groan. His cock was so hard it hurt. He loosened his grip and tried again, his knees almost buckling at the sensation.

He leaned back to let the water run down his chest and cover his hand. The wet suction was like having her mouth circling him, pulling hard as she sucked him in and releasing as she drew back.

Jack clenched his fist and tapped it against the wall. He was so close his spine tingled, every muscle in his body tensing. He opened his mouth, sucking in air and hissing it out with every movement of his hand on his cock.

His balls tightened, drawing up and preparing to blow. He jammed his fist into his mouth and bit down, grunting through his orgasm as the full force of it hit him and dropped him to his knees.

He stayed there, on all fours in the shower, until the lukewarm water turned to ice and his cock stopped throbbing.

Jack turned off the water and got out, then realized he didn't bring any clothes into the bathroom.

"Fuck."

He drew in a breath and let it out slowly. He had no choice but to go out there in his towel and grab something to wear. He was not putting his dirty clothes back on when he just took a shower. He'd have to take his chances in a towel.

He opened the door quietly, hoping Pilar was not in her room. All the clothes they kept in the safe house were in the dresser in the bedroom. Because they all assumed none of them would be dumbasses and go into the damn shower without a change.

Jack scanned the area and didn't see her. But the bedroom door was closed. Of course.

He took a breath and tightened the precarious knot he made in the towel that barely covered his junk. With one hand on the towel, he knocked on the bedroom door.

And waited. He strained to hear movement inside the bedroom. Was she taking a nap? Or did she leave?

He knocked again, a little louder. He definitely heard footsteps shuffling to the door.

She opened it and gasped. "What... Why don't you have any clothes on?"

He sighed heavily. "Because all my clothes are in here. I forgot to grab them when I went to get in the shower."

"Oh," she said, sounding a little disappointed. She stepped back to let him in. Pilar went to the bed, right in Jack's path to the dresser. When she realized he was following her, she moved a little faster, hustling to the bed and curling up in the center.

Jack opened the top drawer, thanking God he chose that one and wasn't bending over in his barely there towel, and pulled out a pair of sweats, a clean t-shirt, and a pair of black boxer briefs. He wasn't planning to leave the house again, so he left the socks in the drawer and turned back to Pilar.

She was staring at his ass, now his cock. Her cheeks turned an adorable shade of pink as she averted her eyes back to the book opened in front of her.

"What are you reading?" Jack asked, trying desperately to return to some semblance of normal between them.

"My Bible," she said simply, not taking her eyes off it again.

"Oh, um, cool. I'll just go get dressed."

She nodded and turned a page, still ignoring him.

Jack left the room, but purposely left the door open. He went into the bathroom again and quickly got dressed. When he walked out, his stomach growled, reminding him that Pilar was fixing breakfast when he went outside.

Shit. He walked into the kitchen and sighed. There was no sign of food anywhere. Whatever she cooked was gone.

He opened the fridge, hoping something delicious

appeared overnight, and grinned. She saved him some breakfast.

He turned to the bedroom to say something to her and saw that she'd closed the door again.

Well, damn.

PILAR NEEDED TO GET A GRIP. It was a little bit of man flesh. Nothing special. And he wasn't parading around trying to get her attention. He forgot to take clothes into the bathroom. When he was hiding from her. Because he thought she was going to attack him or something.

Ugh.

She flipped the page and tried to stay focused on her Bible. The words always gave her comfort, but she wasn't finding any at that moment. She was trapped in a cabin with a man who found her repulsive because her ex kidnapped her brother. The Bible wasn't working. There weren't any stories in there that helped her figure out how to deal with that situation. She closed her Bible and put it back into her bag. She thought about unpacking, but she wasn't moving in, so she just sat on the bed and tried to relax.

If it was a normal Tuesday, she would be at school, working with one of her students. She hated the idea of not being there, but she had no choice. She called in before they left the F-BOMB offices the day before so her boss would know she wasn't going to be in for the rest of the week, but that was all she could do. It was going to cost her her job. Which meant all the students she was used to working with were going to have to transition to Ms. Beck.

Ms. Beck was a good therapist. The kids would do well with her until they hired someone else to replace Pilar.

She picked up her phone and spun it around in her hand. Maybe she could call Ms. Beck and talk her through a few things.

No. Jack and Mr. Dunn said no phones.

But they were in the middle of nowhere. Why couldn't she make a call?

She groaned and turned her phone on and called Joann. If it was quick, Jack would never know.

"Pilar. Where are you?" Joann answered in a hushed voice. "You're going to get fired for this."

Pilar nodded. "I know. But I had no choice."

"Are you okay?"

Pilar shook her head. "Yeah, I'm fine. Listen, I wanted to talk to you about Ricky Norwood."

"Seriously?"

"Yeah, you're seeing him today, right?"

Joann cleared her throat and said, "Yeah, in an hour."

"Good. Do you have his file?"

"Yep, right here."

"Okay. Here's the thing, he's been regressing. I've been working with him weekly all year, but for some reason, the last month, he's gone backwards. Almost back to where he was at the beginning of school. Read through all my notes from early in the year and see if you can help bring him back to where he was a month ago."

Pages flipped as Joann scanned the pages and pages of notes on the student.

Pilar loved her job. She worked with a variety of students in the elementary school. She focused on the older students in grades three through five. Joann always took the younger kids. They worked well together to transition students and when they covered for each other, but Pilar never let Joann get too close even though the other woman tried.

Pilar wondered if it would have been better if she'd let Joann in. Would Joann be safe? That was always her fear. Joann had a husband who taught at the high school and two kids. The thought of any of them getting hurt because of her was unbearable, so Pilar kept her distance.

"I see a few things I can try. He liked to paint when he was in second grade. It's been a few years, but maybe he'll be willing to give it a shot."

Pilar breathed a sigh. "Thank you, Joann. I'm sorry I've put so much on you. If the school board allows me to come back after taking time off connected to a holiday, I will, but I know it isn't likely."

"Well, I hope they do. I'll speak on your behalf if you want me to."

"You'd do that?" Pilar asked, unable to keep the shock from her voice.

Joann laughed. "Of course. You're a truly gifted therapist. The kids love working with you. I've seen improvements in these kids since you've been here. They love you, and you deserve to be here. No matter what's going on."

Pilar choked back the emotion in her throat. "Thank you, Joann. I really appreciate that."

"Of course, Pilar. Please stay safe."

"Safe?" she asked.

"Yeah," Joann said, "I know the only reason you'd risk your job is if you were in danger, Pilar. You're an amazing person and a wonderful therapist. I will fight beside you for your job, and I will make sure they know exactly how dedicated you are. We'll get you back here."

"Thank you, Joann. That means a lot."

"Absolutely. We'll talk soon."

Pilar hung up and stared at her phone. She couldn't help but smile. Maybe there was hope for her. Joann thought highly of her, which meant she might be able to get her job back.

Of course, that meant she needed to survive.

She turned her phone off and dropped it back into her bag. Hiding in the room was even worse than hiding in the woods. She needed to get outside for a few minutes. Maybe go for a walk.

Jack was on the couch when she walked out of the bedroom. He looked up at her with a grin. "This is amazing," he said, holding up the plate she fixed him for breakfast.

"Thanks. I hope it's okay that I used all the food I did."

He shook his head. "Hell, yeah. Anything you want is fine." He paused and shoveled in another bite. "You doing okay?"

She nodded. "Just going a little stir crazy."

"Yeah, I understand. Unfortunately, we can't get out."

"Can I walk around outside, though? Maybe go for a walk in the woods?"

Jack shrugged. "We can probably do that. There's a little stream not too far from here. We have the property on both sides so no one should wander up into here. I'll go with you."

"You don't have to."

Jack looked closely at her for a minute as though deciding what to say. She waited, trying not to be impatient. She needed to go, to get away from him, and he was trying to come with her. Do his job.

"I'd like to, Pilar. Just in case. And it'll be nice to get out of here for a little while."

"You were outside earlier," she blurted, then instantly

regretted her words. The memory of him dripping with sweat, swinging the axe, heated her skin.

He nodded. "I did. But that's very different from taking a walk."

She shrugged, knowing she wasn't going to get her solo walk. She'd have to settle for a walk with Jack. Through the woods. To the stream.

How romantic.

9

———

JACK LED THE WAY THROUGH THE WOODS CAREFULLY, TRYING to make sure he didn't go too far off a trail. He was painfully aware of Pilar following him, her steps much less sure than his.

"You doing okay?" he asked her when they were about halfway to the stream.

"Yep, I'm great," she said.

Jack had no idea why he refused to let her walk on her own. He told himself it was for her safety, but he knew that wasn't the whole truth. He wanted to be around her. Even knowing he shouldn't, he wanted to be.

He also liked to push her. When he pushed, she pushed back. That intrigued him. She was strong, and he'd never known a woman with that kind of strength. Or maybe he'd never bothered to get to know a woman well enough to find that kind of strength.

If he'd simply met Pilar and slept with her, he wouldn't have learned any of the things he knew about her. Like how she loved to be outside, but hated the outdoors. Or how she loved to cook, but seemed more than content to let someone else cook for her. Or how her eyes glowed when she was happy or scared or turned on.

He paused to look at the trees so he could adjust himself, and Pilar ran into his back.

"Why did you stop?" she asked, glaring up at him.

"I was just looking around," Jack said, not meeting her gaze. He was a trained professional, but something about her made it hard for him to school his features and not reveal everything.

"Are you lost?" she asked, a thread of panic in her voice.

Jack shook his head. "Nah, we're good. We're almost there."

Pilar nodded and waited for him to start moving again, then fell in line behind him. Jack made his way to the stream quickly, pushing away all thoughts of getting Pilar naked.

He turned his mind to solving the problem they were faced with. Juan still claimed to have information for them. Something he said would secure his safety and Pilar's and take down the cartel. He hadn't told any of them what it was or given an indication of where it was.

The meeting with Carlos had been Juan's idea. He wanted to draw the cartel out. Dunn agreed with him, but Jack wanted to do things a different way. He was outvoted, and the meet happened, but from there everything went wrong.

Juan was never supposed to be taken. Carlos wasn't supposed to see Pilar, let alone speak to her. The point of the meeting was to prove that the cartel was afraid of Juan and what he had. If they were, Dunn promised Juan his and Pilar's safety.

Jack still didn't know exactly what went wrong. He was tasked with watching Pilar since Juan was going to disappear into the crowd to meet with Carlos. When he approached her, Jack had no idea there was a problem. Not until Carlos walked up.

Dex was supposed to be watching Juan. He was the one who was on him, keeping eyes on him, making sure the meeting went as planned. Obviously, something else happened.

"I'm sorry about this morning," Pilar blurted.

Jack looked at her. He almost forgot she was there. Her eyes were clamped shut and her entire body was tense. And he had no clue what she was talking about.

"What about this morning?"

Pilar sucked in a breath. "When we woke up. I didn't mean to touch you. I wasn't trying to grope you or anything. I know I'm not your type, and I wasn't—"

"Whoa, what? First of all, I never thought you were trying to grope me. I was the one who crossed the line. I should have taken you to bed. I mean, walked you there." He exhaled a rough breath. "I shouldn't have fallen asleep with you on the couch. I should have made sure you were in the bed. Alone. And as for being my type? How would you know my type?"

Pilar rolled her eyes at him then. She gestured to him and scoffed. "Please. Men who look like you give women like me a passing glance before they move on to the thin chica behind me. I just wanted you to know I'm not trying to hit on you or anything."

"I'm still confused by this conversation. I never thought you were hitting on me. And I don't know why you feel the need to tell me all this."

"Because you've been weird since you went outside to get the wood. And I'm guessing you noticed me checking out your muscles and got worried that I would try something since we're here alone and all that. I just wanted you to know that you're... safe or whatever with me. I won't touch you."

Jack huffed a small laugh. He was fantasizing about her, jerked off in the shower because of her, and she was apologizing to him.

He stepped up to her. She took a step back, fear flooding her gaze. He moved closer. "Pilar."

"Hmm?"

"What if I want to touch you?"

Her eyes widened, those gold swirls making him crazy again. "Why... why would you want to do that?"

Jack cocked a grin at her. "Because you are my type, Pilar. Strong and smart. It helps that you have these sexy curves that I can't keep my eyes off of. I wasn't hard this morning because of some random woman I was dreaming about. I was hard because I woke up and felt your arm on my dick and smelled your hair and wanted you."

"You did?"

Jack nodded.

Pilar nibbled her lip. "Then why were you so weird after you went outside?"

Just that quickly, all those feelings came rushing back in. Jack took a step back, needing distance between himself and Pilar. Distance gave him clarity. It always had. It was one of the reasons he was so good at his job. Sitting in a quiet spot, just him and his gun, gave him time to process things. He'd always been like that. He got by with making jokes and keeping people laughing because then they never looked too closely at him, but he was a mess.

After he got out of the shower, he felt more like himself again. He let go of the fears he convinced himself were reality, and even though he knew he wasn't any good for Pilar, after seeing the way she ignored him when he was getting clothes, he knew he could push his emotions aside. She didn't want him, so he didn't have to worry about being wrong for her. Desire that was one-sided couldn't go anywhere.

But it no longer felt one sided.

"I—"

His phone buzzed loudly in his pocket. Loud enough that she heard it and looked at his shorts. Jack dug out his phone and answered. "What?"

"Where are you?" Dex demanded.

"At the stream. Why?"

"Movement. East line."

"That's not us."

"Nope," Dex agreed. "Get back now until we know what it is."

"Ten-four."

Jack hung up the phone and reached for Pilar's hand. She backed up a step, out of his reach. "We need to go," Jack said, ignoring the painful snub.

"Why? We just got here."

"Something tripped one of the alarms on the property. Until we know what it is, we have to go."

Her eyes widened, and her entire body stiffened. It was almost funny that her reaction to being scared was similar to her reaction to being turned on, but Jack didn't comment. Instead, he turned and started back.

Pilar didn't say anything on their walk back, but she kept pace with him. They were back at the cabin in less than half the time it took them to get to the stream. Both were sweating and exhausted. Jack was on high alert, listening for anything that meant there were people out there instead of just animals.

Since they bought the place a few months before, they'd had everything from deer to illegal hunting to drunk college kids on the property. Jack knew better than to assume it was as innocent as any of those when he was harboring a client there.

They made it inside with the door locked before Jack's phone rang again. He grabbed it quickly, his eyes on Pilar's. "Yeah?"

"Two men. Moving toward you. They're going quick, but they obviously don't know where they're actually going. Get out now."

"Get your bag, Pilar. We have to go now. Take everything you brought with you."

Pilar rushed to the bedroom to grab her bag while Jack searched the cabin. "I can take them out."

"No," Dex said. "We're on our way now. Your job is to protect her. We'll go after them, see what info we can get out of them."

"But—"

"Jack, keep her safe. She doesn't need to be in the middle of a firefight. She already almost lost it when she found a fucking flower. How is she going to react if she sees someone get shot? And are you going to be able to focus if you're also watching her? We see two. That doesn't mean more aren't out there."

"Okay, okay. We'll go."

"Now?" Dex pressed.

Jack grabbed a bottle of water for each of them and called out to Pilar.

"Coming. I'm coming."

"They're getting closer, Jack. You need to get the fuck out of there."

"Let's go," Jack said to Pilar, hanging up on Dex and rushing Pilar out of the cabin.

He opened her door just as a shot rang out, hitting a tree not far from them. Pilar screamed and ducked. Jack shoved her into the truck and drew his gun. He fired back in the direction the shot came from and rushed around the truck.

Another shot whizzed by as he got in. More peppered the side of the truck as Jack threw the truck in gear and peeled out. The back door took a heavy thud of a bullet.

"Keep your head down," Jack shouted to Pilar.

She huddled on the seat, her bag at her feet, crying. Jack drove as fast as he could down the narrow driveway, praying no other men were on the road waiting for them or in the woods surrounding the driveway.

The shots from the men at the cabin died out, too far away to reach the truck. Jack kept his eyes on the road and his foot on the gas. He slowed down as he approached the road, which made Pilar whimper.

"It's okay. I just need to make sure there's no traffic coming."

She didn't reply, just cried quietly.

One car was parked on the side of the road when Jack pulled out. He couldn't tell if anyone was in it or not, but he wasn't taking any chances and raced away from the cabin, leaving it to the rest of the team. They'd collect what they could from the men who found their safe house and hopefully pull a few of them in for questioning.

Jack's phone hadn't stopped ringing since he hung up on Dex. When he finally felt like they were safe, he dug it out. "Yeah."

"Jesus fucking Christ, Jack. I thought you were dead." Slade.

"Just needed to focus."

"Everything okay?" Slade asked after he relayed that Jack was still alive.

"No. Those fuckers were on us. Shot at us as we left the cabin. The two you guys picked up had to be farther away. These two got there first."

"How many were there?" Dunn demanded.

Jack was obviously on speaker now. "I saw two, but doesn't mean that's all there was. A white sedan was parked at the road, but I doubt that's where those guys came from. Probably more."

"We're five minutes out," Dunn said. "We'll check it all out."

"Good. Any clue how they found us?"

"Not yet."

"Where are we supposed to go?"

"Go to my place," Slade said. "Howler's there. He'll let you in."

"Okay, thanks," Jack said with a laugh. "Get those fuckers."

"Hooyah," everyone on the other end of the phone said.

Jack hung up and checked his mirrors again. Still no one tailing them. They got away, but they were lucky. Jack couldn't think of any way they would have found them, unless Carlos had them followed. If that was the case, he would have sent men last night. When they were more vulnerable.

Jack glanced at Pilar, who was finally quiet but still curled in a ball. Jack reached over and put a hand on her back. She jumped.

"Hey, sorry," he said. "We're okay now. We're safe."

She shook her head. "I'll never be safe."

"You're safe with me, Pilar. I won't let anything happen to you. I got you."

She didn't respond. Jack rubbed her shoulder, hoping he was bringing her some kind of comfort. She'd feel better once they were at Slade's. When she had something to drink and eat, a shower, maybe a nap. She was strong. She'd be okay.

He hoped.

JACK PARKED in front of a red brick ranch and turned off the truck. Pilar was still in shock from what happened at the cabin, and she had no idea where they were.

"This is Slade's place," Jack said. "He's one of my team-mates. He just bought the place because he has a dog who likes to make a lot of noise. His old neighbors complained, so Slade moved out here so Howler could do his thing."

"Okay," Pilar said, barely hearing him.

"Let's get inside," Jack said.

Pilar scanned the yard, terror overflowing her body once more.

"We're safe here," Jack said calmly.

"You said we were safe at the cabin. The *safe* house."

Jack nodded solemnly. "I know. And we should have been. I have no idea how those guys found the place. We're completely off the grid out there. No cell phones, no elec-tricity, no records. We even registered the place through a shell corporation so it would be harder to track. It makes no sense."

Pilar nibbled her lip. "I used my phone."

"What?" Jack asked, turning to her. "I told you not to."

She shook her head. "No, you said there was no service. You didn't say I couldn't because it wasn't safe."

"I didn't think you'd try to use your phone. You turned it off."

She nodded. "I wanted to check in on my students."

Jack sighed and pinched the bridge of his nose. "Okay. It's fine. At least we know how they found us. Where's your phone now? Is it off?"

Pilar nodded. "I turned it off again after the call. I'm sorry. This was my fault?"

Jack shook his head. "No. I should have told you not to use your phone because they could track it. I'm the one who's supposed to be keeping you safe."

"I'm sorry, Jack."

He smiled faintly at her. "Let's get inside. No one knows we're here."

Pilar nodded, but she waited for Jack to come around to her side of the truck before she got out. She looked around as they walked to the front door, just like Jack did.

On the porch, Jack pulled out his keys and unlocked the front door. "We all have keys to each other's places. Just in case," he explained.

Pilar walked inside and was nearly bowled over by a brown and white dog running at her. Just before they collided, the dog's back legs gave out and he skidded to the side. His tongue lolled out, the dog panting and grinning up at her and Jack.

"That's Howler." Jack dropped to the floor and gave the dog a full body rub. "Who's a good boy? Did you know we were coming? Is your daddy taking good care of you?"

Howler licked Jack's jaw and howled. He definitely lived up to his name.

"He's adorable."

Jack nodded. "Yeah, he's pretty great." Howler scrambled

to his feet and looked expectantly at them. "He wants us to follow him."

"Seriously?" Pilar asked with a laugh.

"Yep. He's the host. He likes to show people around."

Pilar grinned and followed Howler into the house, past an office and half bathroom to the kitchen and living room beyond. Howler plopped down next to two blue dishes with his name scrawled on them.

Jack shook his head. "You're going to be a hundred pounds, dude. Slade will kill me."

Howler looked up at Jack and howled, not accepting no for an answer.

Jack covered his ears and went to the drawer near the bowl. He opened it and scooped out some food. Howler licked Jack's leg, then dropped his butt to the floor and gobbled up his food.

"The only thing he does better than howl is eat," Jack said.

Pilar nodded, watching the dog. It must be nice to only have to worry about someone feeding you and not think twice about someone trying to kill you.

She sucked in a sharp breath, the knowledge that one of those bullets could have killed her fresh in her mind.

Before she could think anything else, warm, strong arms wrapped her up tight and led her to another room. Then she was scooped up and curled against his chest. Jack's manly scent filled her lungs as he held her and rubbed her back.

And Pilar finally let go.

10

———

Jack didn't know what to do. He'd never held a woman as she cried. He was usually the reason they were crying.

Grabbing Pilar and carrying her to the living room was instinctual. The rest was not. He held her and tried to think of something to say that would make her feel better, but there was nothing. The situation sucked, and until it was over, she was in danger. Which meant no words would solve anything.

"We're going to get him, Pilar. We're going to stop him. He's not going to hurt you again."

She kept crying as though she didn't hear him. With how loud she was, it was entirely possible she hadn't. Jack just held her, stroking his hand up and down her back and rocking with her, hoping being there was enough.

"This is all my fault," Pilar finally whispered.

Jack shook his head. "No, Pilar, it's not."

"I'm the one who made a phone call. I didn't listen to you. He found us because of me. We almost got killed."

Her sobs began again, so he pulled her in closer and wrapped both arms around her, holding her tight. "You can't think about that. We had eyes on the place the whole time. We got out of there. We're safe."

"I won't do it again," she blurted, pushing back from him. Her eyes were wild with fear. "I won't use my phone. You can have it." She started to break from his hold, but he tightened it.

"Relax for right now. You said your phone is off. There's no reason to go get it."

"What if he can track it anyway?"

"He can't, Pilar."

"Well, what if he knows about this place? What if he knows where all of you live? We're not safe here."

"Shhh," Jack whispered, drawing her back into his embrace. She was trembling with terror, and her attempts to get away created a major problem for him. He needed her still or she was going to find out exactly what she was doing to him.

"Jack," she said, trying to push free again. The movement brought her hip into contact with his aching cock, and she froze. "Jack?" she said again, more curious this time.

"I'm sorry," he said. "You're a beautiful woman and you're wrapped up in my arms. I can't control him."

"Jack," she said a third time, her voice dipping into a sultry tone that had him groaning.

She pulled back to look at him. He let her go, meeting her gaze with his. He wasn't going to hide the way she made him feel. She already knew, so pretending it wasn't happening was childish and stupid. Jack wasn't either of those things. He was a thirty-six year old man who loved women. And the curvy one in his lap was making him remember all the reasons he enjoyed losing himself in one.

"Jack," she whispered, moving in closer to him.

He held his breath. He was not going to kiss her. He couldn't. It wasn't right. She deserved better.

Her eyes slid closed as she eliminated the gap between them. Her hands eased up his chest and around his neck into his hair to hold him steady. She tilted her head to the side and pressed her lips to his.

He didn't react. He couldn't. If he kissed her, he'd be breaking every rule they had. Don't get involved. Keep your dick in your pants. Never fuck the client.

Then she sighed, that little noise that said she understood and was disappointed. Her entire body sank with the realization that she was wrong about him, and she started to pull back.

The second their lips parted, Jack had to have her back. His hands pressed against her back, bringing her lips into contact with his again. He enjoyed the touch for a second, then needed more of her. He pried her lips apart with his tongue, licking his way into her mouth for his first taste of her.

She bit down, nipping his tongue. He didn't care. She could be pissed off at him for being an ass later. At that moment, he needed to taste her.

He growled and thrust his tongue into her mouth, letting the sharp bite of her teeth fuel him. He groaned and plunged in again, jerking her body flush against his so she could feel how hard he was.

She moaned at the contact and wrapped her tongue around his. Her arms tightened around his neck, and her body got in on the action, tensing again as he explored her mouth and ran his hands up and down her back.

Her hand slid down his chest to the hem of his shirt. He shifted his weight so she could pull it up. Her warm hand pressed flat against his skin, making his muscles jump. He tasted her while she explored his chest, running her hands up and down his muscles until he felt like Adonis.

"You're so sexy," she murmured.

He cupped her ass. "You've been driving me crazy, Pilar. You have to know that."

She scoffed. "I'm the only woman around. I know I'm just here."

He shook his head and kissed his way down her neck. "You're the only woman I saw at the parade yesterday. My cock is aching for you and only you."

She laughed but didn't say anything else. She simply grabbed his face and brought it back to hers for another kiss.

Jack let her control the kiss for a while, but it wasn't enough. He eased her from his lap and stripped off his shirt, then lowered her back onto him, straddling his hips.

"Oh, God," she groaned when she settled against him.

He thrust up into her, and her head fell back. He leaned forward and licked her collarbone. She gasped and grabbed his head, holding him in place. He nipped her flesh and kissed his way across her neck, holding her upright with his hands on her back.

She rocked against him, grinding herself on his straining cock. Jack knew he wouldn't be happy until he buried himself inside her and rose to carry her to the bedroom.

They were halfway down the hallway when Howler let out a bark that made Jack nearly drop Pilar. His claws scratched the floor as he ran and fell and ran again to get to the front door.

"Fuck," Jack said, setting Pilar on the floor. "Bedroom is the second door on the right. Bathroom is right before it. Come out when you're ready."

"What? Why?" she asked, her voice breathy. Her eyes

were shining gold and questioning him. Then they shuttered. "Oh. This was a mistake."

"Pilar, no," he said firmly, cupping her jaw and forcing her to look at him. "I want you so badly I'm not sure how to walk. This isn't about you. Slade's here. That's why Howler went nuts."

"Slade? The guy who lives here?"

Jack nodded.

"Oh, crap."

Jack nodded again.

"Okay, I'm sorry," she said and turned away.

Jack grabbed her arm and yanked her back to him. Surprise tilted her off balance and she fell against him, her hand pressed against his bare chest. "We're not done, Pilar."

"We're not?" she asked. The gold flecks shined in her eyes again.

Jack shook his head and slowly lowered his head. She stared up at him as he came closer. The second their lips touched, her eyes fluttered closed. He thrust his tongue between her lips for a kiss that tortured both of them.

Far too quickly, Jack pulled back. He gently pushed Pilar toward the bedroom and bathroom just as Howler's barks escalated.

Jack went back to the living room as Slade called out, "Where the hell are you?"

"Right here," Jack said, drawing his friend's attention.

Slade stopped, his eyes narrowed at the sight of Jack's bare chest. He looked toward the hallway, where Jack came from, and lifted his eyebrows.

"I don't want to hear it," Jack said.

"Then you better put something on because the rest of them are right behind me. Dunn's going to rip you a new asshole if he thinks you're fucking her."

Jack grabbed his shirt and yanked it over his head, taking a minute to calm the anger racing through him. "Nothing happened."

Slade's gaze dropped meaningfully to Jack's junk.

Jack set his hands on his hips, not bothering to hide. "Look—"

"No, Jack, you look. I get it. She's a beautiful woman, but you're not in a place to handle something like this. Women in dangerous situations fall for the guy protecting them all the time. There are books written about it. You're not the guy to handle something like that. Don't fuck her. It won't be just physical for her."

Jack nodded, knowing his friend was right, but hating it anyway. He didn't have time to answer before the door down the hall opened and Pilar walked out. She saw him standing there watching and grinned.

He watched Pilar until she was at his side again. Then she turned to Slade and flashed him a grin that had Jack wanting to punch his friend.

"Hi. I'm Pilar Luna, although you probably already know that. You're Slade?"

Slade nodded. "I am. Justin O'Keefe, but they all call me Slade. You can call me whatever you'd like."

She laughed softly and grinned. "Thank you for letting us come here. And for helping find my brother. It means a lot to me."

Howler went over to Pilar and dropped onto her foot. She looked down and laughed.

"Sorry about him," Slade said. "He gets very possessive of beautiful women."

Pilar laughed again, and Jack was sure he was going to have to kick Slade's ass.

PILAR NEEDED A BREAK FROM JACK. Being close to him made her brain foggy and her body needy. She didn't have the same reaction to Slade, or Justin as she called him, so she stuck to his side while he took Howler outside.

"This is a great place," she told Justin.

He nodded. "It really is. I was lucky to find it. Most of the homes in the area are either in the middle of the city or way out in the middle of nowhere. I needed something close enough to work that I could be there in ten minutes, but far enough out that this crazy guy didn't have my neighbors filing noise complaints."

"Oh, why would anyone complain about him?"

Justin laughed. "Because he has a tendency to howl. Whenever he feels like it."

"No," she said, laughing.

Justin nodded. "Yep. He doesn't care if anyone else is asleep or anything else. I guess I should have warned you about that before you decided to stay here."

She laughed again. "It's okay. I've never slept much. Not in the past few years."

Justin gave her a small smile. "Hopefully we can change that for you."

She grinned. "You guys already have. Last night I slept on the couch with Jack and it was the best sleep I've had in years."

Justin nodded but didn't comment. Pilar could tell there was tension between them when she walked into the living room, but she wasn't sure why. She had no right to ask, so she just went ahead as though everything was normal, but she waded right into the middle of it if Justin's stiffness was any indication.

"Jack said there's a big group of you that work together. I met Mr. Dunn. How many others are there?"

"Mr. Dunn?" Justin said with a grin. "Did you call him Mr. Dunn?"

Pilar nodded, wondering why that wasn't appropriate. "Should I not?"

Justin shook his head and laughed. "No, it's fine. The rest of us call him Dunn, but we all go by our nicknames or last names. He hates his nickname."

"What is it?"

"Pres. Or Mr. President. He likes to be in charge and can get people to do anything. A lot of the time, he talks you into thinking it was your idea. He's a hell of a leader, though. If he ever had the interest, he'd make a hell of a president, but he hates the thought of answering to people like that. You calling him Mr. Dunn is just really fucking hilarious to me." Justin looked up at her and winced. "Sorry. Really funny. I didn't mean to swear."

Pilar grinned and shook her head. "If you'd ever met my brother you'd know swearing doesn't bother me."

Justin ducked his head and avoided her gaze. Was he hiding something? She couldn't tell.

"Well, still, I try to be more respectful. We should probably get back inside. Everyone else just pulled in."

Pilar didn't have time to ask how he knew there were people there. He whistled for Howler to come back and the three of them walked inside.

To a house full of people. Pilar grinned at the noise and excitement. There was a flash of panic at being around so many strangers, but then she saw Jack staring at her and she felt better.

She went to Jack, careful to keep her distance from him.

He didn't seem like the PDA type, and she wasn't either. "There are a lot of people here," she said quietly.

Jack nodded. "If it's too much, I can tell them all to get out."

She shook her head. "It'll be fine. My family used to have get togethers like this when I was little. It was nice. It's been a long time, though."

"How old were you when your parents died?" Jack asked.

"How did you know they died?"

Jack sipped his water. "Ah, you said they did. You said Juan is your only family left."

Pilar nodded. She forgot she said that. "That's right. Sorry. I was in college. My third year. My mom got sick and my dad was taking her to the hospital early one morning. He fell asleep and ran off the road."

"I'm so sorry. I didn't know," Jack said.

She smiled sadly. "Thanks."

He nodded. "So, do you want me to introduce you to everyone? Then you can put names to all the faces?"

Pilar nodded and let Jack lead her to the kitchen first. Two men stood shoulder to shoulder, one with glasses and the other with his arm around the woman at the stove.

"Hey, guys, this is Pilar. Pilar, Archer and Jaymes are brothers. Lily is the one who keeps us fed. Somehow, Archer talked her into marrying him next month. And Kelsea is a professor of psychology and dating Jaymes."

"I'm not going to remember any of that," Pilar said with a laugh. She shook hands with everyone. "It's nice to meet you all, though."

"You, too. What do you do, Pilar?" Lily asked.

"Um, I'm an occupational therapist. I work at Fallsview Elementary."

"That's not too far from us," Lily said. "We all live in an

apartment complex off 72nd Street, but we're on the end near the Boulevard."

Pilar nodded. "There's a lot to do in that area."

Lily grinned. "That's why Jaymes and I moved there."

Pilar tilted her head. "Wait, I thought he was Jaymes," she said, pointing to the guy kissing Kelsea.

The five of them laughed. "Jaymes and I went to college together," Lily explained. "We've been best friends for years and got apartments in the same complex. I met Archer last summer, and he moved in with me when he decided to stay in the area."

"Ah, that makes sense now."

Jack nodded. "It's a long story."

Pilar grinned. "I think I'm all caught up."

"Let me introduce you to the rest of them," Jack said, guiding her away.

All the men looked roughly the same. Big, lots of muscles, and kind smiles and eyes. She didn't know what was more confusing, keeping straight all their names or trying to understand what she was supposed to call them. Jack introduced the guys by what he calls them, but Pilar had no idea if that meant she should call them the same.

When Lily announced dinner was ready, none of it mattered anymore. Everyone filled plates with lasagna and salad. She said she threw it together when she heard they were all coming over that night. Pilar was impressed. She could handle cooking for two, but cooking for a crowd was something she would need time to plan for.

Lily and Kelsea took seats at the table in Justin's dining room and called Pilar over to join them. She smelled an ambush, but she figured she had no choice and went to sit with the only other women in the group.

At least she knew neither of them was sleeping with Jack.

11

"They don't tell us anything about their jobs, but we're assuming Jack's protecting you," Lily said. "Are you okay?"

Pilar nodded, touched by the concern in the eyes of the other women. It was clear they knew each other well, and if they were willing to welcome her into their world, she'd take it for as long as the offer was there.

"I guess I don't know what I'm allowed to tell you, but my brother was kidnapped yesterday by my ex."

"No shit," Kelsea said. "Wow. That's horrible. And I know shitty exes."

"You do?" Pilar asked.

Kelsea nodded. "Yeah, but that's another story. I'll tell you that later. Why did your ex take your brother?"

"I think he's trying to get to me. He wants me back, but he's... I didn't know when we were together, but he was in the cartel in Mexico. So was my brother, but Juan isn't involved with them anymore. But Carlos is dangerous. I hate sitting here and not doing anything."

Lily nodded to the other room where the guys were all

huddled together. "They're working on it. I promise you, when these guys get together, nothing will stop them."

"And they'll keep you safe," Kelsea added.

"Absolutely," Lily agreed.

"Thanks. Jack's been great so far." Lily and Kelsea exchanged a glance that had Pilar worried. "What?"

Kelsea shook her head, but Lily leaned forward. "Jack's not the kind of guy who sticks around. And I don't mean that to scare you off, but you don't know him. He's a great guy, but if I had a sister, I wouldn't want her to date him."

Pilar shook her head and forced a smile. She hated being so transparent. Usually she did a better job at hiding her thoughts and feelings, but she'd been so overloaded with them that she had a hard time covering up how she felt about Jack. "I don't have any thoughts about that. I know he's just here to protect me."

"Are you sure?" Lily asked. "I mean, I understand if you want him. He's crazy hot, and he can make anyone laugh. It's hard to resist guys like him."

Pilar pressed her lips into a grin. "I'm not going to have any trouble resisting Jack. When I'm terrified, sex is the last thing on my mind."

Lily and Kelsea exchanged another look that said they weren't buying it, but they didn't keep pressing Pilar for information.

Pilar hated lying to them, but she didn't know either of them. She wasn't even sure what their last names were. She wasn't going to tell them that the only man she'd slept with was Carlos, and that she didn't want to die knowing he was the only one who gave her an orgasm or made love to her. She had no designs on Jack long term, but he wanted her, and she wanted him, and there was no reason they couldn't

get it out of their systems, then go back to finding her
brother and being strangers.

JACK TRIED to keep his mind on the task at hand, but he was
getting distracted by the beautiful brunette sitting in the
other room. Pilar didn't look thrilled by the conversation she
was having with Lily and Kelsea, which put Jack on edge.
What were they saying to her?

"Are you listening to me?" Dunn asked, bringing Jack
back to the whole point of the conversation.

"Yeah, boss."

Dunn gave him a hard look that said he knew Jack was
full of shit, but he didn't say anything else about it. It
wouldn't make any difference if he did, and they both
knew it.

"They obviously didn't find what they were looking for
at the cabin," Dunn said. "And they were smart."

"We're smarter," Dex said. "We'll get them."

"The car?" Jack asked.

English shook his head. "Stolen. And clean. We think
they used it to get there, but they had to have realized we
couldn't cover all the woods. It looks like they made a
focused attack knowing someone would set off censors
somewhere."

"They were willing to risk it, though," Dex added. "They
wanted something and they think she has it."

"I don't think she has any clue," Jack said. "I've talked to
her a few times, and she's convinced Carlos took Juan to get
to her."

"Can't say I blame the guy," Dex said, his eyes veering off
to stare at Pilar.

Jack growled, drawing the attention of the entire group. When he realized what he did, he schooled his features and tried to play it off as nothing.

Too bad he was in a room full of professional lie detectors.

"Is something going on with you two?" Dunn demanded.

"No, sir," Jack said, avoiding his gaze.

"When I got here, he was shirtless and coming from the bedroom," Slade provided.

Jack threw him a stare intended to harm. Unfortunately, he couldn't throw a punch, too.

"What were you doing?" Dunn asked, his voice harsh and unforgiving.

Jack looked up into the black eyes of his boss. He and Dunn knew each other in BUD/S. They went through together, and when they were placed on the same Team, Jack was happy to have a friend.

He no longer thought it was such a good thing that they knew each other so well. Jack saw the fury in Dunn's eyes. Dunn warned him not to trust Pilar. He carried his own baggage from overseas back home and was shoving it in Jack's face. Something Jack was not willing to take.

"Would you like the exact details or is a general description enough for you, Pres? I know it's been a while since you've gotten laid, so maybe you need a diagram," Jack said, getting right up in Dunn's face.

To his credit, Dunn didn't blink. The room was eerily still as everyone waited for his reaction. Jack was so close to him, he could feel his friend's breath on his face. They were nose to nose, eye to eye, chest to chest.

Jack knew he should take a step back, but he wasn't going to look like a pussy in front of anyone. And he wasn't going to let anyone tell him who he could fuck. If he wanted to nail Pilar on the dining room table while everyone ate dinner, and she was on board with it, he damn well would. But the only one who had a say in Jack's sex life was Jack and the woman he was sleeping with. Not his boss. Not his friends. No one.

"Do you really think it's a good idea to get involved with her?" Dunn asked quietly. "We don't know what the situation is here. Juan came to us, and this op went sideways because he didn't follow protocol. Now you're doing the same thing and fucking the woman you're supposed to be protecting. Is that smart?"

Jack scoffed. "Are you asking me or are you asking yourself?"

Dunn closed his eyes and took a step back.

Jack should have felt good for winning, but he felt like shit for throwing it in Dunn's face. "Dunn."

He shook his head and turned and walked out the back door into the darkening night.

The rest of the team turned to face Jack. Dex glared at him, then followed Dunn outside. English, Jaymes, Mason, and Rocky stepped away. They were the smart ones staying out of the whole thing. Slade and Archer moved toward Jack.

Great.

"I don't want to hear it from you," Jack said with a finger at Archer. "You have no room to talk about this subject."

"That's exactly why I'm talking to you about it," Archer said, hands on his hips.

"Would you have listened if we told you not to screw her?" Jack asked.

Archer smirked. "You did tell me that."

"And you didn't fucking listen," Jack retorted.

Archer's smile grew. "Hell, no, I didn't listen. And if I had it to do all over again, I still wouldn't. But you're not me."

Jack snorted. "No, I'm not. Because I don't have the guilt of killing my best friend hanging around my neck."

"Just the guilt of killing the last woman you fucked," Archer said, his eyes understanding but firm.

"Fuck you."

Archer shrugged as if it didn't bother him at all. It probably didn't. He found out he wasn't the one who killed Rodney, his best friend and their teammate. His guilt was gone. Jack's would never disappear.

"Listen, it sucks. She had no right to put that on you. It wasn't your fault, but until you can believe that, it's going to hang on you and follow you into every relationship you have." Archer wasn't backing down.

"I'm not getting into a relationship with her," Jack hissed.

"You were just going to fuck her in my guest room?" Slade demanded.

"Listen, guys. I appreciate what you're doing here, but I don't know why it's necessary. None of you get a vote here."

"Does she know?" Archer asked.

Jack glared at him.

Archer wasn't letting him off that easily.

"No," Jack finally admitted.

"She needs to. I think you know that. And Dunn deserves an apology," Slade said.

Jack didn't like either, but he knew they were right on both.

DUNN AND DEX came back in a few minutes later. Dunn

didn't even look at him, but Dex glared hard at Jack. He deserved it, too.

Jack wanted to pull Dunn aside and say something, but he didn't have time before they had to dive back in to what was going on.

"We need to figure out our next step. We have footage of the guys at the cabin, but we can't track them. There aren't any cameras in the area off our property, so there's no way to know where they went or even what they were in. We're kind of in the dark here," Dex said, taking the lead.

"Still nothing on Juan?" Jack asked.

Dex shook his head. "Nothing. His phone is off, his trail is cold. Our best option is to draw them out since they're not talking."

"How can we draw them out?" Jaymes asked. He wasn't an official member of the team, but he was involved in just about everything they did. After the months they all spent working with him, Jaymes had become one of them. Jack didn't think of Jaymes as just Archer's brother, but as his, too. He was smart and an asset when he could be there and help.

"We need to think they can have what they want," Dunn said, his dark eyes drilling straight into Jack's.

"You can't do that," Jack blurted. "No."

Dunn glared at Jack. "This isn't personal, Jack. I've been thinking we need to do this since yesterday. It has nothing to do with what you said."

"She's not trained," Jack argued.

Dunn shrugged. "The problem is we don't have a lot of options. We're on a time crunch, and we all know it. If we're going to get Juan back, we have to tip our hand. They won't crawl out of their holes unless they think it's worthwhile."

"We can't trade," Jack said, his throat closing up at the thought of Pilar going back to Carlos.

"I'm good at being the asshole, so I'm going to be it again. The only reason we're doing this is because he has information for us. We've been operating under the assumption that whatever this is is good enough to put everyone away forever. That's why we're risking our lives here. Not for him, and not for her." Dunn paused to let everyone absorb his statement. "That said, we're not in the business of turning over innocents to psychos."

Jack nodded with the rest of them.

Dex glanced at Jack then said, "When do we need to do this?"

"The sooner the better. We don't know what they're doing to him." Dunn met the eyes of the men in the group. They'd all been through the same training. Slade was held prisoner for almost two weeks. They'd seen and done their fair share of gruesome things. Which meant they had active imaginations about the things Juan could be going through.

"Is there anything to say he turned on us?" Arched asked quietly.

Dunn shook his head. "No proof, but no proof otherwise, either. We're going into this under the assumption that something changed when Juan went to meet Carlos and he either let himself get taken or he was surprised by the whole thing."

"At what point do we fill Pilar in on the whole operation?" Archer asked.

Dunn stared straight at Jack. "We're not there yet. Jack is convinced she's innocent in all this, but if she's not, we could be playing into their hands."

"Do you really think she's a criminal mastermind?" Jack spat.

Dunn raised an eyebrow. "No, but she grew up with one and fucked another. I have no idea who she is. Do you?"

Jack shut up, hating Dunn in that moment.

"All right, let's take a step back. Jack thinks she's innocent. He was the one who saw her freak out yesterday. And he survived the night. She made a phone call about work, which we verified. She didn't reach out to Carlos or anyone else. If she's hiding something, she's excellent at pretending. I don't see it. Her emotions are all over her face," Slade said.

As a group, they turned to look at her. Jack smiled when her cheeks turned pink and she ducked her head.

"Jesus guys, really?" Dex said. "Everyone look at the woman at once. Let's really freak her out. As if this isn't enough."

Jack didn't look away when the rest of them did. She smiled at him, her cheeks flushed again. He couldn't stop his own lips from turning up.

"I have to agree," Dunn said, drawing Jack's attention again. "The little I talked to her yesterday, she didn't strike me as that skilled. I don't think she has any idea what's going on. And she honestly believes Carlos is simply after her."

"So, maybe we fill her in a little bit. Tell her some of what's going on. Maybe tell her Jack was there to meet Juan because he said he had something to give us, and when he ran into her and she said he was gone, Jack realized something happened. Maybe she'll know. Or maybe she can come up with something he might have been willing to turn over." Dex met the eyes of the rest of the team, looking for approval.

Archer nodded. "That's better than sending her into the lion's den."

"I agree," Dunn said. "For tonight, we'll let her try to

relax. I think she had enough to deal with today. I'll be back first thing in the morning to talk to her."

Slade nodded his agreement, and the others followed suit.

"How late are you guys working tonight?" Lily called from the table.

"Not much later. Why?" Archer asked.

"Because Kelsea and I are going to head home soon if you guys are going to be much later. We're tired and have to work tomorrow," Lily said.

Archer looked at Dunn, who nodded. "We're done."

"Everyone get some sleep. We need to be on high alert tomorrow if we reach out," Dunn said quietly.

Jack stepped to the side while everyone filed past him, none of them saying much to him. He was always the guy who brought light and humor to the group. Instead of doing that, he was wrapped up in his own head and pissing everyone off.

Especially his friend.

"Can we talk?" Jack asked Dunn before he walked away.

Dunn crossed his arms and faced Jack.

"I shouldn't have said any of that. I was an ass."

Dunn nodded.

"Nothing?"

Dunn shrugged.

"Fine. You're right. I'm messed up and I shouldn't get involved with her. It was stupid, but... hell, I have no excuse."

"Does that mean you're not going to do it again?"

Jack glared at him. "I didn't fuck her. I was going to, though. If y'all hadn't shown up when you did, I would have."

"Why?" Dunn asked.

Jack shrugged. "I haven't wanted a woman since Meredith. Not because I was in love with her, but because I thought I read them all wrong. I didn't trust myself."

"But you trust yourself with her?" Dunn asked, his eyebrows pulling together.

Jack shook his head. "No, but I trust her."

"That's risky."

Jack nodded. "I know. But it's different. She said she's not interested in anything. I think she's running just like I am."

Dunn shook his head. "That's not a good reason. It sounds like we're going to have two casualties."

Jack glanced at Pilar, who was watching him talk to Dunn. "She's stronger than me, man. She'll walk away and break me if I let her. She's not going to get hurt here."

"You getting hurt isn't a better option."

Jack smiled. "No, but I deserve it."

Dunn shook his head and got in Jack's face. "Meredith isn't on you. She never should have put it on you. You were up front with her, and she chose to ignore what you said."

Jack shrugged. "Maybe, but that doesn't mean it was right. I've never gotten attached. Fundamentally, something in me is broken."

"That may be, but you're still family."

Jack nodded. "Thanks. I'll try not to be a dick again."

Dunn snorted. "You will be, but I get it. I have my moments."

Jack smirked. "Lots of them."

Dunn flipped him off and turned to follow the others outside. He waved to Pilar on his way by, and nodded to Slade.

And then there were three.

12

THE MOOD IN THE ROOM CHANGED AS SOON AS THE DOOR closed behind the others. Pilar glanced between the two men she was left with and had no clue what they were thinking. She wanted to ask, but it was clear to her that the entire group had a connection she couldn't understand.

The community she grew up in was close, but everyone kept to themselves when it came to personal things. Her parents never talked to any of their friends about anything going on that mattered. Pilar always wondered if her parents would still be alive if they had. If someone was willing to help when her dad got too exhausted to drive her mom to the hospital.

Jack had that. He and his friends knew everything about each other. They could read each other, and as Pilar stood between Jack and Justin, she could tell they were having a silent conversation.

"I'm going to clean up the kitchen," she said, moving into the small area to the side. Lily took care of most of it, but Pilar had to do something, and getting out from between the two men seemed like a good idea.

She opened cabinets until she found places for the items left out and tried to ignore the whispered argument going on behind her. When she heard her name, from Justin, her entire body lit up with embarrassment.

She assumed he knew what he walked in on earlier, but Jack didn't say anything about it. Of course, Jack didn't say anything about anything while everyone else was there. He kept his distance from her.

Without a word to either of them, Pilar walked down the hallway she headed down earlier and ducked into the bathroom. She turned on the light and fan and sank down onto the closed toilet. She hadn't taken the time to process everything that was happening. She lost it the day before when Juan disappeared, and she cried like a baby when they were shot at, but she didn't think about it outside those two moments. Alone in the bathroom, knowing the two men outside were arguing about her, she lost it.

She put her head in her hands and let the tears fall. It was possible they would hear her, but at that moment, she didn't care. She let out all the fear and anger and frustration she felt. She sobbed and whimpered and prayed. She begged God and all the angels listening to bring her brother back safely, to remove Carlos from her life for good, and to find the kind of connection she witnessed with Jack and his friends.

She hated herself for asking for the last one, but she wanted it almost as much as she wanted the other two. When she was out of contact with Juan, she felt so alone. She wanted someone to talk to, but she knew letting someone in was dangerous with Carlos out there. She let him intimidate her.

She didn't want to live in fear anymore. She wanted to live her life. Stop hiding and step out into the world. She moved down the street from one of the most beautiful sights in the world, and she'd only been there once. Instead of marveling at the amazing things around her and enjoying the world she was a part of, she was hiding.

She was sick of it. And changing it was going to start immediately.

Pilar dried her tears and splashed cold water on her face. She realized she hadn't taken a shower since the morning before. She had a man to seduce, which required a good shower and a sharp razor.

She smiled at her reflection and left the bathroom. She snuck into her room and grabbed her bag, then went back to the bathroom and got to work. Her life was about to begin.

SLADE GLARED at Jack when the bathroom door closed again. "How can you think about fucking her when she's hysterical like that?"

Jack sighed. "I'm not thinking about it. Will you back off?"

Slade shook his head. "She seems nice, and yeah, she's gorgeous, but she's a client, or related to a client, and might have information we need. She's off-limits."

"I got the spiel from you and everyone else already. I get it."

"So you're not going to go after her?" Slade asked, narrowing his eyes.

Jack shook his head again. "No, I'm not. I haven't been this whole time."

"Your shirt just slipped off?"

Jack grinned when he thought about the way Pilar tentatively tugged his shirt up so she could touch his chest. Slipped sounded about right.

Slade whacked him on the back of the head.

"Ow! What the fuck?"

"Keep it in your pants," Slade growled.

The bathroom door opened again. Both men froze, knowing it was for the best if Pilar didn't hear their conversation. They waited until another door closed, but that didn't happen. Instead, she appeared at the end of the hall looking like a fantasy come to life.

Pilar's dark eyes met Jack's, but she addressed Slade. "I'm getting a little tired. I wasn't sure where I should sleep, though."

Slade grinned and walked toward her. "I'll show you the room you can sleep in. Jack's going to sleep on the couch. My room is right next door to yours."

Jack knew Slade mentioned the sleeping arrangements for his benefit instead of Pilar's. Asshole. He was cockblocking him. It was probably for the best, but Jack hated it.

Once Slade got Pilar settled, he took Howler out, then headed to his own room, with the promise that he'd cut off Jack's balls if he went into Pilar's room.

Jack was pretty sure he actually would, too.

Jack used the bathroom and brushed his teeth, then stripped out of his clothes and settled on the couch in his boxer briefs. He preferred sleeping naked, but he wasn't going to do that to Slade. In reality, he could have gone home, but he felt better staying close to Pilar. She was his assignment.

He punched the pillow behind his head and tried to settle on the couch. The house was too quiet without other people around, so Jack turned on the TV for some background noise and reached for his phone. He played a game and finally felt himself starting to drift off when a door opened down the hall. He froze, listening for whoever it was. Soft footsteps came his way.

He turned to look as she came into view. Her soft smile had him wide awake again.

"You okay?" he asked.

She shook her head.

Jack sat up and patted the cushion next to him. He pulled the blanket around his waist back so she could curl up on the couch, much like they did the night before. "What's wrong?"

She shrugged and settled next to him. She was silent for a long minute, as though deciding what to say. "Carlos was the first man who gave me any attention. He made me feel like I was more than just a brain. I was a woman when he was around. It was hard to ignore."

Jack didn't really want to hear about her relationship, but if she needed to talk about it, he would listen. It would make it easier to keep her in the untouchable part of his brain.

"He was the first man I slept with. He wasn't the first person I kissed, but he wasn't far from it. The other boys I dated were from my neighborhood and almost like brothers to me, but Carlos felt different. It was easy to agree to everything he asked."

"Did he ever force you..." Jack couldn't finish his sentence.

Pilar shook her head. "No. But I know now he would have. He's an evil man. Once I found out who he was... Juan was livid I kept my relationship with Carlos from him. He told me to leave and never come back because Carlos would kill me."

"I'm sorry you had to go through that."

She smiled and nodded. Her eyes blazed with gold. "He's the only man I've slept with, and I need that to change."

"Pilar," Jack groaned.

She shook her head. "No. I need you to listen to me. I don't know you well. After all this is over, I'll probably never see you again, but I'm sick of being afraid of life. I need to know there are good things in this world again, and you're one of those good things."

"I'm not," Jack blurted. The shock and hurt in her gaze had him rushing to explain. "I'm sure Lily and Kelsea filled you in on who I am. They probably told you to stay far away."

"It doesn't matter," she said.

Jack smiled. "The last woman I was seeing killed herself because of me."

Pilar gasped.

Jack nodded. "It's true. When I told her I was leaving on deployment, she said she couldn't live without me. I thought she was full of shit and laughed. I told her we never said we were forever, but she never believed it. I knew she was getting attached, and that's not some cocky asshole thing. I should have called things off earlier than I did, but I guess a part of me knew she was unhinged and if I waited until I was leaving the country, she couldn't show up at my place and try something."

"It's not your fault, Jack," Pilar said softly.

Jack scoffed. "It is, though. All the signs were there, but I ignored them. I told myself she was fine, and that she'd move on. She never did. And now she never will."

"And you think it's your fault."

He nodded. "I know it is."

"That's not how depression works. It sounds like she was depressed, and she wasn't getting the help she needed.

Depression is an ugly thing that lies to you. I studied a little about it in school. Depression is to blame for her suicide, not you and not her."

"I was the catalyst."

"If you weren't, something else would have been."

"I should have gotten her help," Jack said, voicing the thought he'd had since he found out what happened.

Pilar shook her head. "This wasn't on you. It's hard to spot, even for those close to the affected person. You have to let go of this."

Jack huffed a laugh and looked at her. "You're the one I should be comforting."

She shrugged. "I'm still hoping we'll get to that."

He shook his head. "I can't, Pilar. I want to, but I can't."

"Why not?" she asked, not mad but curious.

"I'm supposed to be protecting you. Keeping you safe. Not taking advantage of you."

"What if I take advantage of you?" she asked, her voice dipping low and sexy.

"Pilar," he groaned.

She looked up at him with wide eyes full of emotion. "I'm not looking for a relationship, Jack. I promise you, I'm not."

"That has nothing to do with it."

"Is it your dark secret? Are you afraid I'll lose it, too? That I'm depressed or something?"

He shrugged, her words hitting close to home.

"I wouldn't be allowed to work with kids. I see a therapist weekly because it's not always easy to hear the things kids say and help them. What else you got?"

He smiled at her confidence. "It's not right, Pilar."

She curled up against the side of the couch and dragged in a breath. "Okay. I'm sorry. I'm throwing myself at you, and you don't know how to tell me you don't want me. I'll just go back to my room. I'm sorry."

She got up to leave. Jack knew he should let her walk away, but he couldn't. She had to know the whole truth. "I want you, Pilar. So bad I ache for you. But Slade told everyone what he walked in on. You deserve better than me. Every single one of them agreed. I've never had a real relationship. The women I fuck are just that, nothing more. You're too amazing for something like that."

She stood with her back to him while he talked. He wanted to see her eyes, to read her, but she kept her back to him. "I don't want flowers and romance, Jack. Carlos did that. He sent me flowers and took me out. He promised me things. He brought me into a fantasy world. I can't trust anymore. I thought I loved him, but I never knew him. I gave my body to a man who put a bullet in another woman. After he raped her and beat her up. A woman I knew. A woman who could have been me."

Jack went to her and wrapped his arms around her, leading her back to the couch. He pulled her onto his lap again and let her cry. He held her, wishing he could take all her pain away.

When her quiet tears finally quieted, she lifted her head and looked up at him. Tear-stained tracks ran down her cheeks and soaked the edge of her t-shirt. Her dark eyes glistened under the glow of the TV. Jack's arms were around her back, and hers around his waist.

With every second she stared at him, Jack grew harder. He catalogued everything from the softness of her shorts to the smooth feel of her bare legs against his. The gentle stroke of her thumb on his side, as though she was comforting him. The way her hair glowed, and the gold in her eyes.

"I won't let him hurt you," Jack said fiercely. "He'll never touch you again."

"Will you, Jack? Will you touch me?"

"Pilar," he groaned again.

She shook her head. "Just for tonight, Jack. Let me erase Carlos from my body. Don't let him be the only man I've been with for another day. Please, Jack."

He couldn't say no, but he shouldn't say yes. He didn't say anything, just stared into her eyes. When she rose and straddled him, he let her. And when she leaned in and pressed her lips to his, he let her. And when she ran her hands down his back, he let her.

13

—————

Pilar felt alive for the first time in forever. Fear and distrust and disgust weren't clouding her thoughts or her mind. All that was left was desire for the man beneath her. The man who'd been driving her crazy for just over twenty-four hours.

She still couldn't believe she'd only met Jack the day before. The old Pilar never would have been alone with a man she didn't know well, let alone attacked him more than once and asked him to have sex with her. But she wasn't that person anymore. She couldn't be. She had to live her life again.

She rocked her body against his and tilted her head to the side. It was obvious from the ridge in his boxer briefs he was enjoying himself, but he wasn't engaging with her. His hands were stationary on her back, his lips tight together and unmoving under hers.

Pilar wasn't willing to give up, though. She could climb off him and walk away and go through another night without knowing what it was like to be stretched and filled by another man, or she could kiss and touch Jack until his tightly held control snapped and he became an active participant.

She chose option two.

She ran her hands down his chest, letting her nails slide over his skin. He trembled under her touch, but still didn't part his lips. She couldn't force her way inside, so she decided to put her tongue to use elsewhere.

Pilar slid from his lap and kneeled on the floor at his feet. He stared down at her but didn't speak. She leaned in and kissed his stomach, then one pec, then the other. She circled his nipples with her tongue, hoping it was something he enjoyed. Her experience with men was limited, but she read enough to know what could work.

She bit his nipple and was rewarded with a groan. She laved it, circling the tight peak, then nipped him again. Her hands roamed his upper body, tracing the muscles and learning every inch of him.

She kissed her way across to his other nipple and repeated the process, earning another groan. She licked and suckled his flesh as she moved up, climbing on top of him again and settling over him. When she wrapped her arms around his neck and sealed her lips to his, he cupped her ass and dragged her roughly against his body.

She sighed and darted her tongue out to run along his lips. He sucked her tongue into his mouth, then tangled it with his own.

With his control officially snapped, Jack took over. His hands slid up her back, lifting her shirt as he went. He groaned when he reached her shoulders without any barrier. He broke their kiss to pull her shirt off. He stared at her breasts as soon as they were visible, then watched as he put his hands on them.

"So beautiful," he murmured before taking one taut

nipple into his mouth. He sucked hard, drawing her breast in with the nipple and pressing it up to the roof of his mouth.

Pilar rocked slowly against him, needing the friction from his cock. Jack went from one nipple to the other, as though he couldn't decide which one he wanted to taste more.

"Ride me, Pilar. Take what you need from me," he growled in one of his switches.

The scratch of his whiskers on her breasts was almost as good as his tongue and his cock. She was quickly losing her mind.

"Faster, Pilar," Jack groaned. "I want these beautiful tits in my mouth when you come the first time."

"First... time?" she gasped.

"Hell, yeah. If I only get one night with you, I'm going to make it last."

The rough timbre of his promise sent her over the edge. She gasped and came with a shudder. Jack held her tightly to him, his mouth wrapped around her nipple the entire time.

When she started to come back down, Jack switched to the other side. "Now, we need one with this nipple. Do it again, Pilar."

"I can't," she moaned.

Jack flicked her nipple with the tip of his tongue. "Again, Pilar. I'm dying to be inside you, but I want to make sure you're ready for me. One more, Pilar. Then you can lie down."

His hands guided her hips in a fast rhythm over his cock. He lifted up and pressed against her, bringing her right to the edge and over even faster the second time.

"That's it, beautiful," he said. "So sexy."

Pilar was limp in his arms as he guided her to her back on the couch. He stretched out over her and pressed hard against her, making her gasp.

"Ah, you do have more in there. I need a taste of you, Pilar. Your tits are so sweet, but I need some of this pussy in my mouth. Are you okay with that, beautiful?"

Her panties flooded with his dirty words. Her cheeks heated as she nodded.

Jack ran a finger over her cheeks. "What's with this? Are you embarrassed by the way I talk to you?"

She shook her head and nibbled her lip.

"I think you are, but I think you like it. Do you like when I talk to you about your wet pussy, Pilar?"

She bit her lip and nodded.

"And these beautiful tits? You like that, too?"

She nodded again.

"Do you want me to tell you how hard my dick is right now?"

She gasped with excitement and nodded.

His eyes sparkled in the dim light of the room. "Oh, Pilar, you dirty girl. You like to hear all those naughty words. You love it when I tell you my dick is already pulsing for you, aching to sink into your wet pussy, to stretch you out. You've never been with a man like me because I know that other asshole had a tiny dick. You're going to feel me for days, Pilar. And when you touch yourself next time, you're going to remember how good it felt when I was inside you. Aren't you, Pilar?"

She hesitated and nodded.

"You touch yourself, Pilar?"

She nodded again.

"I do, too, beautiful. I did this morning in the shower. And you know what I was thinking about?"

She shook her head.

"You, Pilar. How fucking sexy you are. I wanted you the minute I saw you, and this morning I lost it. I've been hard since I carried you into bed yesterday. I didn't want to leave you there alone. I wanted to climb into that bed with you and fuck you until you forgot about everything outside of us. Would you have liked that, Pilar?"

She nodded.

He smirked. "Are you going to say anything, or just nod?"

She nodded, and they both grinned. "I love your voice," she whispered. "I... I guess I like dirty talk."

"Have you ever done it?"

"Talked dirty?" she asked.

He nodded.

"No."

"Try it. My mouth is going to be busy for a few minutes. Tell me what you like. How good my mouth feels on your pussy."

She moaned softly and arched into him.

Jack closed his eyes and swore softly. "You're gonna make me come in my underwear like a teenager, Pilar."

"I want you to come inside me."

"I will, beautiful. For right now, it's your turn again."

HE EASED HIS WAY DOWN, dragging her shorts and panties off as he went. When she was stretched out bare in front of him, he had to close his eyes and disassemble and reassemble his MK II before he could look at her again.

"Are you okay?" she asked softly.

Jack looked up at her, his gorgeous curvy woman

stretched out like a buffet for his next meal. There were so many inches he wanted to taste. He nodded and focused on his target, the apex of her thighs and the wet pink skin waiting for him.

"You're stunning," he said.

Her cheeks went pink again.

"I'm not a virgin, Pilar. Not even close. I've been with more women than I can remember," he said.

Her eyes shuttered, her smile faltering, and he rushed to finish his thought.

"I'm not trying to make you feel bad. I'm only telling you so you know that when I say you're the most beautiful woman I've ever been with, you know it's not an empty compliment. You're gorgeous, Pilar. I love every inch of you, from your pink toenails to your pink nipples to your pretty pink pussy. I think pink is my new favorite color." He traced a finger through her slick skin, and she shivered. "This color pink right here."

"Oh, God."

"I hate to ask you this, Pilar, but we need to be quiet."

She nodded. "I'm not loud. I live with my brother. I have to be quiet."

Her eyes dimmed just enough to tell Jack she was retreating into her head again.

He nipped her thigh, and those gold swirls glowed in her gaze again. "Focus on me, beautiful."

He spread her wide with his palms on the inside of her thighs and his thumbs on her wet flesh. He blew lightly on her, enjoying the way her pussy tightened at the cold. He ran his thumbs through her slick folds, drawing her come up to her clit.

She arched toward him, offering herself up. "Touch me, Jack. Please."

"Where do you want me to touch you?"

"Inside. I want your finger inside me."

"Just one?" he asked, looking up at her face to see the answer.

Her eyes widened. "How many can you fit in there?"

He shrugged. "My dick is about the size of three of my fingers, so I'm hoping at least that many."

She licked her lips and nodded. "I can't wait to feel you inside me."

He ran a finger around her entrance, ignoring his throbbing dick. He wanted to sink into her and lose his mind, but she was barely not a virgin. He had to be careful with her.

He eased a finger inside and groaned at how tight she was. She whimpered and lifted her hips toward him. "So good," she whispered.

"You're so fucking tight, Pilar. I can't wait to stretch you out, to feel every ripple of you as you come on my cock."

"Yes, please. I want to do that."

Jack chuckled. "Definitely."

Her body loosened as Jack pumped his finger slowly in and out of her. He watched her body, slick come flooding around his finger with every stroke.

"I need to taste you, Pilar. Are you ready?"

She nodded and propped herself up to watch. He held her gaze as he lowered his head. He withdrew his finger all the way and added a second one, thrusting in with both as he pressed his tongue to her clit.

Her head dropped back to the arm of the couch. Her entire body tightened, then relaxed and drew him in deeper.

"Oh, God, Jack. That feels so good," she whispered.

"Tell me more," he said against her flesh.

"Your tongue, oh, God, your tongue. I need a vibrator

that works like your tongue. I'm so close, Jack. So close. Fuck me with your fingers. Inside. So good. Jack. So good."

He followed her instructions with a smile and sucked hard on her clit when she clamped down on his fingers. She came hard, her body going completely rigid before she bent at the waist and shook with the force of her orgasm.

"More, Jack. Please. More. Let me feel another finger so I know I can take your dick inside me."

"Jesus, Pilar. That mouth. So damn sexy."

"I'm done being scared. I know what I want, and right now, I want you to shut up and lick my pussy."

He smirked as he sucked hard on her. He added his third finger, easing it in as she stretched around him. She lifted her hips with every gentle thrust, clearly impatient. She wasn't the only one. His cock throbbed against the edge of the couch, demanding playtime.

Jack nipped lightly at her clit, and she opened up enough for all three of his fingers to slide in. She moaned at the feel. He teased the spot deep inside her, getting her attention.

"What was that?" she asked, gasping for breath.

"A secret. But we're going to save that for when I'm inside you. Are you ready for me?"

"Yes, please, yes," she said.

Jack wiped his mouth on the back of his hand and grabbed a condom from the pocket of his pants.

"Did you know this was going to happen?" Pilar asked.

Jack shook his head. "No. I never dreamed it would. I always keep a few with me."

Her eyes shuttered just enough that he knew he said the wrong thing.

"I hoped it would, Pilar. I told you I wanted you."

His words worked, and thankfully, she didn't unpack

them. If she had, she would have remembered he hadn't been home since they actually met. But that didn't matter at the moment.

He rolled the condom on and positioned himself between her thighs. He looked up and held her gaze as he eased inside her. She lifted her hips to welcome him in. When he felt her resisting, he withdrew just slightly, then rocked inside again. Slowly, her body relaxed around him until he was fully seated inside her.

"Oh, my God, you feel so good," she whispered. Her brown eyes glowed as she stared up at him.

Jack didn't trust himself to move yet. He clenched his jaw as he held back the desire to lose himself and take her.

He'd been with more than a few women. He clicked with them, in or out of bed. But with all of them, he knew walking away was going to be simple. A nice-knowing-you and a wave and he'd be gone.

As he held himself still on his friend's couch, buried to the hilt inside a woman he'd only known for a day, he was feeling something different. Something he couldn't explain or understand. Something that made him want to wrap her in his arms and never let go.

He told himself the feeling would pass and ruthlessly shoved it to the side. He withdrew, almost to the point where he fell out, then thrust back into her gently. She hummed her approval, and he did it again. With every stroke, he fought to hold it together. He was so close, he thought he was going to come on every stroke, but he had to wait.

"Harder, Jack. I want to know the secret," she whispered, reaching up and setting her hand on his cheek.

He looked down at her. Her eyes were wide and trusting. Her skin flushed a beautiful shade of pink. Her nipples were red from his teeth, her breasts scratched by his whiskers. He looked farther to where her rounded belly sat between them and down to where he entered her. Her legs spread wide to let him in.

Just having her wasn't enough. She asked him for one night. To erase the murderous scum she was with before. He couldn't do that. It wasn't enough. He couldn't just fuck her and be done. He had to own her. To possess her. To have her in a way he hadn't. To show her how she should be loved. Even if he couldn't be the one to love her after their night was over.

Jack pulled back, then slammed hard into her. She gasped. Her eyes snapped shut. He did it again, not giving her time to adjust. Her eyes flipped open.

"More," she whimpered, begging.

Again and again, he thrust into her. He choked back his own need to come, ruthlessly shoving down the build-up as he fucked her hard. She whimpered unintelligible sounds, her eyes slammed shut as she raced toward her orgasm.

Her hands reached up and circled his neck. She clawed down his back to his ass and dug in. He bit his cheek to keep the roar inside.

She was close. He could feel it. He grappled for her leg, draping her knee over his elbow and keeping up his relentless pace. She gasped, her eyes flickering open long enough to catch his gaze, then slamming shut as her channel clamped down hard on his dick.

She rose up and bit his shoulder, screaming into his flesh as her body pumped him for more and more.

Jack stopped breathing as he drove into her one last time, finally letting his own release come. He buried his face in her neck and grunted through his orgasm, his whole body shaking from holding back for so long.

They both went slack, collapsing together on the couch,

still entwined, and Jack still inside her. He told himself it was like any other time he had sex. He was tired. He'd move in a minute. She'd go back to her bed.

But for the first time, he didn't want her to leave as soon as they were done. He wanted to wrap himself around her and hold her close all night. He wanted to wake up with her in his arms and keep her safe.

But none of it was going to happen.

14

Carlos stormed into the room, slamming the door against the wall with a satisfying crack. He wanted to do the same thing to that fucker keeping Pilar from him.

He stalked across the room and threw the pictures at Juan. "Who is this man? Who is he?"

Juan looked up at him. His lip was split with dried blood trailing from it. His nose sat at an angle, more dried blood around that. His eyes were purple and bruised, one barely open. He smelled even worse than he did the day before. He listed to the side slightly, as though he couldn't sit up straight.

The sight made Carlos want to grin. It wouldn't be long before Juan cracked and gave them what they wanted, whether they had Pilar or not.

"I apologize," Juan said through clenched teeth. "I'm unable to catch things at the moment."

Carlos snatched one of the pictures off the floor and glanced at it. It was the one where the man's face was visible. He was shielding Pilar, crowding her against the side of the SUV. He stuffed it into Juan's face. "This man. Who is he?"

Juan leaned back to look at the picture, and a smile crossed his face. "Why do you want to know?"

"Because he had his hands on Pilar. He needs to die for that."

Juan chuckled, a rough sound at first that grew louder the longer he laughed. The sound grated against every one of Carlos's nerves. He didn't have time for mockery. He swung, connecting with Juan's swollen cheek with a satisfying crack.

Juan immediately groaned, and his laughter stopped. His head drooped to his chest.

Carlos grabbed Juan's ridiculous blue hair and yanked, lifting the man's head until their eyes met. "You are not man enough to resist me. Tell me who he is."

Juan spit blood in his face, covering Carlos. He dropped Juan's head and stepped back, frantically wiping his face and clothes.

"You're going to pay for that," he growled.

"What are you going to do? Beat the shit out of me? Check my pants, asshole. You already did. I'm never going to give up my sister."

"Then you will die."

Juan shrugged. "We both know I'd die before I'd give her to you, and if he's the one protecting her, you won't find her."

"I already found her once."

Juan nodded, his head barely making it up. "I guess you did, but you have no leads now. And you're more worried about finding Pilar than you are about what I have, which means you're going to get a call soon."

Carlos narrowed his eyes. Juan knew far too much about the operations they ran. He was smart. What pissed Carlos off was he was also right. They would come after him if he didn't deliver on what he promised. Juan and all his information. Tied up in a bow.

"Then how about we talk about what you have," Carlos said, wiping the last of the blood from his cheek onto his sleeve. He needed to throw away his shirt, which pissed him off. He hated wasting clothes. He rarely got his hands dirty anymore, but he relished the thought of doing so with Juan and Pilar. He volunteered for the job, knowing he could take out all his frustrations on them. He was holding some back for Pilar. She deserved to know how she'd hurt him.

"Are you ever going to stop being so predictable?" Juan asked with a smile and a shake of his head. "I really thought you'd have taken over by now. You were on the fast track when I left. Clambering for a seat at the table. And now you're here, covered in blood. I thought you'd do more with yourself, Carlos."

Carlos wanted to hit Juan again, but that was the other man's intention. He could take the pain. He'd pass out and stop having to talk. But Carlos didn't have time to wait for him. He needed answers.

"Where did you hide it?"

"Hide what?" Juan asked.

"The information you stole."

Juan shook his head. "I don't know what you're talking about."

Carlos balled his fists. He wasn't known for his patience. "Where is Pilar?"

"Probably fucking the guy in the picture. He has quite the reputation."

Carlos's blood boiled. The pictures he had showed the man protecting Pilar, but not touching her the way a lover would. "She's mine."

Juan scoffed. "She was before, but she's not a child. She's

a woman, and you sent her running into the arms of a man who fucks every woman he meets. Pilar's probably screaming his name right now."

"No, she wouldn't. She's mine."

Juan shrugged and slumped over with the movement. He winced, but found the strength to glare up at Carlos. "She doesn't think she's yours. She left your psycho ass when she found out what you are. She ran so fast, she left a dust trail. She'll never come back to you."

"She will," Carlos declared. "If I have to force her, she will."

Juan smirked. "Nah, not once she's been with a man like him. He's going to keep her safe from you."

Carlos saw red. He couldn't lose Pilar to a gringo. Or any man. The man in the pictures had murder in his eyes. He wasn't a good man. He had secrets, and Carlos was going to learn them. He would have Pilar again.

"She's mine," Carlos said. "She'll always be mine."

Juan shook his head. "You missed your chance, amigo. She's moved on. Which means you're not getting anything you came here for."

Carlos lost it. He swung, letting his fists take the brunt of his anger. He beat Juan until the man stopped grunting and slumped to the side, held upright only by the restraints that kept him in his chair.

Carlos felt marginally better, but he still didn't have answers. He needed answers soon, or he'd be the one tied to the chair.

NAILS SCRATCHED THE FLOOR. Fast. Racing. Toward him. A soft thud, then footsteps followed.

Jack tried to make sense of it, but his brain was foggy. He was exhausted.

"Jack!" a voice called out. "Jack, wake up! Pilar's gone."

"What?" Jack asked.

"Pilar. She's not in her room. She's gone. Get up." Slade's voice.

Slade. F-BOMB. Pilar. The pieces were slowly fitting together. For some reason, Jack wasn't worried. Why?

"Pilar," he said.

"Hmm?" she replied, her arm tightening around his waist. Her bare breasts were against his chest. Her warm heat cradling his hard cock.

"What the fuck?" Slade again.

Jack finally opened an eye and saw Slade standing over them, phone in his hand. "Dude! Are you taking a picture?" Jack dragged the blanket up to cover Pilar. Her breasts were pressed against his chest, but nothing covered them above the waist.

"I... No. Fuck, Jack. What did you do?"

She kissed his chest. "I think that's pretty obvious."

Jack snorted and kissed the top of her head.

"Jesus. Are you two drunk? Or high?"

"Tired," Pilar said, pulling the blanket tight around her shoulders. "Didn't get much sleep."

Jack grinned and palmed her ass. His hand was under the blanket so Slade couldn't see. He knew there was a reason he was supposed to stay away from her, probably a hundred, but sometime during the night, he stopped caring. All that mattered was Pilar and being what she needed.

She moaned softly and wriggled closer to him. Her hand slid between them and wrapped around his cock.

He saw stars.

"Jesus. You two need to break it up. This is a job, Jack.

Not your personal fuck time. And that's my damn couch, dude." Howler whimpered. "I'm taking the dog out. When I get back in, please... don't be naked on my couch."

Jack nodded and waited until the door slid closed behind Slade, then groaned. "You're going to kill me."

Pilar giggled. "I'm sore, but I want you again."

Jack pulled back and looked at her. "Shower?"

She grinned. "It's economical. Saves time and water."

"Yeah, we're saving the earth."

"Exactly," she said.

They scrambled off the couch and ran down the hall together. Jack turned on the water and realized he forgot a condom and raced back, grabbing his bag and bringing it into the bathroom.

They made quick work of cleaning each other. When Jack dipped his hand between her thighs, she was slick and ready for him. "I love the way you respond to me. This tight pussy wants me again. Are you ready for me, Pilar?"

She moaned and spread her thighs so he could slide a finger into her. "Yes, Jack."

He pumped his finger into her, enjoying the way she whimpered, and grabbed the condom. He tore it open with his teeth and spit the wrapper outside the shower. "Help me with this," he said, holding it up for her to see.

She grabbed it and looked at it. "I've never..."

"Pinch the tip," he said, showing her what he meant, "then roll it down my cock."

She did as he instructed. She stroked him a few times in the process, making him groan.

"I need to be inside you," Jack said, dipping his head to catch her lips. He nipped her lower lip, then plunged his tongue inside her mouth. She wrapped her arms around his neck and gave in to the orgasm he worked out of her. Her knees went weak, all her weight falling on him to support. He held on to her, loving the feel of her body slipping against his.

When she opened her eyes and smirked up at him, he nearly lost it right there. She was so gorgeous after she came. The gold in her eyes burned brighter, and her smile made him feel like the sexiest man alive.

"Turn around, Pilar."

"Why?" she asked.

"You'll see."

She did as he asked. He pressed up against her back, sliding his hands up to cup her breasts. She moaned and lifted her arms to circle behind his neck. He pinched her nipples and dipped his hand between her thighs again.

"Do you want me inside you? Can you take it?"

"Yes, Jack," she moaned, spreading her thighs for him.

"Good. I can't wait to feel you come on my dick again."

"Like this?" she asked.

He nodded and tugged her nipples so she bent forward slightly. "A little more," he urged.

She did as he said, leaning forward.

"Put your hands on the wall. Or you can touch yourself."

She put her hands on the wall. He was a little disappointed. He lined up and slid his tip inside her. She spread her feet as wide as they could go and he slipped in a little farther.

"Can I feel it? Where you go in?"

"What do you mean?" he asked, his hands holding her hips.

"Can I touch?"

"Fuck, yeah."

He waited until her fingers grazed his dick to slide in

again. As he moved, her body shook and she let out a low moan. "Oh, God, Jack. That's... wow. Do it again."

Most of the women Jack had been with over the last decade were experienced. They slept with men in bars and men on vacation and men they were friends with. They were eager to have sex in all kinds of interesting ways, but they'd been there, done that in every situation.

Being with someone so inexperienced was a rush. She was learning about her body and how amazing sex could be. Everything was new and different.

After Jack disposed of their first condom the night before, Pilar snuggled up to him on the couch and told him about growing up in Mexico. Her accented voice made him forget about the danger she was in as she talked. He enjoyed learning about her.

When she asked how long they needed to wait until they could have sex again, Jack's greedy dick rose to the occasion and filled her once more. They fell asleep after that time, but Jack woke up hard and throbbing a couple of hours later when Pilar rocked her bare ass against him. He thought she was awake and teased her with his fingers. She woke up ready for him and they had slow, lazy sex. The fourth time, she wanted to try being on top, which he was happy to give her. The woman was eager to experiment, and he was a happy teacher.

But feeling her fingertips on his dick with every stroke inside her had him ready to go off without her.

"Touch yourself, Pilar. I'm not going to last long with your fingers there. Press your thumb to your clit and make yourself come."

She shook her head, the dark ropes of her wet hair swinging. "Harder, Jack. I want to come from just you."

He groaned and slammed into her. She moaned, her pussy tightening around him.

"Again."

He squeezed his fingers on her hips and did it again. And again. And again. Her fingertips slid lower until her hand just about wrapped around him. He lost all sense of himself and pounded into her, their wet, naked flesh slapping together. The sound echoed off the bathroom walls, driving him on.

"Yes, Jack. Oh, God, yes."

Her breath hitched, and she tightened more, drawing him in deeper. He adjusted his grip on her and shifted his angle, and with one stroke, she cried out and came hard.

She lifted up on her toes. Her hand on the shower wall pushed hard to keep her from falling face first. The hand between her thighs shook.

"More, Jack, please. More."

Jack was at the edge of his consciousness, barely able to hold his own orgasm back. "Touch yourself, Pilar. I don't know how much longer I can last."

He continued to slam into her, sending her close to the edge, but he came before she did, thrusting hard and deep and holding himself in her as he released inside her.

Jack wrapped himself around her, holding her body tight to his. She didn't say anything, but he could feel the tension in her, the tightness from needing to come again.

As soon as he thought he could support her, he released her. She smiled up at him. He kissed her, plunging his tongue into her mouth and sliding his hands all over her body. She whimpered against him, still so sensitive.

Jack kissed his way down her body until he kneeled at her feet. The spray from the shower forced him to close his eyes, but he could smell her musky scent.

"Jack."

"I need another taste of you, Pilar. And you need to come again. I know you do."

She sighed and tilted his head back, leaning forward to kiss him. He ran his hand up her thigh and teased her while they kissed. When she pulled back on a gasp, he lifted one of her legs and set it over his shoulder.

"Oh, yeah. There's that beautiful pussy. It's been far too long."

She giggled.

Jack licked her from bottom to top. She grabbed his head, holding him in place. He kissed her thigh and said, "Hold on to me however you need to. I can support you, Pilar. I won't let you fall."

She nodded, her eyes on his.

Jack kissed her thigh again, then set to work making her come. He teased her with his fingers and tongue, bringing her right up to the edge before he pushed her over. One wasn't enough for him, and he immediately dragged her into another orgasm. She tugged his hair and scratched his shoulders and even punched the wall at one point.

Jack was in heaven.

Once she was done, they washed each other again, then turned off the lukewarm water. They wrapped up in towels and worked around each other in the small bathroom to get clothes on. Jack's clothes were far too big on Pilar, but she just needed to get to her room where her clothes were. His t-shirt looked damn good on her. Especially since she wore nothing beneath it.

Jack finally opened the door to the bathroom. He kissed Pilar once before she ducked into her room, then he went to face Slade.

"You're a fucking idiot," Slade said as a greeting. "I told you not to fuck her."

"And you're not my keeper."

"I am today. You're in my house."

"You're right. So maybe we should leave."

"You know you can't leave. Dunn's already on his way over here to talk to her."

Jack breathed out a sigh. "Did you tell him?"

Slade's eyebrow went up. "You're afraid of him? You weren't last night."

Jack glared at Slade. "I'm not afraid of anyone."

Slade shook his head. "I didn't tell him. But you need to. You're not thinking clearly anymore. You can't do your job when you're emotionally involved."

"I'm not emotionally involved," Jack argued. As soon as the words left his mouth, he knew they were lies. He did care about Pilar. He always cared about the women he slept with. At least a little. Even the women he picked up in bars he cared about. For a few hours at least.

"Jack," Slade said.

"No, don't. Okay. I get it. I'm fucked up, and Pilar deserves better. Did you ever think that maybe I know that? You found us out here. She came to me. And I wasn't strong enough to say no to her."

"Because you're emotionally involved."

Jack blew out a breath and ran a hand over his hair. His t-shirt felt tight all of a sudden, like it was choking him. He needed to keep Pilar safe. It was the only thing that mattered to him. He couldn't turn that task over to anyone else.

Finally, Jack faced his friend and teammate and admitted the truth. "I'm not letting her go."

They stared at each other for a long minute. Everything was quiet, even Howler. Then a knock at the door set off the dog and drew the attention of both men.

Saved by the boss.

Pilar leaned against the door and smiled. She was sore everywhere, but she'd never felt better in her life. Jack was exactly what she needed.

She chewed her lower lip, though. It was obvious his friends didn't want them together. She got the feeling it went deeper than Jack's past and his ex, but she didn't know what held him back from getting close.

She grinned again. He was pretty damn close to her all night. And in the shower. The memory of him on his knees had her thighs trembling again. Wetness filled her, slicking between her bare thighs. She really needed to get dressed.

She went to her bag and pulled out panties and a bra, then stopped. She wanted to keep Jack's tee on. It smelled like him. She lifted it to her nose and inhaled deeply. Definitely keeping it on. If she was smaller, she'd wear it without anything under, but that wasn't an option. She had far too many curves and too big of breasts to go without a bra for the day. Especially around a bunch of men she really didn't know.

She dressed quickly, adding a pair of pink capris to the

black tee. It fell almost to her knees, but she didn't have time to do anything about it before there was a knock on the door.

"Yeah?" she called out.

"Dunn's here," Jack said through the door. "He needs to talk to you."

Her heart plummeted, and she sank to the bed. "Juan," she whispered. Her throat filled with regret and fear, stopping her from answering. For a few hours, she forgot how she met Jack. Forgot about her missing brother and her evil ex. Forgot about the world outside the sexy man who gave so freely of himself and his body to her.

Jack knocked again, but Pilar couldn't answer. She wasn't ready to hear that her brother was dead, or that they gave up, or something similar. She wouldn't rest until she found him and Carlos. Until Carlos paid for what he did.

"Pilar. Are you okay?" Jack again. His voice sounded concerned, maybe even bordering on panic.

She shook her head, but he couldn't see her. She just sat there, imagining the worst case scenario. She wasn't ready to hear it.

The doorknob rattled, and a few seconds later, the locked door popped open. Jack stood there, looking every bit of a badass. His dark eyes scanned the room quickly, assessing every inch for a change before they landed on her. His blue tee stretched tight over his muscles, muscles that were corded with tension. Jeans hugged his legs and cupped his dick like a lover, like she did not long before.

After what felt like entirely too long but was probably only a second or two, Jack dropped to his knees in front of her. "Pilar? What happened?"

She pushed the tears back. "Is he dead? Is that why Dunn's here?"

Jack shook his head and brushed her damp hair back from her face. "No, baby. He's not. We haven't found him yet, but if he was dead, they would have made sure we knew it."

Pilar didn't know why, but it made her feel better to know that. She was well aware that Carlos made people disappear. If he didn't want them to find Juan, they never would. But Jack was so sure that she believed him.

He slid his hands up her thighs and cradled her hips, staring up into her eyes the whole time. "Dunn wants to talk to you. I didn't mean to scare you."

She smiled at him. "I know. I felt guilty because I forgot about Juan, you know? I was so worried about living my life that I forgot all about him. How horrible does that make me?"

Jack shook his head. "Not horrible at all. Sometimes we have to grab whatever happiness is out there and ignore the shitty things in order to survive. It doesn't mean you love him any less or don't want to find him. It just means you were taking care of yourself for a little while."

She smirked. "I think you were taking care of me."

Jack snorted. "We took care of each other. Many, many times." He nuzzled her neck and kissed her jaw, then pulled back. "Sorry. I know we said last night only."

He rocked back on his heels and stood effortlessly. She immediately felt the loss of his support and reached for him.

He took her hand and tugged her to her feet, both of them laughing when she collided with him.

"I know you don't want forever," she said, "but I wouldn't be opposed to another night."

He narrowed his gaze at her. "Let's go talk to Dunn."

She pressed her lips together and nodded. She knew rejection when she heard it. He didn't want another night, but he didn't know how to tell her that. He was worried she'd lose it.

She wasn't that woman, and she never would be.

Pilar straightened her shirt, feeling silly for keeping Jack's tee on when he was clearly done with her, and followed him out of the bedroom.

Dunn and Justin were in the kitchen, drinking coffee at the dining table, a tablet between them that they were both studying. They looked up when Pilar and Jack walked into the room. Dunn slid Jack a look Pilar couldn't read, but one that said he wasn't happy, then grinned at her.

"Good morning," Dunn said.

"Good morning," Pilar responded. "Um, Jack said you need to talk to me?"

Dunn nodded and closed the tablet, setting it on the table in front of him. "I do. Would you like coffee or something? Jack and Slade are going to make breakfast while we talk if that's okay."

Pilar glanced at Jack, but his back was to her. Justin smiled slightly at her, then got up to help Jack. She didn't want to get in between them to get a coffee so she shook her head and lowered herself onto Justin's vacated seat.

"Did you find Juan?"

Dunn shook his head. "I'm sorry, but no. Not yet. We're going to keep looking for him. I wanted to talk to you about something else, though."

She tilted her head, wondering what else he'd be interested in.

"We know you think Carlos is really after you. That he took Juan to get to you. We're still trying to figure that part out. Can you tell me about meeting Carlos and your relationship?"

"You don't believe me?" she asked, hating that she was so

nervous. She felt like she was in trouble for something, but she didn't know what for.

Dunn shook his head. His eyes were kind, but there was a control about him that put her on edge. She didn't know how someone could be emotionless, but that was the impression she had of him. She was sure it was there somewhere, but it wasn't out front with him. Dunn was careful about everything he said and did, probably even what he wore and drove. His black tee and charcoal cargos were likely intentional so he could blend into the background. Black was neutral. It didn't stand out. And neither did he. Which meant he was looking for something if he was talking to her.

"Carlos and I dated a few years ago. He came to my house with Juan once. We sort of hit it off. I didn't know what he did, I didn't even know what Juan did. I thought they worked for a shipping company. I was home for the summer from college, and we dated the whole time I was there. A few days before I had to go back to college, I decided to tell Carlos I was in love with him and ask him to come with me to Texas, where I was going to school. I didn't want to be apart from him for months."

Dunn nodded and smiled, patiently waiting for the rest of the story.

Pilar took a breath. "My brother found out we were together before I could talk to Carlos, and Juan flipped out. He told me I didn't know anything about Carlos. I went to tell Carlos what Juan said and that I loved him, but when I got to his house... I saw him kill a woman. I was outside, and he didn't know I was there. I went home and told Juan. I was scared. Juan made me leave Mexico that night and go back to my aunt and uncle's house where I was living during college."

Dunn tilted his head. "And all this time, Carlos didn't know where you were?"

Pilar shook her head. "He knew where I was. He called me for months, begging me to give him another chance. He couldn't leave Mexico by orders of his boss, but he tried to stay in contact with me."

"Did you talk to him?"

Pilar shook her head again. "No. I declined all his phone calls and deleted the messages."

"And you never told anyone about it?"

"No. I took a video of what Carlos did that night, but Juan had me send it to him and then deleted it from my phone. He said it was to keep me safe. I knew if I went to the police, they would tell me there was nothing they could do. Carlos was in Mexico, and they couldn't make him stop calling me. Eventually, I changed my number."

"But you stayed in touch with your brother, right?"

Pilar shook her head. "No. Once Juan told me what he really did for a living, I stopped talking to him. The cartels ran our town, our country, my whole life. We hated them. Juan and I talked about getting out all the time when we were growing up. About escaping the torture and terror of living like that. We didn't want to have families and raise kids in that world, so we planned to leave. That's why I went to college in Texas."

"And stayed in the States?"

She nodded. "Yes. By the time I graduated, I knew I couldn't ever go back. Juan found me a couple of years after graduation and convinced me to move up here. He found my job for me and promised me he was done. That he'd walked away from the cartel."

"And you believed him?"

"Absolutely. He's my brother. Why would he lie about that?"

Dunn sighed heavily. "He lied about being in the cartel. Why wouldn't he lie about leaving?"

Pilar shook her head. "No, you don't know him. He wouldn't lie to me. He knows I can't handle that."

"Maybe you're right. I hope you are. I guess my question is how did he get out? The only way I've ever heard of people getting out of anything like that is turning over evidence and going into witness protection or a body bag. Sorry." He ducked his chin and looked up at her.

But his words did something to her. For two days, she was convinced it was all about her. That Carlos was after her. But in the years since she left Mexico, Carlos had never come after her. The one time he did, he ended up with Juan, then confronted her on the street. He could have taken her if he wanted to. There was no reason he couldn't.

She looked at Jack. He was staring at her. He was the reason. If he hadn't been there, Carlos probably would have taken her. But why?

"How did you know I would need help?"

He shrugged and cleared his throat. "You just looked like you did."

"What if he wasn't looking for me? Why did he come to the cabin?"

"We think Juan might have something that Carlos was sent to retrieve. You might be his reward. If he gets what they need from Juan, his bosses will get you back to Mexico for Carlos," Dunn explained far too calmly.

"As his slave. No. I can't. I'd rather die than go with him. I'll kill myself if I have to be with him." Fear pushed everything else out. Carlos would rape her, beat her, probably eventually kill her. He would punish her for the rest of her life if he captured her.

"We're not going to let that happen," Jack said, his voice low and menacing.

Pilar looked up at him, but Jack was glaring at Dunn. Dunn ignored him, keeping his focus on Pilar. She was missing something. Maybe a few things.

"Do you have any idea what Juan might have on the cartel? What information Carlos could be here to retrieve?" Dunn asked.

Pilar racked her brain and shook her head. "No. I... I don't."

"It could be anything, Pilar," Dunn pressed. "Probably more than the video you took. Something on a computer or his phone. A notebook where he has something written down. It could be anything with lots of information about the cartel's activities."

"I... no. I have no idea."

Dunn glanced at Jack and Justin, then scooted closer to her. "Take a minute, Pilar. Maybe something he won't let you see. Or something he always has with him. If we can find whatever it is they're looking for, Carlos won't be able to take you. You'll be safe. And we can take them down."

She nodded, thinking over Juan's behavior over the last year. He didn't have much. He kept his clothes in a small dresser in the living room since he slept on the couch. He didn't have a favorite anything. Shirt, hat, pants. Juan didn't own a computer, and he never used hers.

"My apartment was trashed. Wouldn't they have found what they were looking for?"

Dunn shook his head. "Not if they didn't know what it was. Or where it was. If Juan stashed whatever this is in a vent or in a utility hatch or something, they might not have found it."

"Wouldn't you?"

Dunn shook his head again. "We have no idea what we're looking for. At the time, we didn't even really know we were looking for something. Like I said, it could be as small as a computer chip or as big as a box of files. We have no idea. We're just trying to understand Juan's patterns. Get a better idea of what he might have and where so we can get it before they do."

Pilar nodded and kept thinking. She wished she'd spent more time with her brother over the last year. Asked him more about what he was doing and how he got away. She was smart, and she knew it wasn't easy to walk out on a group like the Castillo cartel, but she stuck her head in the sand and trusted that he did it without consequences.

Now, she had to figure out what Juan had on the cartel that Carlos was after. She had to keep him safe. Bring him back.

"Wait... you said if we find this, it'll keep me safe. What about Juan?"

Dunn exchanged a look with Jack and Justin. One that spoke volumes.

"You don't think he has a chance at getting out of this alive, do you?" she whispered.

Dunn met her gaze with his own level one. If there was ever a time when she needed steady, it was at that moment, but instead of calming her, it pissed her off more. He was giving up on her brother. He was letting Juan die so he could save her.

"A lot of people will live if we bring them down."

"And my brother's life doesn't matter?" Pilar screamed.

"Every life matters, but if we can't find him, we can't save him."

"So find him," Pilar growled. "Find my brother. And don't tell me you don't know where he could be. Set a trap, make a call, tap into everything out there, do all that fancy shit people do on TV. Find my brother."

"We've done what we can, Pilar," Jack said. "We're not giving up, but we've done it all."

"Well, except one thing," Dunn said.

Pilar waited with bated breath for him to elaborate. Instead, Jack growled and Justin cursed. She looked between all three men, anxious for someone to tell her what the hell they were talking about.

"What is it?" she finally yelled, dragging the attention of the men back to her.

"Give Carlos what he wants," Dunn said.

"What he wants?" Pilar asked. "But the only thing he wants is..."

She met Jack's gaze. The pain in his finished her sentence.

"Me."

16

———

JACK WAS GOING TO THROW UP. HE KNEW WHAT THEY WERE asking of Pilar, and he just stood there. He didn't tell her no because he knew what was at stake. He couldn't tell her yes either, because he knew what was at stake. There was no answer.

"You wouldn't be in any danger," Dunn told her.

Jack almost laughed. They all knew exactly who Carlos was. Even if they hadn't been working on this case for months, they had time to dig into who he was. But they had been on the case for months, and they knew. They knew everything about Carlos and what he'd done, both proven and rumor. And they knew Pilar would be in danger if she went anywhere near him.

Pilar gave him a smile, but one that didn't reach her eyes. They were dark and sad. "I'm always in danger. There's no way to stop it."

"We won't let him hurt you," Dunn said. "You won't be alone."

She lifted her gaze to Jack's again. "Will you be there?"

Before Jack could answer, Dunn did. "We'll all be there.

Carlos knows we won't send you in there alone. He's smarter than that."

"I need to understand this whole thing better," she said, shaking her head. "What exactly would the point be?"

"We think Carlos knows what he's looking for. Or has some kind of an idea. We think he might say something to you that will tell you what it is."

"He's not going to let me go. Not once he has me," she said, fear making her voice shake.

"He's not going to have you," Jack declared. "You'll be in the same room, but he is not ever going to have you again."

She nodded but didn't meet his gaze. She stared at the table, tracing a scratch with the edge of her nail.

"You don't have to do this," Dunn said. "If you're afraid, you don't have to go in there."

"No," she said firmly, glaring at Dunn. "I'm not going to be afraid of him anymore. I'm not going to live my life in fear. I've let him take too much away from me. Do you know, I've never felt like I was safe. All this time, and I've just been waiting for him to come back and take me. It was so easy to believe he was here for me. God, why did Juan take something from them?"

Jack knew the question was rhetorical, but he still felt compelled to answer. "He wanted you both to be safe."

Pilar snorted. "So much for that. He's being held captive by the son of a bitch who wants me dead."

"We'll keep you safe, Pilar," Dunn said again. "I promise you."

She nodded. "Now what?"

Jack was impressed by her strength. He wanted to tell her, but it wasn't the time. She needed to stay focused if she was going to come face-to-face with Carlos again. The last time she did, she almost lost it. This time, she would be prepared, but it wouldn't really be easier.

Dunn laid out a plan. They didn't have Carlos's phone number, but they had confidence he would reach out or show up if Pilar was somewhere he could get to. Obviously, they were tracking her, so it was simple to turn on her phone and let Carlos come to them. They had to make sure civilians were safe, so overly public places weren't ideal. Plus, it would limit the options for the rest of the team. They needed to know they could shoot to kill if necessary without risking the lives of anyone innocent.

Once Pilar was on board with the entire plan, Dunn put out a call to the rest of the team. All their other jobs were on hold until they had this case wrapped up, so everyone was available to meet them. They agreed to meet just after lunch, giving them four hours to get ready.

Dunn nodded to Jack when he was finished with his phone calls. Jack was watching Pilar but hadn't moved from his spot in the kitchen. Slade was at the table talking to her, so she was okay. As okay as she could be.

"Yeah?"

"You going to be okay with all this?"

Jack shrugged. "I don't have a choice. It's the job, right?"

Dunn glanced at Pilar and Slade. "Slade told me."

Jack nodded. "I figured he did."

"It's your life."

Jack snorted. "That's your way of saying I'm fucking up."

Dunn shook his head. "No, it's not. It's my way of saying I get it. I don't like it, but as you pointed out so eloquently last night, my vision is cloudy."

Jack narrowed his eyes. He definitely didn't expect that.

"You know I need you on overwatch. I know you want to

be next to her, but you're the only one that can take him out from a distance."

"Rocky's got a good shot," Jack argued.

Dunn nodded. "He does, but not as good as yours. If he grabs her and tries to take off, I don't want the expert shot to go wide and hit her. I need the expert taking the shot."

"Do you think he's going to?"

Dunn glanced at Pilar again. "Yeah. I think he'll try. He's unpredictable and emotional. And if he wants her, he's going to be stupid."

Jack looked at Pilar. His chest hurt thinking of her with that monster. He knew he wasn't perfect himself, but he wasn't ever going to willingly hurt a woman, not an innocent one. He'd read enough about Carlos over the last week, once they knew he was the one coming, to know he was truly evil.

"I know you don't want to hear it again, but for what it's worth, Meredith wasn't your fault. Don't put that on yourself right now. You getting involved with Pilar is different. She's strong. She'd kick ass if she needed to. She walked away from a man she thought she loved because she found out he was a killer. And she walked away from her brother. Meredith obviously wasn't well. Kelsea can tell you that. People don't commit suicide because of a breakup unless there's something else. She wasn't okay, and she didn't let anyone know so she could get help. You can't take that blame on any longer."

Jack finally looked up at his friend and boss. He took in the weary expression on Dunn's face and the sadness in his eyes. The tension in his body and the unease in his stance. "Neither can you," Jack finally said.

Dunn questioned him with his eyes.

"About Ashaki. She didn't turn on us because of you. You need to stop blaming yourself for her."

Dunn rolled his eyes.

"I mean it. It wasn't your fault."

"What about Brady? Maybe I'm not to blame for what either of them did, but I should have seen it coming. I was blinded by both of them."

Jack nodded. "You were. Because they knew what they were doing. They tricked all of us, and intentionally. Both of them were just like Carlos. Do you blame Pilar for Carlos?"

"No, of course not," Dunn said quickly.

"Then you can't blame yourself for Ashaki and Williams. They manipulated us and lied. They made us trust them, then turned around and stabbed us. They were planning this for a long time. I'm sorry she died, but she made a deal with people who couldn't be trusted. And Williams? We'll get him. He'll pay for what he did to Rodney and Jaymes, and Lily. He'll spend the rest of his life in a military prison."

Dunn nodded. "Thanks."

Jack clapped his friend on the back. "Let's solve today's problem first."

Dunn nodded again. "Hooyah."

"I'M SCARED," Pilar admitted. She couldn't look Jack in the eyes. He was a warrior. A fighter. He wasn't afraid of anything.

"Me, too."

She looked up at him then. "That doesn't make me feel better."

He smiled and leaned down to kiss her quickly, dispelling her earlier fears that he was pushing her away. "I don't want you near him. I don't like this."

"Do you think something's going to happen?"

He shrugged. "I always think something's going to happen. That's why I do what I do."

"Why?"

He stared straight into her eyes. "So I can stop it."

She shivered at the rough, possessive tone. "I wish you could be the one with me when I talk to him."

He tapped on the wire threaded between her breasts and taped to her. "I'll be listening the whole time."

She nodded. "I know, but it's not the same as having you next to me."

He traced the wire with his fingertips, probably to make sure it was secure. His light touch lifted goosebumps on her skin. She swayed toward him, wishing they could forget about Carlos and just go back to bed. Things were better when they were wrapped around each other on the couch. She was safe in his arms.

"I'll be watching every move he makes, and every move you make. I'll be the one to take him out if he tries anything."

"Like taking me?"

He didn't reply. He spun her around and checked the transmitter clipped to the back of her bra.

"Don't you have newer technology?"

"Yeah, but we think he'll be prepared for it and be able to jam our signal. This is old school and easily defeated, but you have to expect it."

"What if he expects it?"

Jack spun her around again and tilted her chin up. He stared down into her eyes, his swirling with the same need that pulsed through her. "I got you."

Three simple words. Not the three words she ached to hear from a man her whole life, but another three words that meant everything to her. She knew he meant them, and she knew they were true.

He pulled her in slowly, his hands sliding around her bare waist. He lowered his lips to hers and kissed her. They both opened at the same time, but there was no eagerness or desperation. Pilar felt it through every fiber of her being, but in that moment with her lips to Jack's, all she felt was peace. It wouldn't be their last kiss. It was one of many.

She tilted her head to the side and admitted to herself that she was getting attached to him. She knew the psychology behind it, that he was her protector and she assigned a savior moniker to him even though he was only doing his job. It was silly to fall for him, but she cared. He was a good man, and he was a hell of a lover. She needed both in her life, even if they were temporary.

Jack started to pull back from their kiss, but she wasn't done. He laughed when she tugged him back for one more taste. She needed his strength, just for another second.

When she finally let go, he tucked her under his chin and held her. "Nothing is going to happen to you. I got you, Pilar. I got you."

She nodded and held him, wondering if he needed her as much as she needed him.

JACK CLIMBED to his spot on the top of the rocks and scanned the area. It wasn't ideal, but there weren't any tourists out so it was going to have to work.

"In position," he said softly. "All quiet."

He waited a few minutes until Slade walked across the Three Sisters Island Footbridge in front of him, then repeated the same.

"Moving in," Dunn said, his voice audible through the earpiece Jack wore.

They were ready. Dunn was with Pilar. Ford and Dex were at the entrance to the park so they could watch for Carlos and his men to arrive and stop them if they tried to take Pilar with them. English was in the van in the lot, watching everything coming and going from the park. Rocky sat with him, ready to make changes if Carlos came in with tech they weren't prepared for. Mason was patrolling the area, posed as a runner so he could get a look at everyone around.

"In position," Dunn said. "Turning her phone on on your signal."

They all waited for English to say, "Ready."

Jack watched as Pilar pulled her phone from her pocket and turned in on. It didn't take long for her hands to start shaking. She had an earpiece in and could hear them, so Jack spoke.

"I got you."

He saw her chest rise as she took a deep breath and nodded. Her entire body relaxed, which let Jack relax.

"Incoming," Ford said through the earpiece. "Black van, no plates."

Relaxing was out of the question for Jack once he heard those words. He would have felt better if he could stretch out on the rocks and take aim, but they were in a public park. Niagara Falls State Park was not the kind of place he could carry a rifle to. He was limited to only the guns he could conceal, which meant he only had three.

"Parked next to the bridge," Rocky relayed. "Showtime."

Jack watched as Carlos and two other men got out of the van. One stood outside, sunglasses obscuring his eyes. The other guy followed Carlos down the path.

Jack heard mumbled Spanish as the men walked by him, unaware of him as he laid back against the rock and pretended to be another tourist enjoying the sunshine. When they were out of earshot, Jack repositioned himself to watch the bridge again. He drew his MK 23, pointing it at Carlos the entire time he moved toward Pilar.

"I got you," he whispered again.

She drew in a breath and faced Carlos as he stepped onto the bridge.

"Where have you been hiding, mi amore? You knew I was looking for you," Carlos said.

Pilar crossed her arms over her chest, her back stiff. "I'm here now."

"Si, but the question is why? Who is this?"

"He's here to make sure I don't end up over the edge."

Carlos laughed, tipping his head back.

"I have a clean shot," Jack said quietly.

Pilar lurched at his words.

"Hold position," Dex said calmly. "We need to know where Juan is and what Carlos wants first."

Carlos's grin faded as he took in the change in Pilar's body language. "You're not alone. This was a trap?"

"Why did you take Juan Rios?" Dunn asked.

Carlos sneered at him, then focused on Pilar again. "Who is this man to speak to me?"

"Why do you have my brother?" Pilar asked, her voice cracking.

Jack ached for her. He wanted to solve all this, bring Juan back, and get rid of Carlos for her. The rage he felt for the man in his sights was overpowering. The things he'd done. The way he treated people.

"Your brother has something I need."

"What is it?" Pilar asked.

Carlos stared at her for a long moment. He rubbed his jaw, dark stubble visible even from Jack's distance. His tee was pulled tight over bulky arms and a lean body. He clearly didn't mind getting his hands dirty judging by the scrapes on his knuckles. Jack was sure those came from Juan, but he knew better than to voice his thoughts.

The other man turned, looking directly into Jack's eyes. Jack squeezed the trigger gently, ready to fire on command.

"Blown," he whispered, not lowering his gun.

"Hold position," Dex said.

The guy finally looked away. He stepped close to Carlos and whispered something the mic didn't pick up. Carlos nodded.

"It seems our time here is up."

"No!" Pilar shouted. "Tell me what I need to do to get my brother back."

"Your brother stole from us. He took information that he then used to expose parts of our operation. He will pay for what he did," Carlos said, slowly backing away.

Pilar rushed toward him. "You can't kill him, Carlos. He's all I have left."

Dunn grabbed her arm, but she wrenched free of him and got in Carlos's face.

"He's my brother."

Carlos cupped her cheek. "He was my brother once, too. But he ruined that when he sent you away." He grabbed a handful of her hair and yanked hard, tilting her face back.

Pilar screamed.

Jack froze.

17

———

Dunn rushed in, but Carlos pulled a gun, pointing it straight at him.

"You put your hands on my woman. You grabbed her. You should die for that."

Jack no longer had a clear shot, which he was sure Carlos and his man knew. They moved into the trees, where Jack could catch glimpses, but couldn't see enough to know who was who. He had to move.

He scrambled down from his position on top of the rocks, gun drawn. The entire time he moved, he listened to the conversation happening just feet from him.

"He wants what you want, Carlos. He only wants the information Juan has," Pilar said, her voice strained. She whimpered again.

"Did you see the flower I left for you? I wanted to make sure you thought of me when you slid your panties on. I can't wait to slide them off you again. Then I'm going to teach you how to behave like my woman."

"I'm not your woman," Pilar choked out.

Carlos tsked. "Such strong talk. We both know you'll come back to me."

"I'll never go back to you. You're a monster."

Jack finally got to where he could see them. Both men had their backs to him. He could take them out from where he stood, or he could take them down.

They still didn't have what they needed from Carlos. He hated it, but he had to draw out the whole thing.

"Don't call me that," Carlos growled, tugging harder on Pilar's hair.

She clutched at his hand, trying to tug her hair free of his grasp. "Please let go of me."

Carlos spared her a glance, then returned his focus to Dunn, who still stood with his hands up. "Are you the one Juan ran to when he decided to get out? Are you the one he's been working with to bring down my bosses?"

Dunn shook his head. "I don't know what you're talking about."

Carlos snickered. "You probably are. He's working with someone. Three of our transports have been stopped. One storage house was hit. He's telling someone what he knows. And my bosses are too stupid to just change things. They said they've always operated this way, and they aren't going to change because of one rat. We have exterminators to take care of rats."

"No!" Pilar shouted again.

Adrenaline pumped fast and hard through Jack's veins. He moved the last few steps and cocked his gun, pointing it at the head of Carlos's man.

"Let her go," he growled.

Carlos turned to him and grinned. "Nice to see you again. I should have known you were the one with a gun pointed at me. You're not very smart, though. You didn't take the shot when you had a chance."

Jack swung his gun to point at Carlos's face. "Want me to take it now?"

Carlos laughed. "You really aren't smart. I have Pilar. Do you think you can get her away from me?"

Jack kept his gaze trained on Carlos and said, "I got you."

She whimpered her understanding.

Carlos looked between them, realization dawning in his black eyes. "You touched her?" he spat.

Jack smirked. "I did a hell of a lot more than that. I showed her what a real man is like in bed."

Carlos roared and released Pilar to rush at Jack. Dunn grabbed Pilar and spun her behind him, then cocked his own gun a second before Jack fired.

Carlos froze. He turned back to Dunn.

Jack took the opportunity to pull out a second gun and pointed it at the other guy.

Carlos's gaze narrowed. "Still not smart enough to shoot."

Jack just glared at him.

Carlos took a step back. His man retreated with him, one step at a time, until they disappeared up over the hill.

"Clear," Dunn said.

"Got a visual," Mason said. "Not wasting time getting out of here."

English spoke next. "I got them."

Jack finally breathed a little easier but kept his gaze on the path just in case. Carlos was gone, not for good, but for now. Pilar was safe.

"Jack," Dunn said, drawing his attention.

Except she was crying.

Jack rushed to where she was crouched on the cement path and pulled her into his arms. "It's over now. He's gone."

"He's going to kill my brother."

Jack couldn't say anything to make her feel better because anything he said would be empty words. Once again, she was right. Her brother was as good as dead.

PILAR TRIED to enjoy the long, hot shower she took, but it wasn't the same without Jack in there with her. Then again, she wasn't in the mood for sex either. Seeing Carlos made her skin crawl. Knowing what he was going to do to her brother made her want to throw up. Neither had her ready for sexy times.

She stepped out of the shower and started to dry off. She imagined the towel erasing every touch of Carlos's from her. Her head still ached where he tugged on her hair. Maybe Jack would rub her neck later because that hurt, too. She was lucky, though. She wasn't with Carlos. Jack saved her.

One more reason she liked him.

She wiped the mirror off and stared at herself. She replayed Carlos's words for the hundredth time. She couldn't think straight when he ranted earlier because she was in so much pain, but she was clear-headed now. Every time she thought about it, she was confused, though. Carlos sounded like they were looking for some kind of connection. Some kind of accessed file. But Juan was never on a computer. He had a phone, but he had it with him when he disappeared.

She shook her head, then regretted it when it hurt. She needed some medicine. And sleep.

The dull roar of male voices followed her into the

bedroom. She closed the door behind her and faced her the bed. It looked more than a little appealing. Maybe she could make it an early night.

She dressed in a pair of cotton shorts and Jack's tee from the morning. She really didn't want to put a bra on, but she had no choice when walking into a room full of men. They'd get more than an eyeful if she didn't support the girls.

Knowing they were all waiting to talk to her, she gently brushed her hair and took a deep breath. They were still talking when she entered the room, but they all looked up at her.

"Are you okay?" Justin asked.

She nodded.

"Lily and Kelsea are on their way over with dinner if you're hungry," Archer said.

"Thanks."

"Come sit." Jack stood, giving her his seat.

She smiled at him and took the chair, knowing she needed to sit. She wasn't going to last long on her feet. She was exhausted from her lack of sleep and facing Carlos. She preferred the first one to the last.

As soon as her butt hit the chair, Jack's hands landed on her shoulders. She tensed immediately, not expecting his touch.

"I got you," he whispered.

She nodded and took a deep breath. Her first since Dunn walked into the house that morning.

"Are you okay to talk about all this?" Dunn asked.

She looked at him and nodded. "Yeah. I want to get this over with."

Dunn nodded. "We recorded everything they said to you, but obviously, we don't understand most of what he's talking about. Did you know about any of the warehouses or other things he mentioned?"

She shook her head. "No. As soon as I found out who he was, I left. I haven't been in touch with him."

"Juan never mentioned anything?"

She shook her head again. "No. We didn't talk about what he did. I never wanted to know. I idolized him my entire life, and to know he was doing those things... I didn't know."

"It's okay," Jack said soothingly. "We know you'd tell us anything you know that can help."

She nodded. "I want my brother back. I know it seems like it's not going to happen, but I'll do anything to get him back."

The men exchanged a glance.

"What?" she asked.

"Would you turn over whatever Carlos is looking for in exchange for Juan?" Dunn asked.

Jack squeezed her shoulders tight, to the point of pain. She winced and twisted away from him. "Sorry," he said, avoiding her gaze.

She focused on Dunn again and thought about his question. If she thought it would help, she didn't know what she would do. The truth was, Carlos was a loose cannon. He was untrustworthy at best and downright evil at worst. "I don't know," she answered honestly.

Dunn nodded. "Do you know what he's looking for?"

She shook her head. "No. I've been trying to think about it. He made it sound like Juan was online or something if he was getting schedules, but Juan never used my computer."

"Does he have a phone?"

She nodded. "Of course, but he had it with him on

Monday. Jeez, was it really only two days ago? God, it probably feels like a lifetime for Juan."

Everyone was silent around her as she thought about her brother. Two days felt like forever to her. Forever since she'd seen Juan. Since she was happy. Since she thought her life was normal. Whatever the hell normal was.

"English searched and hasn't found a phone. Can you confirm his number?" Dunn asked.

Pilar recited the number she knew by heart, and English nodded. "That's what I have. It's not on. I can't trace it."

"He turned it off?" Pilar asked.

"Carlos probably did when he took Juan. So we couldn't find him," Jack explained. "It's the first thing we search for most of the time. He probably expected it."

She nodded and took a breath. "Is there any chance we'll find him?"

Silence met her question. They all avoided her gaze. Jack stepped forward again, resting his hands on her shoulders. "We're going to do everything we can, Pilar. Everything. We're not giving up, and you can't either."

She nodded, hoping the team of badasses in front of her would come through for her and Juan.

A knock on the door drew everyone's attention. Howler lived up to his name, racing to the door ahead of Justin. He checked before he unlocked it and let Lily, Kelsea, and Jaymes in.

Everyone got up from the table and greeted the new arrivals. Pilar tried to muster up a grin for them, but she knew it was weak. Lily and Kelsea both hugged her, then went to the kitchen with the food they brought in.

"All of you vultures need to back up," Lily said. "Pilar's getting dinner first tonight. She looks like she didn't get any sleep last night."

Pilar glanced up at Jack, who was trying not to laugh. Pilar couldn't help her grin, and they both started laughing.

"Why is that funny?" Lily asked.

Kelsea nudged her and nodded to Pilar and Jack. "I'm thinking it's because it was on target. Jack's looking pretty worn out himself."

Lily studied both of them closely. "Never mind. You don't get to eat first just because you had really good sex last night."

Pilar grinned. "I'll take really good sex over food any day. Although, with the size of my hips, it's obvious which one I have more access to."

Lily and Kelsea laughed with her. "Totally with you."

"Hey!" Archer and Jaymes both said, moving in on Lily and Kelsea.

With kisses and a few quiet words, they turned back to the food, no longer paying attention to Pilar. Jack leaned down and whispered, "All I know is those hips felt fucking amazing in my hands when I was inside you. I'll make sure you get extra dinner tonight so we don't wear down any of those sexy curves."

Pilar blushed and glanced up at him. He captured her lips in a kiss that had her forgetting about all the people around them. And she didn't mind that a bit.

JACK HEARD Howler bark early the next morning. He was wrapped up in Pilar, exhausted from another night with very little sleep, but he still crawled out of bed. Growing up on his parents' soybean farm then joining the military had conditioned him to function on very little sleep and to get up early, no matter what day it was.

Pilar grunted and rolled over when Jack extracted himself. Instead of his usual desire to run far and fast when he managed to get out of a woman's bed undetected, he wanted to climb right back in with Pilar and watch her sleep. That alone told him he definitely needed to get out.

The house was quiet when he made it to the living room, but the back door was open slightly. Jack went to the kitchen and started coffee, knowing Slade would want it as soon as he got back inside.

The pot just finished dripping when Slade and Howler came back in. "What are you doing up?"

Jack shrugged. "I never sleep in."

"Unless you're up all night."

Jack nodded, not meeting Slade's gaze. He poured them both cups and passed Slade's to him. Jack took a sip and grimaced. He hated adding cream and sugar to his coffee, but black coffee was too bitter for the first few sips.

Slade took milk out of the fridge and added a bit to his cup, offering it to Jack. Jack shook his head, and Slade rolled his eyes and put it back, then spooned sugar in and stirred it up. The sweet aroma was tempting, but Jack couldn't do it.

"What's going on?" Slade finally asked.

"Nothing. Why?"

Slade huffed a laugh. "Because if you're up, you're moving. And instead of staying in bed with the beautiful woman you've been wrapped around for two days, you're out here drinking coffee with me."

"And that means something's going on?" Jack asked.

Slade shrugged. "You tell me."

Jack shook his head. He was feeling unsettled, but he didn't know why. He sure as hell wasn't about to say anything to Slade. Not after the way he jumped on him the day before about Pilar.

"I can't believe we lost that fucker yesterday," Slade said after a minute.

Work. Jack could handle talking about work. "Yeah, me too. I don't know how they did it."

Slade nodded. "English doesn't either. He was tracking them the whole time."

"The van was clean. Like it hadn't been touched. I feel like we're outmatched here. Like there's something we're missing."

"Yeah, I agree. That's what scares me about this whole thing. We set a trap, but it's like we walked into one we created. How did that happen? How did they get away when we were watching them?"

"Obviously, they knew we were watching. They had a plan for it."

Slade sipped his coffee and nodded. "Absolutely, but what I don't get is how they did it. English can't even guess what happened to them. It's like they vanished."

"I want to catch that asshole and make him pay for what he did to her."

"That was rough. Just hearing her whimper made me want to choke him out. I can't imagine how you felt."

"I wanted to kill him with my bare hands," Jack admitted. He drew in a deep breath to calm his racing pulse and need for revenge and glanced at Slade.

Who was smirking at him.

"What?"

"So, that's what's bothering you. How much you like her."

Jack shrugged. "She's hot, and good in bed, and it's easier to keep her safe if I'm inside her."

Slade rolled his eyes. "And you're also full of shit."

Jack scoffed. "How am I full of shit?"

"Because you're not fucking her to keep her safe. You're fucking her because you're falling for her. And you're an even bigger ass than I thought if you're going to pass it off as some casual fuck."

"I'm not falling for her," Jack growled. Jack didn't know how to love. He never had. For most people, falling in love was natural, normal, expected. But Jack never thought he'd fall in love. Was vehemently opposed to it. He knew love wasn't in the picture for him. He even went so far as to consider a vasectomy so he didn't have to worry about accidentally getting someone pregnant, but he never went through with it.

Love was for saps who walked away from their duty to protect and serve. Jack already walked away, but he wasn't walking into another commitment he wasn't prepared to live out.

18

———————

When Pilar woke up, the sun was just starting to peek over the trees outside. She decided to get up and get ready for the day. Not that she had anything to do. She was basically spending her days waiting for news her brother was dead and her nights losing herself in Jack. Heaven and hell. Light and dark. Good and evil.

Jack was already gone, his side of the bed cool to the touch, but Pilar heard the low rumble of male voices and knew he wasn't far. She tossed her bag onto the bed and searched for clothes that were clean to wear that day. Much longer and she'd have to go home for new stuff. Just the thought of going back there had her skin crawling.

It also reminded her of Carlos's words. She absently searched her bag as she tried to piece together what everyone said. Carlos knew Juan had access to the cartel's schedules. Dunn was sure she'd trade the info to get her brother back if she thought Carlos would do it. Jack trusted her.

How did she feel?

Pilar asked herself that question as she pulled out a

black shirt rolled up in the bottom of her bag. She didn't remember putting it in there, especially since all her clothes were basically tossed in. She grabbed the edge and unrolled it, gasping when she realized it was Juan's.

Something fell out of the shirt and dropped silently to the bed. Pilar picked it up and turned it over. It was a cell phone. Almost identical to Juan's, but slightly different when she looked closer. This one was more high tech. And hidden. In Juan's shirt. Buried in her overnight bag. Like it was planted there for her to find.

Her first instinct was to take the phone to Jack. He would know what to do with it. She rushed to the door and went to open it, but stopped.

If Carlos knew she had what he wanted, he might trade her for Juan. She could save her brother. Carlos was going to kill him, but if she handed over the information he wanted, maybe he'd release Juan.

Pilar eased back from the door and returned the phone to the shirt. She rolled it back up and stuffed it into the bottom of her bag. She wanted to turn it on, but if Carlos was tracking her phone, the chances were good he was also tracking Juan's phone. She'd lead him right to her, and her bargaining chip would be gone.

She had to think. She had to clear her head and decide what to do. And she had to do it fast before it was too late for Juan.

Jack heard the bedroom door open and had to force himself to stay seated instead of rushing to Pilar. Howler didn't have the same restriction and took off down the hallway. Pilar cooed to him and spoke softly, telling him what a good boy he was.

Slade caught Jack's eye and lifted an eyebrow. Jack rolled his eyes, but the snicker from Slade said he saw right through Jack.

A door down the hall closed, and a few seconds later, the shower turned on. Jack got hard under the table, his mind conjuring up all the sexy images it had of Pilar dripping wet, and not just in the shower.

Howler whimpered, and Jack knew exactly how the dog felt. He wanted to go in, too.

"Howler, get over here," Slade called out, whistling for the dog. Howler bounded into the room, sliding to a stop at Slade's feet. He reached down and rubbed the dog's head, smiling at him. "Pilar's safe. Let her shower in peace." Slade lifted his gaze and leveled Jack with a hard look. "That goes double for you."

Jack grinned. "I'm just sitting here."

Slade shook his head. "Yeah, okay. You've barely taken your eyes off the hallway since her door opened, and you keep reaching under the table. If I step in something sticky, you're cleaning my whole damn house."

Jack grinned. "I'm not gonna waste a good orgasm on you."

Slade nodded. "Are they a waste with her?"

Jack's grin faded. "No. What's with you?"

"She's our job. I could have just as easily been the one watching her. Or Dunn. You're acting like a lovesick puppy." He glanced down at Howler. "No offense to you." He rubbed Howler's head, then looked back up at Jack. "You say you're not falling for her. Fine. You say she's just a job and you're keeping her safe. Fine. You say you're not picturing her naked in there. Fine. But here's the thing.

She is the job. She's the only thing we have right now that could make this job a success. If we can't find whatever it is Juan was going to hand over, you and I both know we fail. This job is huge for us. We're getting big exposure over it. If it falls apart, there's a lot more at stake than one woman."

Jack didn't like Slade's words, but he was right. A year ago, Jack was delivering a similar speech to Archer about Lily, warning him off getting involved with a nice woman who didn't need his baggage in her life. He wanted to tell himself he could get over his past and have a real life, but nothing in his past made him believe that was true.

He'd carry the guilt of Meredith's death for the rest of his life. He'd carry the guilt of the lives he took and the things he did with him forever. He even carried the guilt of lying to Pilar, even as he told himself it was for the best.

Howler scrambled to his feet and took off down the hallway before Jack even registered that the bathroom door opened. He stared at the end of the hallway, waiting for her to appear. It took a minute, but when she finally did, he had to restrain himself once more.

"Hey," she said softly.

"Good morning. I was hoping you'd sleep in today."

Her cheeks glowed pink, and she ducked her head. When she looked at him from under her lashes, Jack hardened. He hadn't felt such a strong desire for a woman ever.

"Want some coffee?" Slade asked, breaking the spell between Jack and Pilar.

Jack knew Slade was trying to watch out for all of them, trying to make sure the job was a success and that Pilar didn't get hurt. With Jack's track record, he couldn't say he was surprised by Slade's distrust.

Pilar nodded and looked at Slade as though she hadn't

realized he was even in the room. Jack had to admit that made him more than a little happy.

Slade fixed Pilar a cup of coffee, then asked how she slept.

"Good, thank you. I really appreciate you letting me stay here."

Slade nodded. "It's part of the job. I'm sorry the safe house didn't work out."

Pilar scowled. "That was my fault for turning on my phone. I didn't realize."

"Have you had it on since you've been here?" Slade asked.

Pilar shook her head. "No, not once. It's killing me not to check in with work, but I'm not taking any chances."

Slade nodded. "That's probably for the best. Obviously, they had your number and a trace on your phone. They showed up pretty quickly yesterday."

Pilar nodded. "And they got away pretty quickly."

Jack felt the same way she did. That his team let her down. Let them all down. Something happened, but they couldn't figure out what it was. English was tracking every vehicle that Carlos and his buddies could have swapped out for their van, but he hadn't found anything. Yet.

"We're still looking. Unfortunately, they left the van in a heavily populated area. They were smart. They knew what they were doing. We couldn't see them get out of the van or where they went when they did. It seems like they had someone local helping them, but we don't know who that could be either."

"So, basically, the only connection we had to my brother, the one and only way we thought we could get him back, was a bust. And now Carlos knows we're trying to trap him, and will be even more vigilant."

"Pilar," Jack started.

She shook her head and stood. "I'm sorry, but I need a break from all this for a few minutes. Am I allowed to go outside without a chaperone?"

Jack nodded.

Pilar looked at Slade for confirmation, then walked to the back door. Howler followed her, and she let him out before closing the door behind her. Jack stared after her until she disappeared from sight.

"This is why you don't fuck the client. Because when she gets emotional, you want to hold her instead of finish the fucking job," Slade growled. He stood and rinsed his coffee cup, then stuck it in the dishwasher and left the room.

Leaving Jack alone. Just the way he liked it.

PILAR WALKED down the steps of the deck and kicked off her shoes. The grass was still cool under her bare feet, soft and damp. April was her favorite month so far in Niagara Falls. Spring was arriving, with flowers blooming, birds returning from the winter, and sunshine appearing more often than snow. Growing up, she never really experienced spring. Summer was hot, and winter was a little bit of a break from the heat, but it never got cold enough to really have much of a spring.

Pilar was really looking forward to spring. Her first winter in the area had been harder than she expected with more snow than she'd ever seen in her life. Spring was going to be a welcome break.

Except she was looking forward to spending spring with Juan. They were going to get to know their new home. They were going to buy Discovery Passes and be tourists in their new town, exploring the different attractions around Niagara Falls. They were going to visit the local beaches on Lake Ontario and were talking about being like Americans and going to a baseball game.

But Juan was gone.

She thought Jack's team was going to find Juan when she met with Carlos the day before. He said they would follow Carlos back to wherever he was staying and get Juan. She didn't understand why that didn't happen. Why her brother had to spend one more night in whatever kind of cell Carlos put him in. Enduring God knew what kind of torture.

Pilar let herself get lost in Jack the night before. He didn't push, but she did. When she was going to bed, she asked him to join her. He didn't resist, but she was the one who initiated it. She didn't want to be alone. All she could think about was what Juan was going through. She needed the distraction. So while her brother was getting the shit beat out of him, she was having orgasm after orgasm at the hand, mouth, and cock of the man who was supposed to be saving her brother.

Pilar hated herself in that moment. She sank to the grass and buried her face in her hands and cried. She'd spent days hiding. Hiding from Carlos. Hiding in a cabin. Hiding her feelings for Jack, because she had some big ones. Hiding her fears. And now she was hiding the one thing that could bring her brother back.

She knew the phone had valuable information on it. It was unlikely Carlos knew about it or he would have told her. He was smart. He knew if she had something that would save her brother, she'd hand it over in exchange for Juan. He would promise her Juan's release if he got what he wanted. The problem was, she was smart, too. She knew Carlos couldn't be trusted. He told her more lies when they were together than she probably knew about years later. He was manipulative and evil. And he would say anything to get what he wanted.

If she handed the phone over to Jack, there was no guarantee they'd get Juan back alive. If she handed it over to Carlos, there was still no guarantee. Which left her right back where she was before she found the hidden phone.

Lost.

JACK WATCHED Pilar from the back door. He wanted to go out to her, but she made it clear she didn't want company. At least, not the human kind. Howler sat next to her on the grass, his head in her lap. She scratched him absently, her hands moving periodically like she was having a conversation with an invisible person. He would have thought she was on the phone if he didn't see both her hands were empty.

The thought crossed Jack's mind to search through her things while she was outside. Maybe something was in her bag that could help them. If Juan hid something, it's possible he would have hid it in Pilar's things so it would be safe if something happened to him.

Almost like he expected it.

Jack didn't want to think Juan was involved with the whole thing, but he had to admit it was the most reasonable option. If Juan set up the meeting so Carlos would take him and make it look like a kidnapping, it would require the team to move in, exposing their hands. Carlos knew his enemy, and if Juan was helping him, it would explain how they got away.

That was the part that bothered Jack the most. They had

Carlos. He was right there. And instead of holding on to him, they lost him. It was as though he was never there at all, but Jack saw him. Had him in his sights. He could have pulled the trigger and ended the whole thing, but they wanted to get Juan back. He was an asset, and taking down the entire organization was bigger than taking down just Carlos.

Or Juan, for that matter.

And Jack was no longer a sniper. He was a civilian with a skillset that he couldn't use on other civilians. He thought they had Carlos that time. That he didn't need to kill him to stop him. He thought they had him.

He was wrong.

The sliding door opened, and Pilar and Howler walked inside. Her cheeks were streaked from her tears, and she made no move to hide it. Jack opened his arms, letting her choose if she wanted to come to him or not.

She hesitated, which killed him, but then stepped forward and buried herself in his embrace. They stood there, holding each other, both lost in their thoughts.

Jack slid his hand up and down her back, trying to tell her he was there. He cupped the back of her head with his other hand, being careful of the soreness left behind by Carlos's treatment of her the day before. If he was willing to hurt her like that in a public place with all of them around, Jack didn't want to think about the things he would do to Pilar if he ever got her alone again.

He couldn't think about it. He had to focus on now. Stopping Carlos, finding Juan, and protecting Pilar. It was the only way to make sure she wouldn't be hurt again.

"Do you think we'll find Juan?" she asked softly, not pulling out of his arms.

Jack stilled. He wasn't willing to lie to her, but he didn't want to voice his fears either. "I don't know."

"Yes, you do," she said, breaking free of him. "And if you won't tell me, it's because you don't think we'll find him. Please, Jack. I need to know if I should hold on to hope."

Jack clasped his hands behind his back and stiffened his spine. "All I know, Pilar, is we're not giving up. No matter what happens, we're not giving up."

She stared at him for a long moment, then sank back into his arms and wrapped herself around him. "I don't know how I can live without him. It hurts too much."

Jack nodded and held her and whispered, "I got you."

19

———

CARLOS SAT IN HIS SMALL OFFICE AND STARED OUT THE window. It was a nice space. The kind of place Pilar would really make into a home. Of course, the flowered couches and plates on the walls were a bit outdated for him, but the place worked for while he was in town.

The couple that lived there seemed to like it. They refused to give up their home when Carlos showed up. The husband was useful, but the wife... well, she was only useful to get the husband to do what they wanted him to do.

Carlos knew the husband would help them. He was the one who told them the route to get away from Pilar's new friends. And provided the vehicle for them to do it. Carlos looked out the front window and knew they hadn't figured it out yet since no cops were on his doorstep.

Cops. He laughed. The cops at home would have helped him out, paving the way for whatever Carlos needed. If he had time, he could have made the same arrangement, but Andres wouldn't let him. He was supposed to keep a low profile.

Carlos was not the kind of man who was supposed to be in the shadows.

He turned back to the computer and scanned through the plans. They had shipments coming through the border all day. So far, none of them were in jeopardy. Funny that Juan was unavailable and all of a sudden, all the shipments were safe.

Carlos made that happen. No one else. He was the one who figured it all out and stopped it.

When he was in charge, he wasn't going to be as stupid as his boss. He wasn't going to do everything online and give the password to everyone in the organization. He was going to keep schedules private, and he was going to mix things up so no one could predict their routes. He wasn't an idiot.

His phone rang, drawing his attention from the computer. One glance told him it was Andres. Carlos straightened, ready to accept the praise he deserved.

"Hola," he said cheerfully.

"Have you stopped the leak?" Andres growled over the phone.

Even from a distance, the old man's voice made Carlos's back stiffen. He wasn't afraid of him. He wasn't afraid of anything. But he was smart, and he knew Andres could have him eliminated if he wanted to. The men Carlos brought with him would gladly put a bullet in his skull if they were instructed to do so by Andres.

"Yes, sir. Juan is in a warehouse with no access to the outside world."

"Has he given us the information we need?"

"Not yet, sir. He's still not talking."

"Then what the fuck is he still doing alive?"

"Sir?"

"If he won't talk, kill him. Or kill his sister so he knows

we mean business. I thought sending you up there would show me what you're capable of. I'm ready to hand over parts of this business, Carlos. Your name was on the list, but if all you are capable of is chasing a skirt and killing product, then why would I give you the business I worked my whole life to create?"

Carlos drew in a breath and stopped the flow of nasty words he wanted to spew. Andres was a stubborn piece of shit who was withholding his future? Fuck no. If he didn't hand over the entire business to Carlos, Carlos would take it from him. He was the best one to run things, and Andres knew it. "I will get everything we need, sir," he forced out through gritted teeth.

"Good. See that we do. Because our trucks getting caught isn't a part of my plan. We've been lucky all they've caught is the drugs."

"Nothing's been touched since I took him. I've proven that he's the leak."

"We knew he was the leak, you idiot. That's why I sent you up there. But we also need the pictures. The files. The list. It's not just about the schedules, Carlos. It's about everything he took from us. We need to know exactly what he has and how he got it, and stop it from being passed to the feds. If they have proof, they won't hesitate to take us all down."

"Understood, sir," Carlos growled.

"Good. Now get it done. Or you can fucking stay there, Carlos. In a bag."

The call disconnected before Carlos could say anything else. He squeezed the phone in his hand until his knuckles turned white and ached. He fucking hated Andres. How dare he threaten him?

No, he was done playing around. Juan was going to give

him the answers he needed. And if not, Carlos no longer needed him.

PILAR WAS EXHAUSTED. All she wanted to do was crawl into her bed and sleep off the last few days. Forget about the hell she'd been through and pretend none of it was real.

But the group of men she'd been surrounded by all day were reminders of exactly how dismal her life was. They were nice enough guys, but she hated each and every one of them in that moment. Because they were sitting around, talking and laughing, instead of out searching for her brother.

There was a part of her that knew that wasn't fair, but the angry part was a lot louder and more forceful and didn't give a shit that she wasn't being fair.

Pilar left the room, knowing none of them would even notice she was gone. Jack was in the center of the group, laughing and telling stories. She resented the fact that he could enjoy himself. He didn't have a brother out there who was being tortured.

All day Pilar debated telling Jack about the phone she found. When she asked him if he thought they'd find Juan, she was trying to figure out what she should do. If he said no, she was going to turn on the phone and hope Carlos noticed and accepted it as a trade for Juan. But Jack's answer made her pause. It wasn't much of an answer, but she trusted him for some reason. She took him at his word that he was going to keep looking for Juan, no matter what.

She needed to clear her head, but she was stuck. Usually, she went for a walk when she needed to get away from everything. Fresh air was cathartic and cleansing for her.

She'd taken a few yoga classes and was still trying to decide if she liked it or not. Most of the time, she couldn't get into the right positions. Her instructor was a tiny woman with zero body fat and didn't understand that a woman with a belly like Pilar's, not to mention the booty she carried around or her wide hips, didn't move the same way.

But Pilar had to admit when she left, she felt calmer. So she figured she'd give it a try.

She closed the bedroom door softly and took a deep breath. She could still hear the voices in the other room, but she had no choice. She needed to try.

She stood still and took some deep breaths, centering and calming herself as best she could. When she felt ready, she lowered to the floor and sat.

She began with some of the easy stretches and moves, the ones she remembered. She tried out the simple versions of the poses she felt most comfortable doing. The warrior pose and triangle pose. Crescent and chair pose. Downward dog and child pose. She added some planks at the end, hoping she did everything correctly even though she was sure the sequence was way off.

She ended on her back, laying down like they did in class, and just breathing. Like she did after each class, she felt better. Centered, focused, and relaxed. Everything around her felt calmer and quieter.

That was when she realized the voices in the next room had stopped.

She took another breath and blew it out slowly. She wondered if Jack was going to stay with her again. As annoyed as she was with him, she felt better with his arms around her.

Pilar sat on the bed and stared at her bag. The phone was calling to her, demanding she make a choice. Every second she had the phone and didn't use it to get Juan back felt like she was delivering the blows herself. She hoped the yoga would give her clarity, but she was still as torn as before.

A soft knock on her door had her spinning to face it. "Come in," she said quietly.

Jack stuck his head in and glanced around the room. "You okay?"

She nodded. "Just needed a break from all the activity."

"Sorry. We forget how loud we are sometimes." He opened the door wider, giving her a view of all of him.

She forced a smile.

"Juan?"

She nodded.

He gave her a sad smile. "I want to find him, too."

"I know. It's your job."

He shook his head. "I want you to be happy."

"Thank you."

He nodded once. "I just wanted to say goodnight."

"You're not... I mean, you... um, okay."

He didn't move away from the door. "I want to stay, Pilar," he said, reading her mind. "I want to walk in here and make love to you all night. But I'm not going to assume you want the same thing."

"Jack," she breathed. Her entire body lit up with his words. She was raw and worn and emotional. Having a sexy as all hell man tell her he wanted her was one more thing to add to the emotional heap that had become her life.

"You have to ask me, Pilar. I have no clue what you're thinking."

She took a deep breath and met his gaze. His forest

green eyes were soft but filled with heat. The stubble on his cheeks left a reminder between her thighs, a reminder that had her clenching them together again. His broad shoulders were covered by the black tee he wore, but his arms were exposed, giving her a clear view of his tattoos, as beautiful and sharp as the man himself. His cock was hard, visible through his jeans, and all she wanted to do was sink to her knees and taste him.

She ran her tongue along her lips, and he groaned. "You're killing me, Pilar. Which side of this door do you want me on when I close it?"

"The inside," she said quietly. "Please."

He had the door closed and locked before she finished speaking. He was across the room in three quick steps, pulling her up into his arms and pressing his lips to hers.

He kissed her like he was dying for her. Like he couldn't wait another second to taste her, touch her, have her. She returned his kiss with equal passion, needing him as much.

She tore at his shirt, lifting it until it stretched across his chest. Jack grabbed the collar and tore it off, tossing it across the room before he pulled her back into his arms and licked his way into her mouth.

Pilar ran her hands down his bare chest and up his bare back. His skin was hot and smooth, with dark hair scratching her palm around his nipples and leading down to his jeans. She slid her hand into his jeans and wrapped it around him, smiling when he groaned and pulled back from her kiss.

"You feel so good. Jesus, I need you."

Pilar stroked him while he unbuttoned his jeans and kicked them off. She loved the way her hand looked, invisible from the forearm down into his red boxer briefs. She watched the bulge grow larger as she stroked to the end, then smaller as only his cock was pressing against the fabric while she stroked to his base.

"Pilar," he groaned.

She fell to her knees in front of him and tugged his briefs down until her hand and his cock were visible. She drew in a deep breath, loving the scent of him all around her. Musky and hot and so very Jack.

She leaned forward and licked the tip of him, smiling when he groaned and slid his hand into her hair. She parted her lips and licked more of him, wrapping her tongue around him.

"Oh, fuck," he groaned, his hand tightening in her hair.

Her scalp was still tender, but she loved how Jack was responding to her and ignored the slight pain. She eased her tongue down his shaft and took him into her mouth.

He groaned again and jerked, sending his cock to the back of her throat. Pilar choked, but he pulled back immediately. She drew in a breath and did it again, prepared for it the second time.

She repeated the motion, back and forth, in and out. She experimented with her tongue, dragging it along the bottom of his cock and circling the tip when she withdrew. He seemed to like all of it.

"Play with my balls, Pilar. Tug on them a little."

She lifted her hand and cupped him. She pulled lightly, and his breath sped up.

"Fuck, yeah. Bite down, just a little, on the way back. Let me feel your teeth on my dick."

She did what he asked again and was rewarded with a second hand in her hair.

He moved his hips faster, fucking her mouth and holding her still with his hands in her hair. He squeezed his fingers, and she winced, the ache from Carlos's roughness making itself known.

Jack stopped immediately and pulled back. "Shit, Pilar. I'm sorry. Come here, beautiful." He tried to pull her up.

She moved back and shook her head. "It's okay. Please, Jack. I want to do this."

He shook his head. "I'm too close, Pilar. I want to be inside you when I come."

"I want to taste you, Jack."

"Pilar," he groaned.

She looked up at him. "Was it not good?"

He narrowed his gaze. "I'm about to blow. It was fucking amazing. Why would you ask that?"

She shrugged and avoided his eyes again.

"Pilar?"

"It's the first time I've done this, okay? I never wanted to with Carlos, but with you... I want to do everything with you."

He sank to the floor and pulled her into his arms. "Oh, Pilar. I want that, too. I feel like a selfish asshole if I come before you."

She shook her head. "I want to do this, Jack. Please. Next time you can be inside me."

"Promise?" he asked with a grin.

She smiled back. "Yeah."

He kissed her until her head spun and she wasn't sure which of them was going to come first. When he finally pulled back, she grinned when he stood before her again.

She took him into her mouth again, repeating the movements that had him ready to blow minutes earlier. His hands stayed at his side, but that wasn't enough for her. She wanted him. All of him. Every bit of the amazing man baring himself to her.

She reached for his hands and set them on her head. He smoothed her hair back from her face and tilted her chin up to meet his gaze.

"You're so fucking beautiful," he groaned. "The only thing that would make this better is if you were naked and I could watch those sexy tits bounce with every move you make."

She leaned back and stripped off her shirt, then unclasped her bra and tossed it aside.

He moaned when she wrapped her lips around him again and sucked him into her mouth. It wasn't long before he lost control of himself and took it from her, threading his fingers through her hair and fucking her mouth.

Pilar loved it. She tugged on his balls and dragged her teeth along his dick and breathed deep, letting the whole experience fill her with need. Her panties were soaked and her nipples hard. Her breasts ached for him to touch, and she was so close to coming that she thought about reaching between her thighs and coming with him.

But she didn't want to miss a moment.

He grunted, his breath coming in pants. His hands moved to the back of her head, pulling her toward him faster and faster.

"Your tits look so fucking good. One day, I'm going to come all over them. Watch my dick squirt all over you. I can't wait to be inside you. Oh, yeah. That tight pussy feels so good. And this mouth, beautiful. Oh, God. Do you want me to come in that hot fucking mouth of yours? Are you ready for me?"

She nodded and tugged harder on him.

He moaned and fucked her harder, faster. His dick hit her throat, but he was gone so quickly she relaxed.

"Oh, God, yes. Pilar. Fuck. Yes."

He grunted and slammed into her throat. His dick swelled, then erupted into her mouth. Her eyes watered as she fought the intrusion, but she held him in. The salty liquid shot down her throat, and she drew in another deep breath through her nose, bringing his scent into her.

He held her there until he stopped trembling, then yanked her to her feet and into his arms. She swallowed and held him and admitted to herself that she was in trouble. She was going to fall for Jack Farrell if she wasn't careful.

If she hadn't already.

20

Jack held Pilar tight. He couldn't let go of her. His entire body trembled with aftershocks of his orgasm, and he needed her to center him.

He'd never felt that way during a blow job. Or sex of any kind. Staring down at her, watching those perfect pink lips take him in, he couldn't control himself. Knowing she'd never done that before should have forced him to be gentle, but he lost it all when she told him how badly she wanted to taste him. Nothing was sexier than a woman who knew what she wanted.

Her hands slid up and down his back, calming him and heating him in equal measure. His dick still throbbed, coming down from the high and ready for another go. Jack told himself it was just because it was so good, but there was a part of him that knew it was more.

"That was amazing," Pilar whispered, her voice breathless and awestruck.

"Did I hurt you?"

She shook her head. "No. I loved it. I... want to do it again."

He chuckled. "I definitely need a few minutes after that one. But I have a few ideas about how I can spend that time."

Pilar snuggled closer to him and kissed his chest. Every touch from her was magic. Like a bolt straight through him that opened up some quiet part of him. Jack felt a need when he was with her, one he hadn't experienced before. He had to touch her and taste her and hold her every chance he had.

He loved his brothers, and being around them was everything to him, but he missed Pilar like a physical ache when they were there. He wanted to pull her onto his lap and hold her every second of the day, but they all gave him disapproving glances when he got too close to her. He didn't want them judging her, so he kept his distance, but it made him ravenous when he finally had her to himself.

Jack cupped her breasts and thumbed across her nipples. Her light touches halted as she sucked in a ragged breath. Her skin was soft under his fingers, supple and smooth. He loved touching her. He glided his fingers across her skin, enjoying the silky feel of her. She stilled, letting him touch her.

Jack took half a step back so he could enjoy the view, too. His lightly tanned hands were pale against her bare olive skin. Her breasts were pink-tinted, a flush spreading across her body at his touch. Her eyes were closed, a ghost of a smile on her lips.

Jack lowered to his knees and rested his head on her chest. She immediately wrapped her arms around him and held him to her. He flicked her nipple with his tongue, and she tightened her hold on him, moaning softly.

"Oh, God."

He twisted his head and took her nipple between his

teeth. He alternated soft bites and gentle flicks with a roll of his tongue until she tipped her head back and clutched his hair so tight he saw stars.

Or maybe that was just because of her.

"You're wearing entirely too many clothes," he said, his fingers working to draw her shorts and panties down her curvy legs.

Her wide hips bracketed his shoulders, giving him a spot to rest against while he manipulated her other nipple. When she was blissful and he could smell her desire, he eased her onto the bed and settled between her thighs.

"Watch me, Pilar," he commanded. "Put a pillow behind your head. I want to watch your face while I eat your pussy."

Her thighs clenched around him at his dirty words. He rubbed his thumbs on her inner thighs while he waited for her to position herself.

With a pillow propping up her head, her eyes locked on his. He held her stare as he kissed one thigh, then the other. He worked his way closer to her, kissing and licking and biting his way up until she was quivering under his lips.

"You like it when I lick you, don't you?"

She nodded.

"You taste so good, Pilar. I love having your come all over my tongue. Are you going to come for me?"

She nodded again. Her eyes were glassy, but she was completely focused on him.

He nuzzled against her mound and breathed deep. "You smell so fucking good, Pilar. I wish I could smell this all the time. All you, beautiful. So amazing."

She moaned and wriggled her hips. Her body shivered in anticipation. Jack's throbbed with it. He wanted to dive in and never come up for air. To lose himself in her forever.

Jack leaned forward and extended his tongue, touching

her with just the tip. She gasped and slammed her eyes shut. "Look at me, Pilar," he commanded again. "I want to see you, beautiful."

She pried her eyes open and met his gaze again. "Jack."

"I got you, Pilar. You're safe."

She sucked in a breath and grabbed another pillow, shoving it behind her so she had a better view.

"You want to see my tongue on your pussy, don't you?"

She nodded. "I can't see over my belly, though."

"Then watch my eyes, beautiful. Watch me as I taste you."

She gasped, and he dove in, licking from her entrance to her clit. She shuddered, and he did it again.

"Delicious. Want a taste?"

She nibbled her lip and nodded.

He rose quickly, throbbing at her tentative acceptance. He plunged his tongue between her lips, letting her taste her own flavor on his mouth. He kissed her hard, letting her suck all the juices from him before he went back for more.

"That was hot as fuck, Pilar. I need you. I need you to come for me," he croaked, on his knees and focused on her.

He dove back in, burying his face between her thighs. She tightened them around his head, but he didn't care. He just wanted her.

Jack licked into her pussy, sucking her sweet come into his mouth and fucking her with his tongue. She writhed on the bed, panting and groaning.

"Jack. Look. Jack. See you," she gasped.

He looked up at her and was bowled over by the raw need in her gaze. She wanted to see him, to watch his eyes as he devoured her. He'd never shared that kind of connection with a woman before. It had been his idea, but with his tongue inside her and her eyes locked on his, it tethered them together.

He gently pressed her thighs wider and caressed her skin with his thumbs. He spread her channel wider, driving his tongue deeper into her. She gasped again, her body shaking, getting ready.

"I wish I could see your tongue disappear into me," Pilar said. "Watch what you're doing."

"Watch me, Pilar," he said, tilting his head to change the angle he entered her.

She moaned again, her thighs tightening once more. He pressed them wider and teased her with his thumbs. He withdrew his tongue and licked up to her clit, pressing the flat of his tongue to it and dragging it up to the tip.

"Jack," she whispered. "Oh, yes."

He pressed two fingers inside her on the next lick, and she came instantly. His cock throbbed, ready to feel the same thing. Come made her body slicker, and Jack added a third finger, stretching her out so she was ready for him.

"More, Jack. Please, more."

He stared up at her face. Parted lips, bright eyes, and flushed skin. She was every fantasy of his come to life. A beautiful, curvy woman stretched out and begging him to make her come. As long as he lived, nothing would be better.

He curled his fingers and pressed against her clit at the same time. She gasped, her body more than ready. He thrust his fingers harder into her, pressing the spot deep inside with every stroke.

It wasn't long before she was trembling and begging him to let her come. He sucked hard on her clit and fucked her with his fingers, slamming into her until she clamped down on him and came with a silent scream and a full body orgasm.

She twitched and thrashed, but begged for one more. Jack was happy to assist. He nipped at her clit. It locked down on his fingers and refused to let them out. He pushed past her resistance and plunged into her.

She whimpered and wiggled, desperate for the orgasm that was just barely out of reach. Jack reached up and plucked one of her nipples. Her head fell back, arching her back as she bowed off the bed.

"Oh, God, Jack. Yes. Yes."

She came again, a hard shake of her body and a moan that told everyone in earshot exactly what was going on behind the locked doors.

Jack didn't care. All he cared about in that moment was getting inside her. Feeling her come all over his dick and emptying himself into her.

He kissed her thighs and withdrew from her as she laid on the bed, limp and smiling. Her gaze followed him to the bag he had behind the door, one Archer brought over the day before with Jack's clothes. He dug through, knowing there were condoms in there somewhere.

Jack finally found the box and yanked it open, only to groan. "Fuck. You can't be serious."

"What's wrong?" Pilar asked.

"No more condoms. We used them all last night. I didn't realize or I would have stolen some from Slade today."

She nibbled her lip and held his gaze. "I'm clean. And I'm on the pill," she said softly.

Jack shook his head. "No. You barely know me. I'm not letting you take that risk."

"It's not a risk. I trust you, Jack. If you say you're good, I know you are. You wouldn't lie to me. I know that."

Her words soothed and killed him at the same time. He wouldn't lie to her, not if he could help it. He would never lie about sex, about his health. But he was lying about her brother.

"Pilar."

She smiled. "I want you, Jack. And I trust you. If you say you've got me, I know it's true."

He rushed back to the bed and pulled her into his arms. He'd never had anyone trust him that much. He held her, trying to calm his racing heart as he held her.

He pulled back and lowered to his knees so he could look up at her. "I've never had sex without a condom, Pilar. Ever. I've never even been inside a woman without one. I'm clean. And it's been a while since I've been with someone. Before you obviously."

She stroked his cheek and slid her hand through his hair. "Me, too."

"Are you sure about this?" Jack asked, holding his breath.

She nodded. "Yes, Jack. I trust you."

He pulled her into his arms again. "I got you, Pilar. Always."

She nodded again, holding him tight.

He kissed her chest, then worked his way up to her lips. She opened to him, drawing him in and kissing him until he throbbed against the side of the bed. The anticipation was killing him. Being inside her was one thing, but being inside her and able to feel every slick surface and every inch of her was going to be another.

She pulled him up as she scooted up the bed, drawing him on top of her. He settled between her thighs, her wet heat begging for him.

"Pilar," he croaked, drawing her attention.

She caressed his cheek and leaned up to kiss him. "Jack."

He drew in a breath and angled his hips. He gritted his teeth as he lined up with her entrance. She spread her knees, widening her opening so he could slide in.

He held her gaze as he eased into her, groaning as he filled her. Her slick channel was like sliding into velvet. She was soft and smooth and sucked him in deeper with every inch he went in.

"Jesus," he breathed. "I'm not gonna last long, beautiful. Holy fuck, you feel amazing."

"I'm glad I'm not the only one who thinks so," she groaned. "My God, Jack."

He withdrew and gently thrust back in. Slippery skin met slippery skin, and they both moaned.

"Again," she whispered.

He stretched out over her, their bodies connected from their hips to their chests, but he needed more. He had to hold her, touch her, feel her. He reached for her hands, drawing them above her head. He threaded his fingers through hers and pumped into her again.

"Jack," she whispered.

He held her gaze, easing in and out of her so he wasn't done too quickly. He wanted it to last. To feel her body drawing him in, her soaked channel flooded with her come, her naked body pressed to his.

If there was a heaven, he was definitely in it.

"Harder," she breathed.

He angled his hips and thrust in on his next stroke. She gasped and ripples massaged his dick. He clenched his teeth and repeated the steps to disassemble and reassemble his guns in his mind to keep from coming before her.

She tilted her hips up to meet his, her legs wrapping

around his back. "Jack." She squeezed his fingers, bringing his attention back to her face. "Watch me, Jack."

She shuddered in the next second, her neck and face flashing pink as her lips parted and she breathed through her orgasm. Her channel milked him, demanding he follow her.

He couldn't stop the sensations rolling through him and slammed hard into her one last time, letting go of every piece of him holding back. He released into her, his come mixing with hers and flooding his entire body with a bone-deep need to possess her. To mark her. To never let go of her.

He lowered his mouth to her breast and sucked hard on her skin. He muffled his shout as he came, every inch of his body marked by her the same way he ached to mark her. He sucked harder, hoping she wasn't mad when she saw what he did. He had to know he left a mark, even if it was tempo-rary. Because the one she was leaving on him was perma-nent, but in the same place. On his heart.

Jack left the room a few minutes later and returned with a damp washcloth. He cleaned between her legs where their come mingled and dripped from her body. She wanted to hold it inside her, never let go of the little piece of him.

He crawled back into bed and reached for her. Pilar rolled over onto him and grinned. She'd never felt so good in her life. He was amazing. Holding back from falling for him was impossible. He brought her out of the darkness into the light every time he whispered a dirty word or did a dirty thing to her. She'd never felt so desired or beautiful in her life.

"What's going through your head?" Jack asked.

His chest rose and fell with every ragged breath he took. She watched his muscles stretch and contract, his tight nipples peaked above the rest of his skin.

"You okay?" he asked, prodding again.

She nodded.

"What's up?"

She grinned. "Just thinking how good you are at that."

"At what?"

"At making love."

He snorted. "It takes two, Pilar. Trust me, it's never been like that for me before."

"Really?"

He nodded and pulled her on top of him. "No. Never. That's you. I still can't catch my breath. You wear me out."

She leaned forward and kissed him softly. Her flavor was still on his lips, but she didn't mind at all. She'd never felt so free with her body. She'd never been allowed to. Things were different with Carlos, and she was afraid to let go with anyone else. Afraid to be alone and let them in. With Jack, everything was good. Safe. Easy.

"Now what are you thinking?"

"That being with you is easy," she admitted.

He pulled back. "You think I'm easy?"

She shook her head. "I didn't say that."

He narrowed his gaze at her. "That's what it sounded like. That you think I'm easy. I'll show you easy."

Whomp.

Her head slammed into his chest, something soft on the other side. "What the hell?"

She looked up into his smirking face, a pillow in his hand.

"Did you just hit me with a pillow?"

He nodded. "What are you going to do about it?"

She scrambled off him and grabbed a pillow. She swung, missing him as he rolled off the other side of the bed.

They faced each other down, one on each side of the bed. She was debating her next move when Jack rolled over the bed and landed right in front of her on his feet.

She swung her pillow again and connected with his back. He smacked her lightly on the side of the head.

"Hey!"

She swung harder, smiling when her next blow sent him to the bed. He dropped his pillow and groaned.

"Oh, my, God. Are you okay?" she asked, rushing closer.

He shook his head. "Can't breathe. Need mouth-to-mouth."

Pilar rolled her eyes and whacked him again.

He grabbed her and dragged her down on top of him, making both of them laugh as they sank into each other again.

21

———

PILAR WOKE UP EARLY THE NEXT MORNING. THE ROOM AROUND her was silent, as was the house. It was still dark outside, telling her brain she should be sound asleep. But instead, she was up. Debating. Thinking. Considering.

By the time the sun peeked through the curtains of the room she shared with Jack, she knew she had to tell him about the phone she was hiding. She should have told him the day before, as soon as she found it, but she was scared. She wanted Juan.

Jack was a great distraction. He made her feel beautiful and sexy. Neither were words she'd ever associated with herself, but with Jack's hands skimming her body, his eyes devouring her, she couldn't deny those feelings.

Just like she couldn't deny that she was falling for him.

"I love you," she breathed, snuggling up tight to him.

"I got you," he whispered back, his voice full of sleep. He tugged her closer, his hand splayed across her stomach.

She froze, just in case he was awake and actually heard her confession.

His arm was heavy across her side, his breathing slow

and even. He sounded asleep, but she wasn't positive. When he drew in a breath and let it out with a soft snore, she finally relaxed again.

She couldn't tell him. It was stupid. She knew once they weren't in forced proximity, he'd lose interest in her. She was the only woman available, so of course he wanted her. She was the only one getting attached.

He squeezed her side and nuzzled against her. The sun was bright outside, a beautiful day brewing, and she was waking up in the arms of the man she loved. She had a good feeling about it. They were going to find Juan. Things were going to be okay. And she'd find a way to get over Jack. She met him four days ago. She'd survive without him. She'd have her brother back.

Jack moved again, his hand sliding across her stomach to her hip, then back. He drew a deep breath, then groaned. He pressed his hips to hers, nudging his hard cock against her ass. She'd never slept naked with Carlos. The one time they passed out together, he woke her up and made her sleep in the other room. She was hurt. She wanted to wake up to him. But every second she spent with Jack made her months with Carlos pale by comparison. Jack was a good man. Kind, honest, caring. Carlos was none of those things.

Jack's hand slid up her stomach to her breasts and cupped one. He rolled her nipple between his fingers and ground his length against her.

"I could wake up like this every day," Jack said, his rough morning voice doing wonders for her.

Pilar was always a sucker for a sexy voice. The kind of voice that told you a real man was attached. Jack had that voice. Rough and scratchy in the morning, deep and authoritative during the day, low and sexy in the dark of night. She could die happy listening to him talk.

"Me, too," she whispered.

"You're up early," Jack said, still fondling her.

She nodded and hummed her approval. "Couldn't sleep."

"We'll find him," Jack whispered. He suckled on her shoulder, running his tongue over her skin. He abandoned one breast for the other and slid his knee between her thighs.

Pilar nodded. "I know. Today's going to be a good day. I have something to talk to you about."

"Oh, yeah? What's that?" Jack asked, his voice teasing.

"I... oh, that feels good," she moaned, unable to think with Jack's hands on her.

There was a sharp knock on the door.

"What?" Jack yelled.

"Need to get up," Justin called back.

"Why?" Jack demanded.

"We gotta go. Now. Both of you."

Jack froze, his body language telling Pilar it wasn't good. "What's wrong?"

Jack unwound himself from her and climbed out of bed. "I don't know. Let's go see."

Jack stiffly got dressed, tucking his erect cock into his boxer briefs before slipping into the clothes he took off the night before.

Pilar followed suit, getting dressed quickly in the first outfit she could find. Her body still hummed, ready to finish what Jack started, but the tension in her wasn't just from an unreached orgasm. Her stomach coiled tight, anxiety settling in to every inch of her.

When they were dressed, Jack opened the door. He led the way down the hall to where Justin waited for them in the living room. "What's going on?"

"We need to go," Justin said, avoiding Pilar's gaze.

"Where are we going?" Pilar asked.

Justin glanced at her, then ducked his head. "We just need to go. Now. Dunn will explain when we get to the office."

Pilar nodded stiffly. Every cell in her body told her to stay put. To run back to bed and pull the covers over her head like she did when she was a kid. Nothing could touch her there. Even better, she could take Jack with her and they could hide together. Lost forever in bed, ignoring the outside world and all the terrors it held.

But she knew it didn't stop the world. Every day people were killed, children were hurt, women abused. She grew up with it in her backyard, at her school, in her community. Hiding didn't make it go away. Eventually, she had to face it.

Pilar drew in a deep breath and nodded. She followed Justin out of the house, with Jack right behind her. Both of them scanned the area, watching for anyone who wasn't supposed to be there. Pilar just walked, rigid and scared. She didn't know what she was walking into, but if it was good news, she was sure Justin would have told her.

The drive from Justin's house to the F-BOMB offices was a little longer than she thought it would be. The last time she was there, she was barely cognizant of where they were going. But this time, she watched every tree they passed, every car that sped by, every person on the street.

Justin pulled into a parking garage, and Pilar still stared out the window, not bothering to look at the address or the sign saying where they were. It wasn't until they were heading into the building that she noticed it wasn't an office.

"This is the hospital," she said, drawing her brows together. "Why... is Juan here?"

Justin nodded, and for the first time, Pilar was filled with hope. She grabbed Jack's hand and grinned up at him. He smiled down at her, but his smile was stiff.

"He's here. Juan is here. I can't believe you found him."

Pilar rambled on while Justin said something to the woman behind the counter. When she glanced at Pilar and offered her a sympathetic smile, Pilar's gut churned again.

"He's not okay, is he?" she asked when Justin joined them again.

Justin didn't look at her, just shook his head.

"Where is he? I want to see him."

Justin drew in a breath. "Someone will take us there, Pilar. He's on his way up now."

"Up? Up from where?"

"Justin O'Keefe?" a tall Black man asked. He wore a pair of dark blue scrubs and frameless glasses.

Justin turned and nodded. They shook hands and exchanged whispered words. The man glanced at her, his light brown eyes sympathetic, then back at Justin.

"What's going on?" Pilar asked, pushing between them.

"Ms. Luna. Let's go back here for a moment," the man said. He reached for her arm, but Pilar pulled back.

"No. Who are you?"

"I apologize. I'm Michael August."

"And what do you do here, Mr. August?"

He glanced at Justin. Justin nodded, and Mr. August looked at Pilar again. "I'm the medical examiner."

"Medical examiner? But that's..."

The three men stood around her waiting for the news to kick in. Her brother was dead. She wasn't there to see Juan. She was there to see his body. He was dead.

JACK WAITED for her to collapse. He could tell by the look on her face she thought her brother was going to be fine, but he knew from the second Slade knocked on the door that Juan was dead. If he wasn't, Slade would have led with that.

Instead of dropping to the ground, Pilar drew in a breath and nodded at Michael. "Let's go."

Michael glanced at Slade and Jack. They both shrugged and followed behind Pilar and Michael. The elevator ride was short. When the doors opened, the smell of bleach hit them in the face. Jack breathed through his mouth as he tried to stop the overwhelming urge to vomit.

They stopped outside the door to the morgue. Michael again glanced at them, but he was the professional. He knew how to handle this. Slade and Jack were military men. They only knew how to kill, not how to explain to a family member that someone they loved was killed.

"I'm sorry, Ms. Luna, but you need to prepare yourself. The man we believe is your brother was hurt badly. It's apparent from his injuries that he was tortured before he was killed."

"Why am I here?"

"You need to identify his body," Slade said. "Since he was technically an illegal, his prints, dental records, DNA... they aren't in the system. We were notified this morning since we have calls out to all the local hospitals and law enforcement about anyone matching his general description. Since you're his closest living relative, you need to be the one to identify him."

Pilar took a breath and squared her shoulders. Jack hated that she had to go through this. That she was going to come face-to-face with Carlos's handiwork, but she had no choice.

"They can come with you if you'd like," Michael said softly.

Pilar nodded. "Please."

Jack and Slade each took a side, offering her their silent support. Michael led them into a small room with one slab. The smell of dead flesh was strong enough to bring back the desire to vomit, but Jack had to be strong for Pilar.

They all stood at the head of the slab, all three men watching Pilar. When she nodded, Michael began to roll back the sheet.

Pilar gasped.

Jack wanted to look away, but he wouldn't let himself. Juan's cheek was sliced open, dried blood covering his cheek. His opposite eye was swollen shut. Blood and mud were caked in his hair, but the bright blue tips were undeniable. From the crookedness of his nose, that was broken, and God knew how many other bones. He had the look of a man who'd been beaten for days. And all they could see was his face. The rest of his body was probably worse.

"That's him," Pilar finally breathed. "That's Juan."

Jack closed his eyes and said a silent prayer for him, and another for justice.

"Where... what..." she dragged in another breath. "I don't know what I want to know."

Slade spoke first. "Dunn has all the details. At least, as much as we know. We can go there when you're ready."

Pilar nodded, her eyes still fixed on Juan's face. "I'm so sorry," she whispered. "I'm so sorry, hermano."

Pilar turned toward the door and left the room. Jack followed her, letting Slade talk to Michael about where to send all the findings. They were going to get Carlos. And Juan would help them.

In the hallway, Jack tucked a strand of hair behind Pilar's

ear. "I'm sorry, Pilar. I thought we'd find him before this happened."

She nodded. "I did, too." Her breath shook as she sucked it in. "I can't believe he's gone. How am I going to survive without him?"

She swallowed roughly and tears streamed down her cheeks. Jack couldn't stand there and let her cry. He wrapped his arms around her and held on tight. She let go, crying into his shirt and clutching him. It wasn't long before she was sobbing in his arms.

Jack led her to the rickety plastic chairs a few feet down the hall and pulled her onto his lap. She curled up into him, letting him hold her while she cried for her brother.

Slade walked out a few minutes later and took one look at them, then looked away. The emotion on Slade's face reflected what Jack felt. They knew Juan. For months, they'd worked with him. They promised to keep him safe. And instead, he'd gotten killed.

Jack didn't have to ask what came next. He was going to tell Pilar the truth. Every last word of it. From why Juan insisted they move to Niagara Falls to why they were at the parade, and everything in between. There was a high likelihood she was going to be pissed at them for lying to her. At Jack.

Her crying quieted a few minutes later, and Jack brushed the hair out of her face. "Are you ready?"

She drew in a breath and nodded. "Yes. I'm ready to kill that bastard for touching my brother. He's not going to get away with this."

Jack nodded. He agreed completely.

PILAR HELD Jack's hand with one of hers and held Juan's phone with the other. She stuffed it in her purse the day before when she debated what to do with it. Now that Juan was dead, she had no reason to consider giving it to Carlos. Jack's team would know how to get into it and be able to get the data off it to nail Carlos and the rest of the cartel. They were going down.

The SUV stopped and Pilar realized they were back at the office building Jack took her to the day they met. Four days ago. Was it really so short? She felt like she'd lived a lifetime since she met Jack. She'd lost her brother, fallen in love, and faced the devil.

Now it was time to destroy the devil. He wouldn't hurt anyone ever again.

Pilar silently followed Jack to the elevator and up to the offices. He scanned them through and led her into a conference room, a different one from last time. He quickly made her a cup of tea and set the steaming mug in front of her. She tried to smile at him, but she couldn't manage it.

Jack took the seat next to her and rested his head on his hands, his elbows on the table. He looked almost as defeated as she felt.

It wasn't long before the rest of the team joined them in the conference room. It was quiet, the group of them not joking or yelling or even talking as they walked in. The silence was eerie and intimidating, to say the least.

"Do you need anything?" Dunn asked when he sat across from her.

"Carlos's head."

Dunn nodded once. "Already on order."

She reached into her purse as she nodded, knowing he was going to deliver exactly that. But she had to help. "Maybe this will make the process go faster."

She held out her hand and revealed the phone in her palm. The entire mood in the room shifted from one of sorrow to one of tension.

"What is that?" Dunn asked carefully.

"I think it's Juan's. I found it in my bag. It's not mine, but it was rolled up in a black shirt at the bottom. It must have been there all along, and I didn't realize it when I was packing. I think he planted it there, knowing what was going to happen. Somehow."

Pilar watched the men as they all stared at the phone, then glanced at her and Dunn. When he finally took the phone from her, slowly as if he thought it would attack, he handed it immediately over to English.

"Get into this, but be careful—"

"Yeah, so they can't track it. Not a problem. It has some sophisticated stuff on it. Might be a retina scan. This is high end."

"Could be what we've been looking for," Jack said, speaking for the first time since they left the morgue.

Pilar glanced at him and found him studying her.

"When did you find it?"

She sighed but held his gaze. "Yesterday."

Every male in the room sucked in a deep breath at once. Except Jack. He just stared at her, unmoving. Untrusting.

"I was going to tell you."

He nodded sharply.

"We have a few things you need to know, too," Dunn said, drawing her attention from Jack. "There's a lot you don't know, and we didn't want you to. We needed to protect your brother, and possibly you, and this country."

"What are you talking about?" Pilar asked. Her pulse quickened as she tried to make sense of what Dunn said. She couldn't. Not without more information. But she could tell by the mood of the room she wasn't going to like what he had to say.

She leaned back in her seat, but felt vulnerable and exposed, so she leaned forward again. She rested her hands on the table in front of her, lacing her fingers together and squeezing them tight. She stared at them as her knuckles turned white, then released so blood returned. Her hair fell in her face, but she flicked it back and met Dunn's gaze again.

"What are you talking about?" she repeated.

"Your brother was working for us. For months. He was giving us information about the cartel and working with us to take them down. Meeting Carlos the other day was part of our operation, but something went wrong. Meeting Jack wasn't a mistake. He was there to keep you safe if anything happened to Juan. It was a requirement of your brother's, or he refused to give us any information."

"Wait, what... I don't get it. What do you mean?"

"Your brother was doing everything Carlos accused him of. He was... basically, a spy. For us."

22

―――――

Pilar's head spun with the new information. Carlos knew. He told her. But Pilar dismissed him as a crazy man. Mostly because he was. But he was right. Juan was working with the US government to bring down Carlos and the entire organization.

And it got him killed.

"How could you let him do this?" she hissed. "You were supposed to keep him safe. Isn't that how things like this work? He promises to give you information and you keep him alive! And you what? Just let him walk away with the most evil man I've ever met in my life. How could you?"

Pilar was more angry than she'd ever been in her life. They lied to her. Every single one of them. They told her they would help her and let her rattle on about Carlos being after her. They tried to make it sound like she was wrong, but she didn't believe them. They knew. They all knew. They knew the truth, and they kept it from her.

"You're no better than Carlos," she spat. "You're liars. All of you." Pilar got up to leave, not wanting to spend one more second in the presence of the men she thought were helping her.

Dunn stood. "We are. You're right. And you have every right to be angry right now, but you're still in danger. If you walk out that door, you and I both know Carlos will find you. He'll kill you and probably do much worse to you before he kills you. None of us wants that, Pilar. Let us finish what we started. Let us keep you safe while we find him and take them out."

She froze at his words, knowing every word was true. She couldn't walk away and expect to live. Carlos could be outside the office waiting for her. She had no way of knowing.

She turned back to the room and her gaze landed on Jack. Jack. She thought she loved him. She opened her heart and soul up to him, along with her legs. And he used her just like Carlos did. He told her things, probably lies, to gain her trust. And all she did was blindly follow the man who was planted in her life to make her trust him.

"Was sleeping with me part of the deal?" she asked him.

To his credit, Jack didn't speak. He didn't even move. He just sat there and stared at her.

"Poor, helpless Pilar. I was an easy mark, wasn't I? Lost without my brother, a man you were supposed to protect. And you let him walk into that monster's trap. Then you fucked your way into my heart. Damn you, Jack. Damn you for making me fall for you. For stealing the little bit of life I had left in me. For taking that from me."

She closed her eyes and fought the tears that squeezed through her lids and poured onto her cheeks. When she opened them again, she ignored Jack and focused on Dunn.

"I don't want him anywhere near me. I don't want to see

him ever again. I don't care who babysits me, as long as it isn't Jack."

Dunn nodded and moved toward her. "Why don't you wait in my office while we figure all this out? Then I'll come get you, and we can take you to wherever you're going to stay."

She nodded stiffly, avoiding the eyes of every other man in the room. It ripped what was left of her heart to pieces to walk away from Jack, but she had to. He wasn't the man she thought he was. She thought she loved him, but she clearly couldn't trust her heart. She fell for Carlos, too. And Jack was just another liar who used her to get what he wanted.

Fuck him. Fuck all of them. She was done with men. For good this time.

JACK COULDN'T MOVE. He couldn't say anything. He was aware of her walking away from him, and it gutted him. Everything she said was right. He let Juan walk into Carlos's trap. He was a liar. He was no better than the man who stole her virginity. He stole everything else from her.

When the door closed softly behind Pilar and Dunn, Jack still sat there. The rest of the room erupted into motion, all quiet, but still motion. English tapped endlessly on his keyboard. Archer and Dex started talking about the situation they were in. Slade joined them after a few seconds. Mason and Rocky stared at him, but he ignored them until they gave up and paid attention to the others.

Jack felt like he was observing his life. Floating. He wondered if that was what death felt like, and if he was about to die. He wished he had. That he could trade places with Juan so Pilar had her brother.

She said she fell for him. She loved him. Holy shit, she loved him.

The phone, though. Why didn't she give him the phone? They could have found Juan before he died if they had the phone.

But would they have? If they had the phone, would they have kept looking for Juan or would they have considered their job done, and the consequences were inevitable.

Jack hated himself for not being able to answer the question. And if he couldn't answer it, he didn't blame her for doubting the answer either.

Dunn walked back in and came right to him. Jack still sat in the chair he fell into when they got there. Pilar's light, floral scent drifted to him as Dunn dropped into her chair. Her face stared at him, smiling and laughing, then moaning and coming, then angry and accusing. Jack hated it. He did that to her. He betrayed her. He hurt her. He loved her.

"Are you okay?" Dunn asked after a second.

Jack forced a smile. "Of course. Why wouldn't I be?"

Jack knew Dunn could see right through him, but he didn't care. All that mattered was keeping Pilar safe.

"You're not going out there if we find something," Dunn said, glancing at English as he typed furiously.

"Like hell."

Dunn shook his head. "You're spiraling. I know it because I felt it. When Ashaki betrayed us and Rodney got killed, I did the same thing. But I ignored it. It almost got all of us killed."

Jack shook his head. "I can't. I can't sit here and not be involved. She didn't betray me, I betrayed her. I'm the bad guy here."

"The phone—"

"If she turned it over, would we still have dedicated all

our resources to finding Juan, or would we have done exactly what we're doing now and tried everything to get into the phone to see if it was the info we needed?"

Dunn held his gaze for a long moment, his dark eyes answering the question before he sighed and looked away. "This is a big case—"

"And he's just one man. I know. I get it. I probably would have supported that decision. But I just..."

Dunn nodded. "I know. I hate this, too."

Jack looked up at him. "She needs to be with you or Dex. Keep her at Slade's, but I want one of you with her there, with Slade and Howler, until this is over."

Dunn drew in a breath and nodded.

Only once he knew she'd be safe could Jack start to think again. English was talking, saying something about the phone.

"Retina scan. It's high end. Not many of these even exist."

"Can you crack it?" Dunn asked.

English shrugged. "I don't know. I've only seen one of these, and I didn't have to break into it."

"What about Pilar?" Jack asked.

They all turned to look at him.

"Maybe she can get into it. If Juan hid it in her bag, knowing all this was going to happen, maybe he set it up so she could get into it."

English shrugged. "Worth a shot." He extended the phone to Jack, but Jack refused to take it. After a long moment, English held it out to Dunn.

"I'll be right back."

Jack felt the same sick wave wash over him. He'd never hold Pilar again. Make her laugh. Sink into her. Lose himself in her. She was gone, as good as dead for him. He lost her, and he only had himself to blame for it.

The room operated around him as Jack sat there. He couldn't think. He could barely breathe. He had a job to do, but for the moment, all he could think about was Pilar. He wanted to help her. To ease her pain over losing her brother. He was the last person she wanted to see, so he had no choice but to give her space.

When Dunn came back, the phone was live and unlocked. "She was one of the users. It played a short message for her from Juan asking her to turn the phone over to us." He glanced at Jack. "It also said he was sorry for lying to her and that he trusted all of us with his life and she should, too."

Jack closed his eyes and sank into his seat again. He sat there while the others worked, pulling all the information from the phone onto the secure F-BOMB servers to upload to Homeland Security.

Dunn took the seat next to Jack again and turned to face him. Jack felt the weight of his stare. "I think you should go to her. Tell her you're sorry. She shouldn't be alone right now."

Jack shook his head. "I'm the last person she wants anywhere near her. She hates me, more than everyone else. I betrayed her. My sins are on a whole different level."

"Don't do this," Dunn hissed. "Don't blame yourself."

Jack laughed mirthlessly. "Why not? It's my fault. I knew getting involved with her was a bad idea. I knew it would end in disaster. I knew she'd hate me when the truth finally came out. And I did it anyway."

Dunn squeezed his fists, looking for an argument, but none came. Jack was right, and Dunn knew it. Jack was to blame for deceiving Pilar. The others warned him, but he made the choice to sleep with her. To hold her. To love her. Lying was bad enough, but lying to her when he was also sleeping with her was worse.

He deserved every last bit of pain he got for it.

"This is a fucking gold mine," English breathed from the other side of the room. "He has contacts in here for people we didn't know were a part of this. And conversations. This alone is going to bring them down."

"So you know where they are?" Dunn asked, forgetting Jack and slipping back into his role as the boss.

"Not yet. With the volume of numbers in here, it's going to take a while to search them."

"Make it half that," Dunn said. "We owe that woman a resolution."

English nodded and bent over his laptop again. The rest of the team surrounded him, watching as more and more information flooded their servers and put nails in the coffins of every person involved with the cartel.

Jack tried to be happy that they were bringing down the organization. They were flooding the United States with drugs, and there were rumors about human trafficking. When Juan first came to them, he wasn't sure they'd ever see anything for the efforts, but Juan came through. He delivered what he promised. And he paid for it.

By late afternoon, it was clear they weren't going to get all the information they needed that day. Juan had a phone number for Carlos, but the phone was turned off, so they couldn't track it. The ME's report wasn't done yet, even though Dunn called multiple times asking for them to rush it, so there was very little anyone could do but wait.

Jack hated that part of the job. It was the same way when they were SEALs. They'd get orders and prepare, then wait until it was time to execute, either on a plane going to their location or in place waiting for things to happen as they expected. Nothing was fast in the hurry-up world they existed in, and it drove him nuts.

"You should take Pilar home. Get her some food and let her rest," Jack said. It killed him that he wasn't the one who was going to take her home. He wanted one more night with her. One more morning. One more time to slip into her body and know he'd never loved a woman before, and wasn't likely to ever love one again.

Dunn nodded and jerked his head to Dex. Dex stood and headed for the door with Slade on his heels.

"Dex?" Jack asked Dunn.

Dunn nodded. "I want to stay here and find as much info as we can. He'll take care of her."

Jack nodded. Their footsteps echoed in the hallway outside the conference room. He wanted to turn and catch a glimpse of her walking by, but he couldn't handle watching her walk away again.

Dex stuck his head in and nodded for Dunn to step outside with them. Jack strained to hear the conversation, but all he could make out were murmurs that told him nothing.

Dunn walked back in a minute later. The door closed harshly in the hallway. Pilar was gone. Probably for good. The only thing Jack had left to do was catch the son of a bitch who killed her brother, and give her the space she needed.

PILAR WALKED into the bedroom she shared with Jack and closed her eyes. His bag was already gone, likely removed by

Justin when he went through the house before she and Dex went inside.

Thankfully, both men were giving her space, but it only made the silence that much louder. She'd gotten used to Jack's steady presence over the last few days. Looking for him when the room was crowded or reaching for him when he was close. She hated herself for wanting to sink into him and let him help her feel better. The only peace she'd had for days was with him. And that was gone.

She finally opened her eyes and looked around the room. It looked the same as when she left that morning. When Justin knocked on the door and interrupted them. The sheets were thrown off the edge of the bed, her bag still on the end, open and spilling out clothes. The curtains were pulled shut, blocking the fading sunlight from brightening the room. She didn't want to see every inch of it.

Pilar went to the bed and sat down. The sheets were cool, but when she laid down, she smelled Jack on them. His scent filled her and made her ache for him. Tears flooded her eyes and she let them fall.

Then she realized she was crying over the man she'd known for days instead of the brother she'd loved her whole life.

She cried harder, thinking about Juan's smiling face and his happy attitude. Since they reconnected, she knew he was hiding things from her. She tried to ask him a few times, but he always deflected her questions. Her one rule was that he wasn't bringing the cartel back into their lives. He promised her he wasn't.

He lied, too.

It was a trend with her. The men in her life lied to her. About everything. Between Carlos making her believe he was a good man, Juan lying about being in the cartel in the first place, Jack not telling her he was working with Juan, and Juan bringing Carlos back into her life, she was exhausted. Too many liars. Too much pain.

Pilar sat up and swiped the errant tears from her cheeks. She was done crying over men who didn't give her the respect she deserved. They treated her like a fragile little girl instead of the woman she was. Well, fuck them.

23

Pilar stormed out of her room and into the kitchen. Justin and Dex were sitting at the table, talking quietly, when she stomped past them. Both men stopped their conversation and looked at her. She ignored them and went to the freezer, where she thought she saw a bottle of liquor.

She was wrong. No liquor in the freezer. Or the fridge. Or in the cabinets she opened and slammed shut.

Howler whimpered, but she needed alcohol. It was rare that Pilar drink, but she wasn't going to sit there and feel sorry for herself. Alcohol would drown her pain for the night since Jack wasn't there. And wouldn't be again.

"Are you looking for something?" Justin asked, startling her. She'd almost forgotten he was there.

"Alcohol. Anything."

"That's probably not a good idea," Dex said.

She smirked at him. "Yeah, you're right. But my brother was killed by my psycho ex today. And the man I'm in love with now has been lying to me and fucked me to get information out of me. Did he tell you about it? Was it like a big group project? Maybe you guys played rock-paper-scissors to see who got to fuck the mark. Is that how it went?"

"Pilar..." Justin tried.

She turned to him and shook her head. "Don't," she breathed. Tears filled her eyes again, and the strain of fighting them off had her mouth flooding. She swallowed and drew in a breath. "Please. Just let me forget for one night."

Justin and Dex had a silent conversation before Justin stood and opened a lower cabinet. He stepped back and revealed a collection of liquor that had her sucking back her tears.

Pilar crouched in front of the cabinet and grabbed one of the full bottles. She didn't care what kind of alcohol it was as long as it worked. She stood and untwisted the cap, snapping the seal. It smelled like rubbing alcohol, but she tipped the bottle up anyway and took a healthy swig.

Then choked.

Justin moved in to take the bottle from her, but she turned away from him.

"Pilar," Dex started. "You don't have to do this."

She smiled at him. "I do. Because I'm in a house with two men who are supposed to keep me safe. Two men who already let my brother die. Two men who are friends with the last guy who fucked me." She took another sip, wincing less the second time. "Did he tell you we did it without condoms last night? In case you didn't get that part of the story. It was good, too. The first time I'd ever had sex without a condom. He said it was for him, too, but I doubt it. I'll need to get tested when this is all over. Make sure I didn't pick up something. Especially if he's the one you always send in to keep the witness in line."

"It's not like that," Dex said softly. "We all told him it was a bad idea getting involved with you."

She laughed. "Oh, that's good. So none of you wanted to take one for the team and thought Jack shouldn't either. He just did that all on his own. Went rouge or whatever. Maybe he thought I was a consolation prize since he let Juan go with Carlos."

The two men stared at her, probably thinking she was unhinged. She was sure they were right, but she couldn't seem to stop herself.

"I told him I loved him. I don't think he knows that part, but you can tell him later. When you're all sitting around and laughing at the poor Mexican chica whose brother died. I told him I loved him. And I do. I hate him for making me fall for him. He's the kind of guy I always liked. He makes me laugh and makes me feel like I matter. Or did. God, it really sucks finding out the man you love is really an asshole who used you." She sipped again, barely noticing the burn anymore. "I guess I'm an easy target. Men take one look at me and think the fat girl is desperate for attention, so I'm an easy mark. I must be, too, because I fall for it. Hook, line, and sinker. Isn't that what you say? First Carlos, now Jack. Two men who made me think they were good. Two men who let me fall in love with them. Two men who'll never love me. And I don't want them to. You know? I mean, why would I?"

Pilar sank onto the couch and sipped the bottle again. Justin and Dex were standing in front of her, looking like badasses even with the frowns on their faces.

"This is good stuff," she slurred. "What is it? I should drink some more."

Pilar turned the bottle up and sipped again, taking an

extra swallow when the first one slid down easily. Dex took the bottle from her when she lowered it.

"Hey! That's mine. I was drinking that," she argued.

He ignored her and carried the bottle back to the kitchen. Pilar tried to get up and go after him, but she felt heavy all of a sudden.

"I'll get it later," she whispered, turning on her side and nuzzling against the pillow. Even that smelled like Jack. She pressed her nose into it and groaned, yanking it from under her head and throwing it across the room. "Get out of my head!"

She found another pillow that didn't smell as much like Jack and snuggled with that, letting the alcohol drag her off to sleep.

"WE GOT HIM," English said, quietly announcing it to the room.

Jack drew in a breath and nodded. It would all be over soon, and then Pilar could go back to her life. The one he wasn't a part of.

"Where is he?" Dunn demanded.

They were all still in the conference room. It was barely past two in the morning. Jack was numb but focused. He needed to finish the job, then move on.

"He's at a house downtown. Not far from where we lost him that day in the park. Son of a bitch. He was hiding under our noses the entire time," English hissed.

"It doesn't matter now. We got him. You got him." Dunn paused and looked around the room. "It's late. Everyone needs their sleep."

The entire room went silent. Jack held his breath,

waiting to calm down before he spoke. It didn't work. "With all due respect, fuck you. We're going after him now. When we know where he is and can surprise him. We all know if we sleep, we'll miss him. And none of us can actually sleep. If we could, we would have hours ago."

Dunn looked around the room at the others, all of whom were nodding in agreement with Jack.

"All right. Let's head out. I'm going to notify Slade and Dex."

Jack nodded. He wished he was the one protecting Pilar, the one with her overnight. The one who had to sit the mission out because he had more important things to do.

The men dressed in silence. The snap of belts, the scratch of velcro, and the click of their many weapons provided all the noise they needed to get focused. Jack wasn't one for idle chit-chat when things got real. He thought it was part of being a sniper, but the others didn't talk either. They were all focused on grabbing the right weapons and protecting themselves before they faced down evil.

"All's quiet at Slade's," Dunn said when he came back into the room. "I notified local PD. Anyone have a plan?" Dunn had his vest in his hand. He looked around the room while he pulled it on, securing it in place.

"You always come up with the plan," Archer argued.

Dunn nodded. "Just wondering if anyone else has any input tonight." He looked at Jack, but Jack just shook his head.

"We're residential," English began. "And not in a war zone. We have to be smart. Assume there are hostages. The couple who lives there are Maria and John Hodgkins. Both sixty-eight. Retired. He used to work for the city as a planner. No kids. No living family that I can find. If they're still alive, we have no clue what shape they're in."

Dunn looked at Rocky. "You ready?"

Rocky, the team medic, nodded. "Always. Gear is in the truck."

"What else do we know about the area?" Dunn asked.

English clicked a few more keys. "Tight. All the houses are close together. Less than ten feet in some cases. It'll be good for cover, but shit for sneaking up if someone has a dog or is up. From what I can tell, most of the people in that area are older, lived there for decades."

"Hopefully that means they're all retired and not up in the middle of the night," Archer said.

Everyone else nodded in agreement.

"Who's going in?"

"Me," Jack said immediately, drawing the eyes of every other man.

Dunn's eyebrows went up, but he didn't argue.

"Me," Archer said, followed by Rocky and Mason.

"I'm at your disposal," English said.

"What are the risks of not having eyes on the place?" Dunn asked.

English shrugged. "They could run, but that could happen no matter what."

"Yeah, but the bastard could get away if he does," Jack spat.

"True," English agreed. "But we're smart. We're going to surround the house, get heat signatures, do some recon before we bust in there. We're not going to just walk up to the front door and ask if they'll hand over the murderer."

"All right," Dunn said, raising his voice above the others. "English, pack up and come with us. We'll park one truck in front and one on the back street. Find the bodies and surround them, then go in and bring the son of a bitch down."

"Hooyah!"

JACK WANTED THE BACK. He knew the son of a bitch would run. And he was happy to be the man who took his ass down.

When they pulled up to the quiet street behind the target, adrenaline pumped through his blood. He was alert and ready. They were ending this tonight, and setting Pilar free.

"You ready?" Archer asked Jack.

Jack nodded. "Always."

Archer held his gaze for a long minute. When a voice broke into the silence between them, Jack breathed a sigh of relief.

"Four heat signatures inside. One in the basement, likely our hostage. Two on the main floor, one on the second floor," Dunn said.

"Ten-four," Archer said. "Eyes on the prize. We're looking at a bunch of fences over here. No clear path."

The truck was silent while they waited for a response. Jack searched the street, watching for movement that could give them away. It was quiet, almost too quiet.

"If you can't get in, he can't get out. What's Squirrel say?" Dunn asked.

As much as Jack hated his nickname, it was necessary on missions. If someone was listening to them, they didn't want to reveal their identities.

"Nothing high over here," Jack relayed. "Not unless I want to scale someone's roof."

"Not advisable," Dunn said firmly.

"Agreed. So I'm limited."

"All right. You two on getaway. Hulk, behind the wheel. Squirrel, on guard."

"Ten-four," they said in unison.

Jack took a deep breath. He stared at the house stuck between the others. With everything so close together, there weren't many opportunities to get through. The fences were chain-link, giving them a view, but not a clear shot, even for him.

"Moving in," Dunn said softly in his ear. They were all connected through their comms, allowing Archer and Jack to hear everything as the team moved forward.

"Breaching the door."

The snick of the lock was audible, followed by the rapid footsteps of the rest of the team funneling into the house. Dunn went to bat with the judge for the exemption allowing them to enter the home without announcing their presence. They had to operate within the law, which would normally mean announcing their presence before breaking into a house. They argued that if Carlos had even a few seconds of warning, it could prove deadly for the hostage and likely for the team as well.

"Clear right," one voice whispered.

"Clear left," said another.

"Moving to the back."

Jack's pulse raced as the footsteps moved forward. Dunn's contacts at the local police department provided them with blueprints for the house. Jack could picture the house in his mind as they moved through it.

Pop-pop.

Jack and Archer shared a look. Excitement filled him. He

turned his focus back to the house, watching intently for anyone moving around in the back.

"One hostile down."

"Thought there were two on the main floor," Jack muttered.

"Eyes up. Second heat signature is on the move. Second floor," English said through the comms.

Jack stared at the house through his sight. All the lights were off inside and the streetlights prevented him from using night vision. He was at a disadvantage, but he wasn't about to let the bastard go.

"Movement out the back," Archer said. "Second floor. Looks like there's a ladder."

Jack watched as the son of a bitch sped down the ladder and turned toward the house next door.

"Moving east."

"You got him?" Dunn barked.

"Tracking. Looks like he's got a path."

"Don't lose him. We want him alive if possible. Dead works, too."

Jack drew in a breath and stared down his sight. A house blocked his view, then Carlos emerged again, sneaking around the edge of the house just ahead of Jack and Archer.

"I have a shot," Jack said softly.

"We want him alive," Dunn said. "Go after him. Give him a chance to turn himself in."

Archer and Jack pushed out of the SUV silently, both of them moving toward Carlos in the shadows.

Carlos looked around, but the unmistakable sound of gunfire at the house drew his attention.

"God dammit!" Carlos shouted into the night.

The distraction was long enough that Archer and Jack

were able to close the distance between them. Jack found cover behind a truck across the street from Carlos. He kept the man in his sight, holding his position. He didn't have a good shot, but he would if Carlos kept running in the same direction.

Archer moved across the street. He was exposed, in the center of the road, when Carlos turned and saw him.

"Who the fuck are you?" Carlos demanded.

"I'm here to bring you in," Archer shouted back. "Your men are dead. Put down the gun and put your hands on your head."

Carlos laughed, then pulled the trigger. The blast echoed in the silent night, splitting the quiet peace of the street.

Archer dropped to the ground instantly. His still form urged Jack to rush to him, but he held his position, his heart pounding in his chest, his blood thumping loudly in his ears.

Carlos didn't wait for Archer to get up, he just took off down the street. Jack listened to his footsteps until he came into view, then pulled the trigger, not hesitating.

The shrill yelp pierced the air before the thud of Carlos hitting the ground. Jack watched him for a minute, satisfied that he wasn't moving, then rushed to Archer.

"Man down."

24

PILAR WOKE UP THE NEXT MORNING WITH A KILLER HEADACHE, feeling like she spent the night eating cotton balls. She tried to pry her eyes open, but it hurt too much.

"Oh, God," she groaned.

"Take this," a male voice said, right next to her.

Pilar screamed and yanked her eyes open. She couldn't place the voice and when she looked around, she couldn't place where she was.

"It's me, Pilar. It's Dex. You're at Slade's house. Howler is outside the door, whimpering to get to you. You're safe."

Her reality came slamming back to her in a flash. Juan, dead. Carlos, free. Jack, liar.

She groaned again.

"Pilar. Ibuprofen. It'll help the headache," Dex said, drawing her attention again.

She sucked in a breath and closed her eyes. She held out her hand for Dex to set the pills in. She popped them in her mouth and accepted the water, swallowing it all down.

"How much did I drink?"

"Enough to forget. Once you passed out, at least."

"How did I get in here? The last thing I remember is the couch."

"I carried you," Dex said, sounding uncomfortable.

"You did? I'm not light."

"No one is, Pilar. But carrying you in here was nothing compared to carrying a buddy fully loaded with gear off the battlefield."

She looked up at Dex for the first time. The sadness in his dark eyes ricocheted inside her. She knew that pain. She felt that pain.

"I'm sorry for your loss," she said softly.

He nodded once. "I'm sorry for yours." He moved toward the door but paused when he got there. "For what it's worth, I don't think Jack slept with you to get information. He never told us anything you said, or about anything you did."

Dex's cheeks pinked with his last words, and Pilar remembered some of what she confessed the night before. "Oh, God. I can't believe I told you guys all that. I... um..."

"Don't worry," Dex said. "We won't say a word to anyone. But I think you should tell Jack how you feel."

Pilar laughed mirthlessly. "That's never going to happen. He doesn't want me. He hasn't apologized or tried to explain. I was a mark for him. A job. I don't mean anything to him."

"I really think—"

Pilar shook her head. "No, please. Don't try to explain his actions or make excuses for him. I know he's your friend, and I can't handle you telling me he's really a good guy and I should give him a chance. A part of me understands he couldn't say anything because you guys have rules and all, but it still hurts that he lied. He might be a great guy, but he's obviously not the guy for me. And I need to figure out how to get over him." She smiled.

"Sadly, I've done it before. I'll do it again. Alone once more."

Dex hesitated a minute, then nodded. "If you want to take a shower, Slade's fixing breakfast."

Pilar nodded, thankful he didn't push more. It wouldn't change anything to hear how wonderful Jack was. She knew. And it only hurt to imagine him being wonderful for someone else, but she wouldn't hold out hope he'd be the guy for her. She was done thinking she had a chance at finding love. She was just done.

PILAR TOOK her time in the shower. When she was done and dressed, her stomach growled, telling her to quit stalling. She was feeling better than when she got up, but it was going to be a long day with a hangover from hell.

The soft voices of the two men who'd protected her for the last night reached her as she moved down the hallway.

"He should be fine."

"I hate that we weren't there."

"It wouldn't have changed anything."

He sighed. "It just pisses me off. Fuck."

"What's going on?" Pilar asked.

Both men swung to look at her. "You should sit down," Justin said.

"No," she said. Her palms were clammy and her throat tightened. "What happened?"

Justin and Dex shared a look. Apparently, Justin lost whatever silent battle they had because he said, "They found Carlos last night."

"What?" Pilar breathed, sinking into the chair next to her.

"He was in a house in the city. Forced his way in and hid out there," Justin continued.

"What?" she repeated.

"English tracked him down and the team went after him last night," Justin said.

"What?"

"He—"

"Stop," Dex said. "Slade, she's spinning. Stop."

Pilar's head spun as the room collapsed around her. Both men came to her sides, one on her left and one on her right. They breathed with her, forcing her to focus on every breath. After a few, her pulse slowed. She gulped in air and held it then slowly exhaled.

"Are you okay?" Dex asked carefully.

Pilar nodded. "I, um, yeah."

"Pilar?" Justin said.

She finally met his worried gaze and offered him a timid smile. "I'm fine. I... slower this time."

He grinned back and took the seat next to her. Dex sat, too, and between them, they told her what happened.

"They found him early this morning. He was hiding out at a house in downtown Niagara Falls. He'd forced his way in."

"Did he... did he kill the people who lived there?" she breathed.

Dex and Justin exchanged a look and nodded. "The wife, yeah," Dex said. "The husband was still alive. Barely. He'll be okay. Physically, at least."

"Oh, my God."

Justin jumped in. "We don't have to do this now."

She shook her head. "No, I need to know."

They traded another look, and Pilar stiffened her spine. She knew what kind of man Carlos was. It was why she left him and never looked back. None of it was a shock to her. And if she didn't get herself under control, they weren't going to tell her everything.

She wanted Jack. She hated it, but she wanted him to wrap his big, strong arms around her and hold her tight while she heard the rest.

Justin finally sighed and nodded. "They've been there since they arrived in town. He had two men with him."

"Juan?"

Justin shook his head. "They weren't keeping Juan there as far as the team could tell. This was just where they were staying." Justin took a deep breath. "He's dead, Pilar."

"Jack?" she breathed, her heart stopping.

Justin and Dex both stared at her wide-eyed. She looked between them, begging them silently to tell her no. Then Dex shook his head.

"No, Pilar. Not Jack. Carlos is dead. Jack's the one who killed him. He shot Archer, and Jack got him."

Her eyes overflowed with tears, and a sob shook her whole body. "Archer?"

"He'll be okay. He was wearing a vest. Knocked the wind out of him and cracked a couple of ribs, but nothing he hasn't been through before," Justin assured her.

"Lily's never going to forgive me."

Dex rested his hand on Pilar's. "Lily knows Archer was doing something important. And she knows it was Carlos's fault, not yours."

"But—"

"No," Justin said firmly. "You are not responsible for that man's actions. Do not take that on yourself."

"But—"

"No," both men said together.

She choked back her protest and nodded.

"Is... is everyone else okay?" she asked, not wanting to ask about Jack, but needing to know.

Dex nodded. "Yeah. No one else got hurt. Dunn took a punch from one of Carlos's men, but he's fine."

"And Carlos is dead? Jack killed him?"

Dex and Justin both nodded. "It's over, Pilar. You're safe."

"It's over," she breathed. "I can't believe it's over."

PILAR COULD TELL Dex and Justin were anxious to get to the hospital to see Archer. She wanted to go, but she didn't want to show up where she wasn't welcome, so she asked them to take her home.

"Are you sure?" Justin asked. "You're welcome to stay here a little while if you'd like."

Pilar shook her head. "I need to find a new job, maybe a new home. I need to move on. Figure out what I want to do now."

"What do you mean?"

She shrugged. "I lost my job by taking this week off. And I'm not sure I can live there knowing Carlos was in my home. Even though he's dead, he's tainted it. And there's really nothing keeping me here. Without a job, and without Juan, and without... I just don't know if staying in Niagara Falls is the right thing for me."

"Where would you go?" Dex asked.

Pilar shrugged again. "Maybe back to Texas. Where my aunt and uncle live."

Dex and Justin both nodded. "Family," Dex said. "I don't blame you."

Pilar's throat tightened at the thought. Her brother was her only family. She loved her aunt and uncle, but leaving them had been surprisingly easy the first time. Returning was because she didn't know where else to go. She had no one else. She wanted to feel tethered. To have someone miss her. To know someone cared.

Pilar packed up all her stuff, hating herself for taking the tee Jack left behind, and Justin grabbed her bag. The three of them walked in silence to the SUV. The drive was just as quiet, with Pilar up front and Dex in the back on his phone.

When Justin pulled up in front of her apartment, she trembled. She didn't want to walk in there alone. She didn't want to face the fact that Juan was gone. She would need to do something with his stuff. Plan his funeral. Say goodbye.

She didn't want to do it alone, but she was. Alone. And she'd be alone forever. The thought of opening up to someone else, to letting another man in, terrified her. The only two men she loved had lied to her. Deceived her and made her feel like she was used. She wouldn't survive a third attempt at love.

Without saying a word, Justin turned off the SUV and the three of them got out. She smiled her gratitude and led the way into her apartment.

Things had been picked up since the last time she was there. Shelves were stacked with books, papers in neat piles, and everything was organized. She looked closely and knew it wasn't how she left it, but it was close enough.

"Thank you for doing this," she said to Dex and Justin.

"We didn't," Dex said.

She smiled. "I know. You were with me. But the team did. Someone had to have picked up."

Dex slid Justin a look and nodded. "Definitely. I'll pass on your thanks."

Pilar grinned, feeling better that she wasn't dealing with a mess. She walked through her home. Her bedroom was clean. Neat. She stopped in front of the drawer that held the flower from Carlos. She drew in a breath and opened it. All her panties were gone, and so was the flower. In its place were packages of new panties, the same kind she wore, untouched by the flower.

She dropped to the bed and sobbed. Dex and Justin rushed in.

"Are you okay?"

"What happened?"

She grinned and pointed to the drawer. "The flower is gone, and so is everything it touched. Thank you. I know Juan orchestrated this whole thing and forced you guys to help me, but this is above and beyond. Thank you."

Again, they looked confused, but both men nodded.

"Are you going to be okay?" Justin asked.

Pilar nodded. "Yeah. Thank you. Please tell Archer I'm sorry. And Lily, too."

They smiled. Justin stepped forward and hugged her. "Call us before you leave town, okay? Tell us where you're going?"

Pilar promised, but she knew she wouldn't. Once they walked out her door, she wouldn't see them again. It was how it needed to be. A clean break.

JACK SAT in the waiting room at the hospital and stared at his phone. When he saw Archer go down, he couldn't think. Once Carlos went down and Jack got back to Archer, he was able to breathe again, but he wanted to kill the son of a bitch all over again. One quick death was too good for the evil bastard.

A door at the end of the hallway opened, and Jack

looked up. Dex strode toward him, looking ready to kill someone, too. When Dex saw Jack, he veered away from the nurse's station and went to him.

"Is he okay?"

Jack nodded. "The doctor's with him now. Lily's back there."

"Are they going to discharge him?"

"He wants them to, but she's refusing. She said he needs to stay one night in the hospital and make sure he's okay. He went down hard. No signs of a concussion, but she's Lily."

Dex grinned. "He'll stay."

Jack nodded. "Yep." He looked past Dex. "I thought Slade was coming."

Dex's face lost all traces of humor. "He stayed with Pilar."

Jack was going to throw up. In one night, he not only lost the woman he loved, but she chose one of his best friends.

Jack nodded, knowing he couldn't do anything about it. He wanted Pilar happy. And if she was happy with Slade, if he was the man she wanted, he wouldn't stand in the way.

He might throw a few punches and call out his supposed friend for moving in on his woman, but he wouldn't stop Pilar from being happy.

"Someone was in her place."

"What?" Jack demanded, fear replacing the anger he felt. "Who? How do you know?"

"She thanked us for cleaning up her apartment. She said it was a mess the last time she was there, and she knew someone on the team did it. Last time we were there, we... well, we weren't gentle. And it's neat now. Too neat."

"I did it," Jack admitted. "I picked up her place."

"What?" Dex asked, turning to look at Jack. "You?"

Jack nodded. "Once Lily got here this morning, she sent

me home with strict instructions not to return until after lunch. I couldn't sleep, so I went to Pilar's and cleaned her place. I wanted her to feel safe when she went home."

"The panties?"

Jack's cheeks heated. "She freaked out, man. When she saw that flower, she didn't want to touch any of them. I tossed them and got her all new. I left them in the package, though. So she knew they were new."

Dex nodded. "She saw. She really appreciated it. We thought someone else might have been after her. I'll let Slade know."

Jack nodded. "I didn't think to warn you guys. I should have. I was just..."

"You were trying to take care of the woman you love. I get it."

Jack wanted to deny it, but he couldn't. It was the truth.

Dex thumbed a text to Slade, then slid his phone back into his pocket. "She's leaving. Said she might go back to Texas where her aunt and uncle are."

It split Jack in two to know his chance with Pilar was truly over, but he nodded. Just like being with Slade, if leaving was what she wanted, he wanted her to be happy.

"She said she lost her job when she had to take time off. And Juan's dead. And she doesn't have any reason to stay here. There's nothing keeping her here."

Jack nodded, keeping his mouth shut. She didn't have a reason to stay. He couldn't give her one because she hated him. As much as he wanted her, he couldn't change anything.

"It really sucks, though, because she doesn't have a job there. It might be hard to get something. If she still had her job here, she could look for something in Texas and finish out the school year here. Take her time. But you know how these bureaucratic systems are. It's policy that if she takes time off connected to a holiday, she loses her job. It's really too bad we can't tell her boss the truth. Or a version of the truth. Something to make him see that she had no choice and shouldn't be penalized for it."

Jack nodded, an idea forming in his mind. Dex was right. She needed a job. And until the school year was over, she wouldn't be able to get something new in Texas. It was for the best if she still had her job here.

"Excuse me," Jack said, standing and searching for the school superintendent's contact information as he walked away.

No one was in the office on a Saturday, but he put a reminder in his phone to go there first thing Monday morning and get in to see the guy. Pilar deserved to be happy. If that meant moving to Texas to be near her family, he'd let her go. But it was logical to think she'd need money until then. It wouldn't change her mind about leaving, but maybe it would help her. That was all he wanted.

Since he knew he couldn't have her.

25

"Ms. Luna. Thank you for coming," Mr. Barclay said with a grin.

Pilar hadn't seen the man smile much in the time she worked for him. She'd only met him a couple times, but he was never smiling. He always seemed nice, fair, but not friendly. To see him smile threw her off.

"I'd like to offer you your job back," he continued.

"What?" she blurted.

Again, he grinned. "Pilar, I wish you could have trusted me and told me what was going on."

Confused, she nodded. "Um, yeah."

"I understand why you couldn't. It makes sense. When your contact was here yesterday, he said it was a matter of national security that you stay quiet. And when he said there could have been a threat to the school if you went to work... You risked your job for these kids. That's the kind of person we need here."

"Um, thank you," Pilar said, trying to piece together everything that was happening.

"Oh, no, thank you. From what I understand, the assignment is done."

Pilar nodded.

"Good. Are you able to start back to work next Monday? I haven't posted for your replacement yet. I was going to work on that this week. I'm sorry about your brother and figured you'd want the week to take care of everything. If Monday is good for you, that would be great."

Pilar nodded again. She'd been trying to figure out how she was going to make ends meet before she left for Texas. Having her old job back made everything possible.

"Excellent. Thank you. And hopefully you can talk to me before something like this comes up again."

Pilar shook her head. "It won't, Mr. Barclay."

"Well, if it does..." he trailed off and grinned. He walked her to the door and nodded at Jessica.

Pilar signed the paperwork Jessica had for her, then she was out the door and left wondering what in the hell just happened. She got her job back, but she had no idea how. Someone must have talked to Mr. Barclay about Carlos and the whole situation. Must have said Pilar was instrumental in bringing him down. She sighed. If she'd turned over the phone earlier, she might have been. Instead, she waited until Juan was dead.

Pilar took a deep breath and pulled out of the school lot. She had a meeting with the funeral home to schedule Juan's cremation and plan the service. She hadn't told anyone about his funeral. No one would care. He was a criminal who sacrificed himself to bring down the people who made him who he was. He wasn't a hero. He wasn't a good person. Not to the rest of the world. But he was to Pilar. He was her brother, and Pilar loved him.

When she finally made it home that evening, Pilar felt

more alone than she had in her entire life. She wanted to crawl under her covers and forget the world, but Lily was on her doorstep.

"What are you doing here?" Pilar blurted.

Lily lifted the pan. "I brought you dinner. I figured you could use something good."

Pilar stood there staring for a long minute. Tears welled in her eyes and her throat closed up.

"Are you going to let me in?" Lily asked with a grin.

Pilar nodded and finally put the key in the lock, then led the way up to her apartment. Inside, everything looked the same as when she left, including the baby powder she dusted in front of the door in case anyone came in.

Lily saw it and grinned. "That's a good idea. I just hid under my covers and pretended the world didn't exist."

Pilar grinned. "I want to do that, trust me."

Lily nodded. "It's normal. After I was kidnapped, I wanted to hide from everything. Pretend nothing could ever hurt me again. But Archer..." Her eyes welled up, and she pressed her lips together in a forced grin.

"Lily, I'm so sorry he got hurt. I'll never forgive myself for—"

"Don't you dare blame yourself, Pilar," Lily said harshly. "This was not your fault."

"But if I wasn't involved with him—"

"Your brother was. He would have been here for Juan regardless of you. That doesn't mean it's his fault either. This is on Carlos. Besides, it's not the first time Archer's been shot. I hate it, but it happens. It's part of the job. And if I'm being completely honest with you, there's a part of me that enjoys it because then I know he's safe for a little while."

Pilar chuckled. "I can understand that. When they told

me Jack—" Pilar stopped herself and pressed her lips together, avoiding Lily's eyes.

"You love him, don't you?" Lily asked gently.

Pilar met her gaze and nodded. "But it doesn't matter. Jack's not built that way. He told me more than once that he doesn't do forever. He was honest with me."

"Yeah, Archer said the same thing. He wasn't willing to think about dating, let alone forever. But it was his idea to get married. Not that I'm complaining. I can't wait to call him my husband. But I never expected it when we first met."

Pilar smiled. She couldn't imagine Lily and Archer not together. Not head over heels for each other. They were connected in a way she'd never seen before. Like they could almost read each other's thoughts.

Pilar never had that. Or anything close. Jack noticed when she wasn't there, but that was the closest she'd had to a deep connection with someone.

"Jack's a good guy, you know," Lily said. "I know you're mad at him, but he wouldn't have lied to you if it wasn't necessary."

"I don't do well with lies," Pilar admitted.

"Well, sure. Who does? But when you're with someone on this team, you have to get over it. Archer doesn't tell me everything, and I know he won't. It was hard at first, but if I knew everything, I could become a target. Hell, I still could. But knowing what's going on doesn't make me safer. And hiding under the covers doesn't either. I have to live my life. I have to take the risk that the man who kidnapped me is still out there, and he could come after me again any time. But I also know that if he does, Archer and the team will do anything to find him and bring me home."

"They didn't find Juan and bring him home," Pilar said softly.

Lily nodded, reaching out to cover Pilar's hand with her own. "I know. And I hate that. They all do, too. Archer has been at work every day trying to figure out where they went wrong and how Carlos outsmarted them. It's making all of them nuts. But that won't bring your brother back." Lily squeezed Pilar's hand, drawing her eyes up. "They genuinely liked Juan. Archer mentioned him to me a while ago. He said he was a good kid trying to make up for what he did. He admired your brother. A lot. They all did. He was a hero in their eyes."

Pilar's eyes welled with fresh tears that weren't going to be contained. She slammed her eyes shut and let the tears fall. Lily sat there, holding her hand and letting her cry. It could have been a minute, or it could have been an hour. Pilar just knew she wasn't alone, and it felt good.

"Thank you," Pilar finally managed.

"It's true, Pilar. I know you hate them for not bringing Juan home, but they hate themselves even more. And I know it's a lot to ask, but if you're having a service, I think they'd like to come."

Pilar sucked in a breath. She'd resigned herself to saying goodbye to her brother alone. To moving on with her life. To not having anyone. Lily showing up shouldn't change that. She still didn't have anyone. Juan was gone. Her parents were gone. And Jack... he was never going to be hers. He never was and dreaming he might be was a foolish idea.

"Jack's kind of a mess lately," Lily said without preamble. "He sat in the hospital for hours, feeling like it was his fault Archer was shot. When he left, I know he didn't sleep even though he told me he did. Every time he left the hospital, he's come back looking more exhausted than when he left. He's not sleeping. He's barely eating. He looks like a zombie half the time, staring at the door when we're together, as though he's waiting for someone to show up. Someone he's gotten used to watching and having near."

Pilar closed her eyes at the onslaught of emotions. She was burying her brother in two days, and instead of being able to focus on him, she was thinking of Jack. The man who pretended to care about her so he could get close to her. The man she fell for because she was so naïve.

"He lied to me, Lily. I don't know if I can get over that. But even if I could, he doesn't want me. He doesn't want anyone."

Lily took a breath and stood. Pilar stood with her. "Jack has never been in a relationship. I'm not sure he would know how. I know I told you to be careful, but I think he's hurting even more than you are right now."

"I just don't know," Pilar said softly.

Lily nodded, letting it go. "I know you don't know me well, but I think we could become friends. I'd really like to if you're up to it."

Pilar nodded. "I could use a friend while I'm here."

"You're leaving?"

Pilar nodded again, her eyes filling once more. "I have no reason to stay here. I'm going back to Texas to be near my aunt and uncle. I don't want to be alone anymore."

Lily nodded. "I get that. I'll miss you, but I understand."

"Thanks."

Lily walked to the door and turned to hug Pilar. "Please don't leave without saying goodbye."

Pilar nodded. "I'll be here a couple of months. Please tell Dunn thank you for talking to my boss."

"Your boss?" Lily asked.

"Yeah, he told my boss what was going on, or some of it, and I got my job back. I really appreciate it."

Lily nodded. "I'll tell him, but I don't think it was him."

"Why not?"

"He's been away. After Carlos, Daniel went to help bring down the cartel. He hasn't been in town for a few days."

"Then who talked to my boss."

Lily grinned. "I think you know."

Pilar stared at her as Lily walked out the door. When it clicked closed behind her, Pilar yanked it back open.

"Lily?"

"Yeah?"

"Juan's funeral is Thursday at noon. At St. Gregory's."

Lily smiled and nodded. "I'll see you there."

Pilar grinned and took a deep breath for the first time in days. She had a friend, and she wouldn't be alone for Juan's service. Maybe everything would turn out okay.

JACK STARED at himself in the mirror and tried to convince himself Lily was right. And Archer and Slade and Dex and Dunn, all of them. He didn't for a second think they were, but he tried. For them.

The tie around his neck felt too tight and the pants he wore hugged him wrong. Everything felt wrong. Especially getting dressed for Juan's funeral without Pilar by his side.

The sharp knock on his door was the only alert he had before Archer and Lily walked into his apartment. He turned to face them and their worried grins both fell.

"You look like you're going to be sick," Lily said, rushing over to him.

Jack forced a grin and met Archer's gaze. "See? I told you she'd be mine one day. All I had to do was fall in love with someone else and feel like I was going to throw up and she'd run to my side."

Archer huffed a laugh, then winced. "Shit. Don't make me laugh. It fucking hurts."

Lily threw Archer a glare over her shoulder. "You should have taken a pill like I told you to. I don't have any sympathy for you."

Jack smirked, and Archer flipped him off.

"I saw that," Lily said.

"It wasn't at you," Archer cooed.

"Doesn't matter. He's terrified. You need to give him a break."

"He's showing up unannounced at the funeral of the guy he was supposed to protect, whose sister he's in love with. Why should he be nervous?" Archer asked with a grin.

Jack returned the finger.

Lily swatted his shoulder. "Stop it. He got shot five days ago. Give him a break."

"Ow! Is there anyone you aren't going to go mama bear over?"

Lily straightened Jack's tie and thought for a second, then shook her head. "No. This day is too important for all of you to let you act like children. All of you are hurting, but none as bad as Pilar. She's my priority today. Which is why I'll kick all of you out if she tells me to."

"You were the one who said we should come," Archer exclaimed.

"And I think she'll want you there, but if I'm wrong, you're all gone." She tightened Jack's tie and stepped back, smoothing her hands over his shoulders. "Now, are we ready?"

Jaymes and Kelsea followed them to the church. The drive was far too quick for Jack. He could have dealt with a trip back to Georgia to visit his parents first. That might have been enough time to get his nerves under control.

Dex and Slade arrived a few seconds after them, and Dunn was already there. Everyone looked at Jack when he got out of the car, studying him to see if he was going to lose it.

He smoothed a hand down his charcoal suit and hoped it was good enough for Juan's funeral. He shoved his hand in his pocket and found the wad of tissues he stuffed in there earlier. Just in case Pilar let him close to her and needed one.

"Should we go in?" Lily asked, looking around at the group of them, standing uncomfortably outside the church.

Dunn nodded. "Yes. We're following you, Lily."

Lily nodded and squared her shoulders. She looped her hand through Archer's good arm and started for the church. The others followed, one by one, until Jack was alone.

Or thought he was.

"You going in?" Slade asked.

Jack drew in a breath and looked up at the church. It was grand and beautiful and sad all at once. A place he felt he couldn't lie. "I talked to my parents the other day. They want me to come home."

"Okay? And?"

Jack shook his head. Slade had a good relationship with his family. His little sister worshipped him growing up. His parents were still married, and happy, and everyone always supported his choices. Jack knew Slade wouldn't understand how he was feeling. "Never mind."

Slade shook his head. "No, you don't get to do that. What's going on?"

"I've been thinking about what I want. Joining the Teams was the best decision of my life, but leaving was tough. After Rodney... And then Williams... Now Pilar... I just don't know where my place is."

"What do you mean?"

Jack sucked in a deep breath and finally met Slade's gaze. "I'm a killer. I hide and shoot. I spent years training myself to eliminate the enemy. As a civilian, I can't do that without answering questions. No one can give me orders to shoot to kill anymore, not without a shit ton of paperwork. So I don't know if I have a place here."

Slade studied him for a long minute. Jack stared at the church and tried not to squirm.

"I think there's something else going on with you," Slade said. "I don't think it has anything to do with your parents, or Rodney or Williams. I think it all has to do with Pilar."

Jack shrugged, not wanting to admit how true that was.

"Love isn't the kind of thing you can run away from. Even if you decide to leave, and I hope you don't, but if you decide that's what's best for you, running isn't going to fix anything."

Jack huffed a breath. "How would you know?"

Slade met his gaze. "Because it's what I did. Before I signed up, I was going to marry my high school sweetheart. Our parents were good friends, and she was close to my sister. We grew up together. Our future was set. But I panicked. Just freaked out. And I ran. I signed up and left and never looked back."

"No. That's not possible. You have a great relationship with your family. And you've never mentioned this," Jack said, his world thrown.

Slade shrugged. "There's a lot about each other we don't know. A lot we hide because it's too painful to think about. I hate the way I treated her, but I can forgive myself because I really believe it's better for her this way. She got married, had a couple of kids. She's good. Your story doesn't have such a happy ending, and you're waiting for the other shoe to drop here."

Jack drew in a sharp breath and nodded. It didn't take a genius to figure out exactly what Slade was talking about. "Meredith."

"You have to let go of her. Pilar isn't like her."

Jack shook his head. "No, she's not, but I didn't know Meredith was like that either."

"Look, Meredith was fun. She was beautiful and sweet, and hiding her pain."

"She wasn't the only one who lied, though."

Slade narrowed his gaze at Jack. "What do you mean?"

Jack took a breath and looked up at the church again. "I told her we were leaving a week before we left. I wanted to get away from her. My lease was up, but we got delayed, remember?"

Slade nodded.

"I didn't tell her things changed. I crashed with Dunn for the week. Meredith saw me out one night. I went to a different place than usual, but she was there. I was with someone else, and I could see she was hurt, but I told myself it was for the best. Things were over between us, whether I left when I told her or a week later, it was over. She killed herself that night."

"Fuck," Slade whispered.

Jack nodded. "I saw her call, but I ignored it because I was at the other chick's place. Hell, I don't even remember her name."

Slade ran a hand over his face, his palm scratching over his beard. The sound rubbed Jack's nerves, putting him on alert. Birds chirped as they flew over the church. The wind rustled through the trees. The soft rumble of cars on the street filled in behind him. He heard it all, waiting for the slam of the front door and his friends being thrown out.

"I liked Meredith," Jack admitted. "I wasn't in love with her, and I knew I wasn't going to get there, but I liked her. With Pilar..."

"It's different," Slade supplied.

Jack nodded. "But I still lied to her. She hates me."

"She was hurt, but I don't think she hates you. She said a lot the night she stayed with Dex and me." Slade avoided Jack's gaze for a minute. "She felt used. And she just lost her brother."

"And now we're at his funeral."

Slade nodded. "Yeah. But she hasn't thrown the rest of them out yet. Let's go in."

Jack took a breath and stared up at the church again. Finally, he nodded and let Slade drag him inside, hoping he was making the right choice.

26

PILAR SAT IN THE FIRST PEW LISTENING TO THE GENERIC service. The priest never met her brother and couldn't offer much in terms of comfort for Pilar, but the strong presence surrounding her helped.

Someone else walked in after the service began, but she didn't have it in her to see who it was. Probably someone who didn't realize the church was occupied. She understood the mistake with only a couple of cars in the parking lot and a handful of people inside.

Pilar stood for the next song, her hands shaking as she opened the book to the correct page. Lily grabbed one of her hands and held it tight. Kelsea was on her other side. Her protectors. They were keeping her upright.

The men sat in the pew behind them. Archer, Dunn, Jaymes, Dex, English, Rocky, and Mason. They filtered in behind Lily when she burst her way into the church. Pilar hated herself for being disappointed when Jack wasn't with them. She didn't want him there, but she needed him. His strength and support. Just once more.

She realized Slade wasn't there either and wondered if he was the person who came in later.

The service was just about finished when Father Jonathan said, "I've been told someone would like to speak about Juan. Pilar, are you okay with that?"

Pilar's eyes filled, and she nodded. The only people there were F-BOMB, so it had to be one of them. She turned to see who stood and lost her breath when Jack strode up the aisle toward her.

She held her breath as he held his head high and stared past her. A part of her ached to run into his arms, but she held herself still. Waiting. Watching. Listening.

"Juan Rios was not a friend of mine. He wasn't someone I spent time with. We didn't get a beer after a long day or share stories about our past. We never watched a game together or had dinner. He wasn't someone I knew. It'll be one of my life's biggest regrets."

Jack paused and looked at her. Their eyes collided for the briefest of moments before he ripped himself from her again. Pilar was mourning the loss of her brother and her lover at the same time, and both were killing her.

"I had the pleasure of getting to know Juan's sister this week. Pilar loved her brother with such entirety that I know Juan was an amazing man. Any man lucky enough to have a woman like her love him is truly blessed, even in death. Juan wasn't perfect. He did things he regretted. He made mistakes, but he gave his life to correct those mistakes. The most important thing to him was his sister. He talked about her every time we spoke. She was his world, and I know he gave his life to protect her. He would have done anything for Pilar. I wanted to bring him back to her. To reunite them. But I failed. We failed. And for that, I'm truly sorry."

He met her eyes, his full of emotion and regret. She sucked in a breath through her tears, praying she wouldn't break down completely in the church. Lily and Kelsea squeezed her hands, and she squeezed back, drawing strength from them.

"Nothing I can say or do will ever change what happened, but Juan gave me something I've never had. Something I never thought I'd have. If I could say one thing to him, I would tell him thank you. Thank you for choosing me to be the one who watched over Pilar. Thank you for trusting me with the person you loved most in the world. Thank you for... Thank you."

Jack drew in a breath and held it, then stepped down and walked past her once more. Pilar turned and watched him. She wanted to call out to him, to go after him, to thank him or hit him or hug him. But Father Jonathan stood and started speaking again.

The door at the back of the church slammed open, then slid closed again. Father Jonathan kept talking, going through his closing prayer and dismissing the group.

Pilar couldn't breathe. She couldn't think or speak or stand. She collapsed onto the pew and dropped her head into her hands.

"Are you okay?" Lily asked softly.

Pilar shook her head. "No. Nothing about this day is right."

"I'm sorry. This is my fault. I really thought you'd want everyone here. And Jack... I asked him if he would say something. Don't be mad at him."

Pilar looked up at Lily with watery eyes. "I'm only mad at him for walking out. I can't do this alone. And I don't want to do it without him."

Lily grinned. "Well, that's the best news I've heard all day."

Pilar huffed a laugh. "You like to meddle, don't you?"

Lily nodded. "Especially when I know the two people should be together. He's hurting, too."

Pilar swallowed roughly. "I feel like... I don't know what. I'm at my brother's funeral and crying over the guy I'm in love with. I'm a horrible person."

Lily shook her head. "No, you're not."

Pilar drew in a shaky breath and held it. Then another. When she didn't feel like she was going to collapse, she stood again. "Thank you. I don't think I could have gotten through this without you here."

Lily grinned, her entire face lighting up. "I'm happy to help."

"Can I ask you one more favor?" Pilar asked.

Lily nodded. "Of course. Anything."

"Can I ride with you to the columbarium?"

Lily grinned and slid her arm into Pilar's. The soft fabric of her black dress brushed Pilar's bare skin. Lily gently pulled her along, following behind Dunn, who carried the small box that held her brother's ashes.

A week ago, Pilar didn't know any of the people there existed. Now, she was friends with them and counting on them to help her through one of the worst days of her life.

"Hey, honey?" Lily said softly to Archer. "Pilar's going to ride with me. Will you guys take her car?"

Archer nodded. "Of course."

"Kels," Lily called out. "Want to ride with us?"

Kelsea kissed Jaymes quickly and joined Pilar and Lily. "Absolutely. The men can fend for themselves."

Kelsea grabbed Pilar's other arm and the three of them

walked outside into the brilliant sunshine. It didn't seem right to bury her brother on such a beautiful day, but she knew Juan wasn't in the box Dunn carried. The beautiful day meant he was watching. He could see her from his new spot in heaven. With her parents, always keeping an eye on her.

At the cemetery, Pilar directed the way through the graves to the columbarium at the center of the wide open space. Juan mentioned once that it was a beautiful structure and that he imagined it would be a peaceful resting place. She remembered the conversation after he died, and a part of her wondered if he knew his past would catch up to him one day. If he was guiding her the entire time. He knew what he was getting into when he went to F-BOMB. He had to know the end could have been coming for him.

Pilar was proud of her brother. Even though he knew, he still pushed forward. He still turned over evidence and met with Carlos and did everything he could to make sure he righted all the wrongs from his life.

Dunn carried Juan's remains up the short hill to the courtyard that overlooked the rest of the stones. His name, new and freshly carved into the granite, gleamed. Pilar traced the letters with her finger, ignoring the rest of the group as they gathered around her.

Father Jonathan said a few words intended to help her feel better, then he removed the smaller box from inside the mini-casket and slid it into the spot with Juan's name on it. When the door closed, locking with a finality that broke her heart, Pilar lost her fight with control and sobbed.

Pilar looked around at the stoic faces of the men who tried to save her brother. None of them shied away from her, holding her gaze as it slid from one to the other. They accepted their part in her pain with a strength she didn't possess.

But the one person she was searching for wasn't there. He didn't come. He was noticeably absent, especially after his words at the funeral.

"Jack," she whispered, the word a question and a plea.

Then he stepped to the side, revealing himself behind Slade and Mason.

She drank him in, devouring him with her eyes. Her breath hitched in her throat, choking off any chance she had at making another sound.

He moved between his friends and stopped in front of her. His pain was visible, a mask that felt like the man she thought she knew. She ached to ease his pain, but she had too much of her own.

He reached for her and she fell into his arms, letting his strength become her own. She held on to him and cried while Father Jonathan screwed on the stone that declared her brother truly gone forever.

JACK DREW IN SLOW, deep breaths and tried not to inhale her too deeply. Her scent danced around him, demanding he suck it in and hold it for himself, but he couldn't. She didn't belong to him. She wanted him, but it wouldn't last. He couldn't risk falling harder and ending up even more broken.

So he held her. And he let her cry. And he supported her when she almost collapsed to the ground. Every one of her sobs was a shot through his heart. He was to blame for her pain, her sadness, her tears. He could have watched Juan that day, but he was too focused on her. Then he lied to her about all of it. Following orders.

"Thank you," she finally whispered, her head cradled against his chest. "Thank you for being here for me."

He nodded once, stiffly, awkwardly. He wanted to say so much to her, but her brother was barely buried. If he ever saw her again, he'd try to work up the courage to say some of the things he wanted to say, but at that moment, it had to be about Juan.

Pilar pulled back from him after a few minutes and looked at the small crowd around them. It pissed Jack off that none of her coworkers or other friends were there. She would have been all alone if Lily hadn't forced them all to go. He couldn't bear the thought.

"I feel like I should offer to feed all of you or something," Pilar said with a small laugh. "Um, I... it means a lot to me that you're all here. That you came. I know you all knew my brother, but I appreciate you all being here."

Slade stepped forward and pulled Pilar into a hug. Jack let go of her so she could hug him back, immediately missing the feel of her against him. Slade whispered his apology, then invited her back to his house.

She smiled. "You don't have to do that."

Slade shook his head. "Lily has a ton of food in the car. She thought you'd be most comfortable at my house since you were there. We didn't want you to be alone today."

Jack waited for her response. He wanted to be alone. To sit in a dark corner and drink until he forgot her name and the way she felt in his arms. The taste of her skin. The feel of her lips under his. The perfection of her body. The sound of her moans and laugh.

"Thank you. All of you. I appreciate it," Pilar said softly.

Slade moved to walk away, and Pilar turned to Jack. "Are you coming?"

Jack started to shake his head, but there was something in her eyes. Something that made him pause. Something that gave him the tiniest bit of hope. Hope he didn't deserve, but hope he craved like an addict. "Do you want me to?"

She held his gaze and nodded. "Yes."

He sucked in a tight breath and nodded. "Then I'll be there."

Pilar smiled and turned to walk away with Lily and Kelsea, the three women leading the way down the path to the cars.

Jack watched Pilar the whole way. The gentle sway of her hips, the pull of the black fabric of her dress across her ass. He couldn't believe he was ogling her in a cemetery where they'd just put her brother to rest, but he was.

He stopped next to Pilar's car and waited for Archer to let him in. Jack hated not having his own vehicle. He could use the few minutes between the cemetery and Slade's house to get his thoughts together, but instead, he rode with Lily and Archer, and Lily took their SUV and made Archer take Pilar's car. Which meant Jack had to drive because Archer wasn't cleared yet.

He should have ridden with Slade.

"She looked pretty happy you're here," Archer said once they were out of the cemetery and back on the road. "Are things okay?"

Jack shook his head and shifted in his seat. Even the car smelled like Pilar. "We haven't talked. About anything. I think she's just emotional today."

"She needed you."

Jack shrugged. "I guess." He didn't want to get his hopes up any higher than they already were. The way Pilar looked at him, the feel of her in his arms, her quiet request that she go to Slade's. It all made him feel like maybe they still had a chance.

Archer was quiet the rest of the ride, following the string of cars weaving through Niagara Falls to the northern outskirts of the city. They filled the driveway in front of Slade's house and made their way inside.

It wasn't long before everyone was laughing, talking, and eating. Slade pulled out trays of food he claimed to have made that morning. Lily's food filled the counters and went into the oven to heat up. It was enough for ten groups their size.

Jack grabbed some food and kept to himself, feeling raw and vulnerable. He ached to go to Pilar, but Lily and Kelsea were surrounding her, keeping her full of food and wine and laughter. Laughter that chased Jack around the room.

He walked down the hall to the bathroom and closed the door. He didn't turn on the light. Couldn't. If he did, he'd see the shower where he kneeled in front of her and licked her until she came, then turned her around and sank into her. Where he kissed her in front of the mirror. Where he wrapped her in a towel and held her.

No, he couldn't see it.

He used the bathroom, washed his hands, and splashed water on his face. He was just about to open the door when her laugh found him again. Locking him in. He drew in a breath and held it, the roaring in his ears demanding he get the hell out of there before he lost his mind.

He left the bathroom and headed straight for the back-yard. He closed the door behind himself and stalked down the stairs into the soft grass. He tugged at the tie choking him until it loosened and gave him a tiny bit of air. Then he fumbled with the buttons until he had a couple free. He rested his hands on his knees and tried to breathe, but he still felt like he couldn't get enough air.

He stripped off his coat and spun to throw it to the ground when he froze.

There she was. Standing no more than three feet from him. Staring at him like he was as crazy as he felt.

Then she grinned, and everything locked back into place.

27

"Hey," Pilar said softly.

Jack just stared at her. His eyes wild and his hair disheveled. His tie pulled loose, but still hanging around his neck. The top buttons of his shirt undone and it half untucked. His jacket in his hand, on the way to the ground.

She couldn't remember when he'd looked more beautiful. She knew it was a strange word to use for a man, but Jack was real in that moment. He wasn't hiding who he was. Pretending to be someone he wasn't. He was just Jack.

"I needed some fresh air," Pilar continued. "Lily and Kelsea seem to think I'm going to lose it and... I don't know. Cry, maybe? I already did that. I'm sure I will some more. There's no way I'll go hungry with them around. Lily asked me to be one of her bridesmaids. I don't really know why since she really doesn't know me, but for some reason, I said yes."

Pilar paused and looked at Jack. He was still staring at her, his green eyes tracking her fidgety movements. She didn't know what to do with her hands, and she couldn't seem to stand still. She was nervous. She'd never been nervous around him.

Then again, when they met, she was half catatonic.

"I thought it was a nice service. What you said… it meant a lot to me," Pilar said.

"Why are you out here?" Jack asked gruffly.

Pilar backed up a step, shocked by his outburst. "I… I wanted some fresh air."

"But I'm out here."

She shrugged.

"Listen, what we had… I know you're hurting right now, and I'm happy to be here for you, but I can't keep doing it. I can't chat with you like we're friends."

"We're not friends?"

He laughed mirthlessly. "No, Pilar. We're not friends. We're never going to be friends."

Tears stung her eyes. She swallowed her pain and took another step away from him. "I'm sorry. I didn't mean to assume—"

"What? That I could dismiss you as easily? I get it. I was an ass. I treated you like shit. I lied, and I slept with you when I shouldn't have. I'm sorry. But every time I touched you was because I wanted to. You can choose not to believe me, but I can't stand here and pretend to be your friend when just being in the same room as you has me…"

"Has you what?" she asked softly.

He finally looked up and met her gaze. The fire in his warmed her, setting every cell in her body ablaze. "Has me dying to claim you. Has me wanting to throw you over my shoulder and remind you how good we were together. Has me aching to pull you into my arms and convince you that I'll never let anyone hurt you ever again."

His breath burst from him in heavy pants. Her brain was

having trouble processing what he said, but her body got it. Her breath pulsed out of her, making space for the need that throbbed through every inch of her body.

He stared at her, begging her with his eyes to say something, but she couldn't. Her lips wouldn't work.

Resignation shuttered his eyes, and he turned away from her. "Just go back inside."

"No," she croaked.

He spun back to her. "Pilar, please."

She shook her head and took a step toward him. "No. Because the only thing that's keeping me together right now is the way you're looking at me. Like you found the same thing I found the first time you kissed me. I thought I loved Carlos, or the man I thought he was. I told myself I did, because I gave myself to him. I let him into my body, but you... dammit, Jack. You're the only one who's ever really had my heart. You had it from the minute I saw you on the street. When you made me smile, even though I was terrified. It's always been you, Jack. And if you don't do exactly what you said you want to do, I'm going to..."

The side of his mouth quirked up. "You're going to what?"

She fought her grin and stepped into his space. "I'm going to have to throw you over my shoulder and embarrass you in front of all your friends when I carry you off and have my way with you."

Jack slid an arm around her back and tugged her body flush to his. "It would totally be worth it," he whispered, his lips a breath from hers. "Because I don't care how I have you as long as I have you."

"You have me, Jack Farrell. You've always had me."

He finally closed the last bit of distance between them and kissed her. She wrapped her arms around his neck and let him take away all the pain and fear and sadness, and replaced it with something much, much better.

Jack.

PILAR COULDN'T REMEMBER the last time she laughed so hard. Lily stood in front of the mirror and puffed her stomach out, frowning at the bump.

"People are going to think I'm pregnant," she gasped. "How did I not notice this before?"

"Because you were too blinded by love. It doesn't matter what they all think. It matters what my brother thinks," Jaymes said, smiling at Lily in the mirror.

She turned and hugged him, thanking him softly.

The laughter and the sweet made Pilar happy she was a part of the small group that welcomed her in and made her one of them.

Over the last month, she'd gotten to know Lily and Kelsea well. And the men of the group. They all had their own fun side, a piece of themselves she didn't get to see when she was a job, but they let out once she was only there as a friend.

Dunn and the team he worked with took down the cartel, stopping the flow of drugs and women into the states. She knew there was more work to do, but she was proud because her brother helped. He did what he set out to do, and he stopped the men he set out to stop. He was a good man in the end.

"Just keep your flowers there," Kelsea said. "No one will notice. Not once Archer starts crying."

Lily burst out laughing. "Oh, my God. He's totally going to cry, isn't he?"

Kelsea sipped her champagne and laughed. "Absolutely. He's such a softie when it comes to you. I'm surprised he managed to ask you to marry him."

Lily smiled at her reflection, a secret in her eyes. Pilar wanted that feeling. To know the man she loved was as head over heels for her as she was for him. She was pretty sure she had that with Jack, but there were always moments that made her doubt.

"Are you okay?" Lily asked, catching Pilar's frown.

Pilar pasted on a grin and nodded. "Of course. I'm with Kelsea, though. No one is going to think twice about your not-a-baby bump once Archer loses it."

"They might think he's pregnant," Kelsea dead-panned.

Lily snorted. "He is the more emotional one at times."

Pilar grinned. Just the thought of Archer getting emotional was enough to make her laugh. He was stoic and firm. He was obviously different with Lily, but there was no way in the world Archer Ford was going to cry. Ever.

"Are you ladies ready?" Jaymes asked, glancing at the door.

They looked at Lily and waited for her nod. "Absolutely."

Pilar led the way out of the room, stopping at the back of the church. Soft music filtered through the closed doors. She stared at them, wondering if she'd ever be the one who wore the white dress.

It would help if she heard those three magic words from Jack first.

Pilar dragged in a breath and pushed thoughts of Jack away. It was Lily and Archer's day. She wasn't going to ruin it because she and Jack were still trying to figure out their future.

Marge from the church slipped through the doors and grinned at everyone. "We're ready when you are."

"I've been ready," Lily said, her eyes on the door. Focused. Happy. Ready to march down that aisle.

Jaymes stood in front of her, his black tux a sharp contrast to the elegant white dress Lily wore. It was simple and beautiful, a white sheath that hugged her chest and draped to the floor. It shifted with her as she walked, revealing the red combat boots she wore underneath, a nod to Archer and a private joke between them. Her dark hair was piled up with tendrils dangling down her back, highlighting the low back of the dress.

"Are you sure you want to marry him?" Jaymes asked with a smirk. "Dunn's still free, and Slade. Dex? English?"

Lily laughed and pulled Jaymes in for a hug. "I love you. Thank you for being here for me."

"You know there's nowhere else I'd rather be. And I know you'll do the same for me."

Lily eyed him, then slid her gaze to Kelsea. "Are you two..."

Kelsea and Jaymes locked eyes and shook their heads. "Not yet, but one of these days," Jaymes said, raw love in his eyes for Kelsea.

Pilar was happy for all of them, but she wanted the same. She was jealous. And she hated herself for it.

"We're ready," Marge said. "You're up first."

Pilar nodded and took her spot in front of the door. Marge opened it, and the entire room turned to look at Pilar. She forced a smile and walked down the aisle.

Jack was standing up front with Archer. He mouthed *I got you* to her when she was close enough to read his lips. She smiled at him, then took her spot.

She stood to the side and watched as Kelsea followed

her, then Jaymes walked Lily down the aisle and gave her away before taking his place next to Jack.

After the readings, the priest stood before the congregation and spoke. "When I first met Archer and Lily, I wasn't sure what to make of them. He was stiff, and she was so full of life that I couldn't see how they would work." The church chuckled. "I can see you all understand what I'm saying. Over the last few months, I've seen a different side to both of them. One that supports the other and lifts the other up. Obviously, I've never been married, but I've been given the privilege to celebrate many weddings. I've seen couples who never came together, and couples who never fought, and couples who were connected on such a basic level that it was hard to imagine them apart. Archer and Lily fall into that last category. They're the kind of couple I want to marry every weekend because I know they'll last. I know they'll fight and make up. They'll love and laugh and cry and pray and always come together in the end. And to have been a part of that, I will forever be grateful."

Pilar wiped her eyes and smiled. She stared at Archer and Lily's linked hands and knew every word the priest said was right. They would last. They had forever. They had each other.

The rest of the ceremony was quick. Archer did get choked up during his vows, whispering the words so quietly to Lily that Pilar could barely hear them. Lily cried, her voice shaking with each word she said to him, but they were loud and strong and confident.

When the priest announced them husband and wife, Archer tugged Lily to him and dipped her back, kissing the hell out of his new bride. The entire church went nuts, whistling and cheering until Archer lifted Lily to her feet.

Lily's cheeks were bright red, but her smile couldn't be

contained. Archer held her tight to his side and marched his wife down the aisle, high-fiving his team on the way past them.

Pilar laughed, watching them go, then looked over at Jack and Jaymes. Jack stepped to the center to meet Kelsea, but Jaymes stepped in front of him and stole Kelsea. Jack laughed and nodded at Pilar.

"Looks like I got you," he whispered in her ear, kissing her neck.

Pilar shivered, the feel of his lips on her skin enough to make her want him. It still surprised her how quickly she fell for Jack. How much she wanted him. She felt like she couldn't get enough, and that scared her.

"Are you okay?" he asked when they were halfway down the aisle.

Pilar nodded and pasted on a grin. "Of course."

Jack tugged her closer to his side. "No, you're not. What's wrong?"

She shook her head. "Nothing. I'm happy for them."

Jack grinned. "It's pretty great, isn't it? I never thought I'd see Archer get married."

"Probably not something any of you planned," Pilar said.

Jack shook his head. "I definitely never planned on it. What about you? Did you dream of getting married when you were young?"

Pilar drew in a breath and nodded. "I did. My parents had a great marriage, and I always wanted what they had. A man who loved me and was always there for me."

They reached the vestibule, and Jack pulled her to the side, away from the others. "You know I got you, right?"

She nodded. "I know."

"And you know... you know that means I love you, right?"

"What?" she gasped.

Jack smiled and cupped her jaw. "My parents are great, but I never thought I'd find love. I never thought I'd find you." He looked around them. "I want this, too. A church. All the people we love. A big ass party. And you in a sexy dress that I get to unwrap."

"Are you…"

He shook his head. "No, I'm not asking you right now. It's Archer and Lily's day. When I ask you, it's going to be all about us. But I wanted you to know I'm right there with you, Pilar. I got you."

Tears streamed down her cheeks, and she nodded. "I got you."

DUNN STOOD at the bar and sipped his one and only drink of the night. He didn't trust himself to have more. Not when he couldn't trust himself at all.

Jack and Pilar danced close, holding each other and swaying to a tune that didn't match the fast beat of the music playing. Dunn was happy for them, but he knew their joy was banked, reserved, less than it should be. Her brother should be there. He should have had a chance to be a part of their future. To have his own future. Instead, he was dead, and it was Dunn's fault.

The list of things he regretted was piling up higher and higher every day. His team put their faith in him, but he wasn't sure he was the right person to lead them. All he'd done so far was nearly get them killed, missed all the signs of what they were walking in to, and lost a CI. Someone they all cared about.

Dunn was lost. It had been years since he felt like his

carefully planned life was spiraling out of control, but that was how he felt. His military career was the one thing he always held his head up high about, but that stellar record was tainted by the betrayal of the man who taught him how to be a frogman. Williams believed the Navy owed him something, and by taking it, he owed all the men who served under him something else.

Answers maybe? An explanation? Dunn knew neither would ever be enough to make up for what Williams did. He took Rodney from them, and he tried to kill thousands of others. There was no excuse, no reasoning.

Dunn finished his drink and returned to his seat. He watched the couples dance and laugh and wondered if he'd ever be able to let his guard down enough to feel the simple pleasure written on their faces.

The last time he felt that free was before he joined the Navy. A lifetime ago. Things were different then. He was different. He made promises to Ashleigh, promises he wanted to keep even though he knew he never would.

There had been women since her, but none that compared. Dunn imagined her with a full life. Married with kids and a big house and a constant smile. He hoped it was true. He wanted it to be true.

"You doing okay?" English asked, taking the seat next to Dunn.

Dunn nodded automatically. He didn't want his team doubting his abilities. He had enough doubts on his own. "All good."

"Good. I never thought I'd see Archer married."

Dunn chuckled. "Tell me about it. Especially the first one. And Jack with only one woman?"

English laughed. "That might be the bigger surprise. Think you'll ever follow them off the cliff?"

Dunn hesitated, then shook his head. "No."

"Yeah? I always thought you'd be the first to fall."

"Nah, not me. I'm married to my job, and after Williams..." He couldn't admit the rest, but he didn't have to.

English's eyes darkened. He nodded and drew in a breath. "Not everyone's like him. And not every situation is. Some guys make it work."

"Not many."

English stared at Archer and Lily, silent for a long moment. "We're not in anymore. It's different now. They wouldn't have gotten to where they are if we were gone all the time."

"I hope it lasts for them. But I know it wouldn't for me. Not now. Not with Williams out there."

"You know none of us blame you, right?"

Dunn's cheeks warmed at being called on his shit. The only thing he hated more than feeling weak was knowing other people saw it. "Yeah, well, I don't agree."

English sighed heavily. "Do you need some time off?"

"No. Hell no. I need to find him and end this. It's been way too long."

"We'll get him."

Dunn nodded sharply. They had no choice. It was only a matter of time before Williams was back. And with the knowledge and skills he had, Dunn knew he would be back with a plan none of them saw coming.

THANK **you** so much for reading Jack and Pilar's story! Jack was always that funny, sweet guy, and it was so fun to watch him fall, and fall hard! And Pilar was absolutely perfect for him.

Dunn is a man who prides himself on his instincts. Too bad those instincts keep letting him down. He's trusted the wrong person too many times, and when his biggest regret shows up on his doorstep, he's not sure if he can trust anything she says. Or if he can trust himself to keep his hands to himself. Get your copy of Failure now!

Are you ready for more? Newsletter subscribers get *exclusive* bonuses like short stories, bonus scenes, and a first look at everything new. Sign up for my newsletter today so you never miss a thing!

Can't get enough alphas? Olivia is a single mom with no desire to have a man in her life. Ethan is an alpha who won't take no for an answer. She's sure she'll regret letting him in, but it isn't long before she's begging for more. Read Curvaceous & Captivating today!

ABOUT THE AUTHOR

USA TODAY Bestselling Author Mary E Thompson spent most of her childhood wishing she had a few less curves. She hid in the pages of books because her favorite characters never cared what size her clothes were. Now, neither does Mary, and she writes stories that celebrate women like her. Real women who have curves, chase dreams, and find love, because we should all be happy, no matter our dress size.

Mary spends her non-writing time with her husband and two kids, watching too much TV, cheering for her hometown football team (Go Bills!), and hiding chocolate from her family.

Visit https://MaryEThompson.com/ to sign up for Mary's newsletter, **Romancing the Curves**. Subscribers get free ebooks and other fun stuff, like exclusive, members only content and giveaways, plus are the first to know about new releases and sales!